SELFIE

STUART JAMES

Copyright © 2021 Stuart James All rights reserved

The characters and events portrayed in this book are fictitious. Any similarity to real persons, living or dead, is coincidental and not intended by the author.

No part of this book may be reproduced, or stored in a retrieval system, or transmitted in any form or by any means, electronic, mechanical, photocopying, recording, or otherwise, without express written permission of the publisher.

ASIN B09B1ZHFX4

Cover design by: Jerry Todd.
Editor: Laura Joyce

DEDICATION.

This book is dedicated to my wife Tara, children, Oli and Ava and my mother and father, Kathleen and Jimmy.
My world.
My life.
Love always.

INTRODUCTION.

Thanks so much for choosing Selfie.
Please, please leave a review. You don't know how much it means to me.

Make sure to keep up to date with projects I'm working on and sign up to my mailing list at:
https://www.stuartjamesthrillers.com
I'll also send you a free short story.

Also, you can follow me on social media.
I love to hear from readers and will always respond.
Twitter: StuartJames73
Instagram: Stuart James Author
Facebook: Stuart James Author.
TikToc: Stuart James Author

Selfie.

Stuart James.

QUOTE.

Justice will not be served until those who are unaffected are as outraged as those who are.
Benjamin Franklin

PROLOGUE

P resent Day.
October.
West London.

'I've got to dash. I'll be late. See you tonight.' Peter Simpson leant forward and kissed his wife on the cheek. He grabbed a sandwich from the worktop, tightly wrapped in cling film and held together with silver foil. His grey hair was slick, pushed back. His suit was immaculate, and his expensive aftershave, often overpowering, filled the kitchen with notes of Jasmine blossom, vanilla and patchouli.

'Oh, what time are you home?' his wife asked. 'Remember we have Ken and Mary.'

'Oh, that's tonight? Damn. And here was I thinking I'd have you to myself.'

Peter stood in the hallway and removed a scarf from the coat stand. He listened to the mild rocking motion, the legs slightly unbalanced as he placed the scarf around his neck. 'I guess around 7-7.30. I can't imagine I'll be any later.'

'Great. It will be nice seeing them.'

Peter listened to his wife's voice as it echoed through the house. He pushed his arms into his coat. 'Right. That's me. See you later. Have a great day.' Peter opened the front door. His wife shouted something from the kitchen, and he stepped back into the hallway.

'Wine. Grab a bottle of red. Actually, two bottles.'

'Two bottles of red. Got it. See you tonight.' He closed the front door and stood for a moment on the steps of their three-bedroom semi-detached house off Fulham Broadway. A light drizzle pushed against his face. It was early. In another half hour, dawn would push through and bring light to the streets. People would spill from their homes like a flood of life, suddenly assembling for one reason: money. He briefly contemplated going back inside and imagined the look on his wife's face as he said, 'Sod it. I don't feel like it today. Let's jump off the chaos for a moment. We'll take it up again tomorrow.'

Peter moved down the steps and stood on the pavement. He glanced left, right, watching the emptiness. Taking a deep breath, he steered his thoughts to the day ahead. The meetings, often sat for hours inhaling the cheap perfume and the smell of stale coffee in the air. The throats being cleared, the false smiles and artificial hugs. *'Let's do this, team. Happy vibes, people. Let's create a little magic.'*

He managed a car showroom, but as more online internet sites popped up, boasting that they can buy or sell your car with no haggling and give you a price within a minute, it made the industry that much more difficult.

Peter knew the time wasters. He could spot them a mile off. The walk-in, sit in the front seat, drive around the block and sod off without so much as a thank you type who lately took up so much of his time. He wished they were honest from the start.

'I'm not interested in the car; to be blunt, there are too many zeroes on the end for my liking. But hey, it makes me feel good. Just let me drive it to the end of the road and back. It breaks up my day. What do you say?'

Recently, he'd contemplated early retirement, moving to the coast with Anna and doing nothing. He knew he'd struggle with the boredom. And besides, they'd miss Phoebe. Peter and Anna's only child lived in East London and, although she was awful at keeping in touch, her being less than an hour away was a comfort in itself.

Peter removed the fob from his trouser pocket and watched his black BMW 8 series wink at him. As he moved towards it, he saw something tucked under the windscreen wipers. *The usual shit,* he thought.

We'll give your house a deep clean. Available for weekly visits or a one-off. Call today. Need to give your garden a long-needed facelift? We're here to help. Call now. We're open twenty-four-seven.

Yeah. The neighbours would love to hear a lawnmower at four in the morning.

Peter moved to the windscreen and peeled the A4 page from the glass. Part of the paper had become soggy and wet. He noticed the writing. The first thing that got his attention was the name. His name. Peter Simpson, written in thick black felt. Halfway down the page, four words: **Look In The Boot.**

Peter stepped back. He brought the paper closer to his face as he squinted his eyes.

Look In The Boot.

He paused, now holding his breath for a brief second. He let it out, pushing his lips as they vibrated together. He inhaled, trying to stem the anxiety which began to envelop his body. It worked at his ankles, rising like a hot flame, slowly engulfing him, swallowing his frame. His skin itched.

Look In The Boot.

The paper flapped as Peter's hand shook. He moved along the pavement, peering into the front passenger window. A folder on the seat. A pen clipped to the edge. The back seat was empty. Peter placed his hand on the cold metal at the rear of the car. He lifted his arm upwards, listening to the groan of the boot hatch, his heart pumping, the anxiously momentarily replaced by fear, which then became adrenaline. Three senses in the space of a few seconds.

Look In The Boot.

The lid was open halfway, and Peter contemplated closing it, moving to the front of the car and driving away.

Look In The Boot.

The door of the boot was now fully open. Peter stared at the blank space as relief washed over him. His breathing returned to normal, and the anxiety evaporated. He leaned his body against the car and sighed, then he screwed the paper tight into a ball, squeezing his fist hard. He stepped back from the car, moving away, his eyes focused ahead. Peter spun a half turn, now facing the house. He moved up the steps and made his way to the front door. As he fished the key from his trouser pocket, he noticed the gap, as if he hadn't shut it properly when leaving. Had someone knocked, Anna opening the front door, expecting to see him?

Peter held the key in his right hand, his palm face up and, with his left hand, he pushed. 'Anna. I'm back.' He called from the hallway. 'Anna. Where are you?' He was troubled by the lack of acknowledgement. A few minutes ago, his wife had been in the kitchen, sat at the breakfast bar. He remembered she'd poured herself a bowl of cornflakes as he left. Peter moved towards the kitchen, continually calling his wife's name. The bowl was on the table, still half full. The chair where she had been sitting was empty, pushed out. He backed away, moving up the stairs. At the top, he pushed open the bathroom door. Empty. Further down, the bedroom door was half-open. Peter reached forward, pushing it slowly. He saw the bed made, a curl at one end of the duvet. His wife's dressing gown was hanging on the inside of the door. Peter called out again. 'Anna. Where the hell are you?' He reached into the pocket of his trousers, grabbing his phone, searching the last number he'd called and pressed the screen. He listened to the dial tone: seven, eight bleeps, then her voice, apologising for not being able to take the call. He pressed the end button and dialled again. Seven, eight, then her voice. Another apology.

Peter stepped out of the bedroom, checking the other rooms, then he walked back along the hall and down the stairs. He pushed the door to the living room. As he stood, his eyes glazed over the furniture. The three-seater sofa to his left. The flat-screen telly on the opposite wall. The long dining table which stretched lengthways across the room. Peter walked to the window and looked out. It was still dark. Above, he watched the blanket of dark clouds, formed together. Compacted and organised with no credible shape. He hated this weather.

Peter walked to the front door and pulled the lock downwards in a sharp movement. He stepped outside, then moved down the steps. As he made his way towards the back of his car to close the boot, he saw the figure, like a contortionist, her body mangled as if folded over. It looked like her face had been smashed with a claw hammer. Her mouth was open, but awkwardly so, as if it had been ripped apart. Her eyes were rolled back, only the whites now visible.

It was Anna. His wife had been murdered and placed in the boot. Peter stood, watching his wife's body. His mind raced with images, the wonderful times they'd had together. His best friend. His soul mate. Peter felt his body begin to tremble uncontrollably. He waited in the hope she'd start to move, glancing at her chest for any sign she was alive, urging for her stomach to push in and out. He knew. As he stood over her body, looking at the appalling state of Anna, he knew she was dead.

Another note lay on her body.

Peter screamed as he lifted it closer to his face.

It read: **You should have done as I asked.**

1

The Next Evening.

Matt peered into the rear-view mirror, watching his daughter as she played a game on her phone. She was unaware, her eyes a mass of concentration. He glanced again a few seconds later. Now, she wore a frown, her eyebrows furrowed, dropped deep on her face. A dull tone played out as she lost a life.

'Are you winning, Lucy?'

'No. I hate this game.'

'Lucy. Hate is a harsh word. Dislike would be a better choice,' Matt advised.

Lucy looked at her father. 'Did you dislike your old boss when you worked for that electrical firm?' she said with a cunning smile. 'I heard you call him the F word on more than one occasion when you're with mum.'

Matt laughed. 'Okay. Maybe hate is a better word than my choice of language.'

He jumped as the phone rang through the speakers. Matt reached forward and pressed the answer button on the Jeep's dashboard. 'Hey. Missing us already?'

'You don't know how much,' Nadia said.

'How's your mum?' Matt listened to his wife as she sighed.

'Well, let's say she's better. She's still sore and unable to walk. It will be sometime tomorrow when I join you both. Is Lucy okay?'

'Ask her. You're on speaker.'

'Lucy. Are you bored yet?' Nadia asked.

'I'm okay, Mum. How is Nan?'

'She's alright, baby. Nan had a bad fall, but she's alive. You can't kill a bad thing.'

Matt laughed. 'What does that mean anyway? It's a stupid saying.'

'Are you near the hotel?' Nadia asked.

Matt pinched the corner of his eyes with the thumb and forefinger of his right hand. 'Another hour, I'd say. The traffic is light. Although looking at the Satnav, it seems there's a couple of red spots further along.' Matt watched the signs. It was another sixty-three miles to their destination.

The Satnav stated just over an hour. The petrol gauge was bordering the red section. He'd have to stop soon and fill up.

Lucy was holding the phone to her face, clicking the side and posing. She flicked her long blonde hair and pouted.

'If you don't know what you look like after fifteen years,' Matt said jokingly.

'I'm playing a game,' Lucy said.

Matt steered the conversation back to his wife. 'So, you think you'll be up tomorrow morning?'

'I hope so. A neighbour is going to pop in, and it's only for the weekend. I'm sure she'll survive. You know how Mum can milk it, though. She'd have me move in if she could.'

'Off you go,' Matt said sarcastically.

'You'd never survive.'

'I'll have you know I'm a great cook. Ask your daughter. Lucy, back me up here.'

'Dad. Do you want to fall out with me this weekend?'

Matt turned for a moment. 'No. Why?'

'I won't answer the last question then. Let's say we know the smoke alarms work in the house.'

Nadia laughed. 'Say no more.'

'Right. Well, that's appreciation for you. You can walk the rest of the way if you like,' Matt joked.

He watched his daughter as she screwed her face and held her thumb to her nose, wriggling her fingers.

Matt stuck his tongue out and blew a raspberry sound.

'You two make me laugh. You'll have a great time. Make sure she doesn't have a late night. You know what she's like in the mornings.'

'I can hear you, Mum.'

'Drive carefully. Call me when you get to the hotel. I love you both so much.'

'Bye, Mum. See you tomorrow.'

'See you, Lucy Lou. Love you. Behave now for your father.'

Matt pointed in the rear-view mirror, laughing silently.

'I can hear you, Matt. Don't wind her up,' Nadia stated.

'Bye now, darling. See you soon. Love you, darling.' He pressed the end call button. Matt heard the clicking sound coming from the back of the Jeep as Lucy continued to take selfies.

'Lucy. Let's play a game. I spy.'

'Dad. That's a baby's game.'

'It is not.'

It is, Dad.'

'Isn't.'

'God. You're so annoying.'

Matt peered in the mirror and smiled. As his daughter looked at him, he forcefully turned his head away. 'I got the last look.' He listened as Lucy sighed loudly behind him.

The traffic was now heavier. The petrol needle sat at almost the last point. Matt had seen a sign a couple of miles back declaring they'd approach a service station in seven miles. He estimated another three or four to go. He listened to the radio. A presenter Matt didn't care much for argued with a caller who had dared to disagree with a point he'd made earlier.

'Dad. I'm hungry.'

'We'll get to a service station in a minute, Lucy. I'll get you something there. How is the bladder holding up? Do you need the toilet?'

'No, I'm okay.'

'Just food, huh, baby?'

Lucy smiled. 'Food would be great.' She leant against the back door and continued to hold the phone to her face. Click. Click.

'What's the pleasure in taking selfies, Lucy? I'd love to know.'

'Oh, Dad. You don't understand.'

'I think I do. You hold the phone in front of your face, pout or pull some other crazy expression and click. Don't you find it boring? Just you in the picture. I always thought a photo is more interesting with other people in it.'

'I'm playing a game.'

Matt spun the steering wheel and jabbed the brakes. He watched as a car ahead swerved from the first lane to the middle of the motorway, almost clipping the front of their vehicle. 'What a prick.'

'Dad.'

'Sorry, Lucy. But he's driving like an arse.' Matt watched the car slow down. He touched the brakes, fearful the driver was going to stop. Matt backed away, killing his speed. Without indicating, the driver in front pulled to the inside lane.

Matt watched the speedometer. Seventy-four miles an hour. He pushed the brake further to the floor. Seventy. Sixty-eight. A sign on the left instructed the service station was a couple of miles along the road. The driver was swerving in front, again, edging over into the middle lane, then back to the inside, like he was playing a game, trying to draw attention to himself. Matt jabbed the brakes further, not intending to get involved in a road rage incident, especially with his daughter in the back. He listened to the clicks coming from the backseat. Lucy, her phone held to her face, pressing the side button.

A few seconds later, the car had dropped behind. Matt focused on the road ahead, watching in the left-wing mirror as they pulled away.

'Are you okay, Lucy? Are you missing mum?' Matt tried to distract his daughter.

She placed the phone on her lap. 'Yeah. I'm worried about Nan, though.'

'Nan is a tough cookie. She'll be alright.' Matt reached forward and turned the control knob anticlockwise to mute the sound of the radio. 'Are you looking forward to our weekend away?'

Lucy paused before answering. 'Yes. I'm excited about the swimming pool.'

'I know. I gathered that.' Matt watched the car in the mirror. Another vehicle had edged between him and the aggressive driver. He glanced at a sign to his left, declaring the service station was half a mile away. Matt flicked the indicator down and moved the Jeep into the first lane. 'Right. This is us.'

The road weaved into a single lane as they passed a truck stop, the main building with fast food outlets and eventually a petrol station.

'Okay, honey. We need to be quick. I'll fill the Jeep. Are you coming inside?'

Lucy opened the Jeep door and stood on the forecourt. She breathed in the smell of petrol, watching her father wrestle with the hose as he pushed the nozzle into the back end of the vehicle. The sound of trucks on the motorway was overbearing. Lucy gawped in astonishment. 'It never seems like we're going that fast,' She stated.

'Yeah. Mad, isn't it?'

Lucy was holding her phone in her right hand, and a voice came over the Tannoy.

'Miss. Can you put the phone away? Pump two. Put the phone away, please.'

Matt looked at his daughter as she placed the phone in her jeans pocket. 'A hundred lines for you and a Friday night detention,' Matt declared.

Lucy laughed as she watched her father with the nozzle, the digits rising so fast she struggled to keep count. The meter stopped at sixty-seven pounds and fifty-three pence.

'Wow. That's a lot of money to spend in just over a minute,' Lucy confirmed.

'Welcome to my world,' Matt announced. He shook the end of the nozzle, making sure to get every last drop into the Jeep. 'Right. What do you fancy?' Matt walked towards the door, and Lucy followed.

Inside the shop, Lucy made her way towards the crisps while Matt eyed the sandwiches, grabbing a ham and cheese with a couple of days left on the best before date. He watched his daughter scanning the rows of food. She ran her hands along the chocolate bars, sweets, and then grabbed two large family bags of crisps and a tuna sandwich.

'Done?' Matt asked.

'Yeah. This will do me.'

They joined the queue. Matt was stood in front, Lucy behind, watching an elderly lady as she struggled to find the back of the reader, tapping her card awkwardly, like a woodpecker knocking its beak against a tree trunk. Matt moved forward and placed the food on the counter.

'Dad. You have to look.' Lucy was checking her selfies.

'Pump two?' the cashier asked, busy multi-tasking, leaning into the Tannoy, ordering a driver to return the nozzle fully to its holder, adjusting her seat and talking with the lady sat next to her.

Matt nodded.

'Okay. With the food, it comes to seventy-nine pounds and thirty pence, please.'

'Dad. Look.'

Matt grabbed his card, inserted it into the machine and tapped the four-digit pin. 'Honey. Wait a second.' Matt heard the beep.

'Thank you, sir. Do you require a receipt?'

Matt nodded his head. 'Yes. Please.'

'Can I interest you in a loyalty card?'

'No. Thank you.'

She handed Matt a receipt. 'Have a great evening.' The shop assistant beckoned the next customer forward.

'Dad. You have to see.'

Matt handed the sandwich and crisps to his daughter. 'See what, baby?'

She held the phone towards her father's face, balancing the food in her left hand.

Matt looked at the photo on the screen. His daughter, with her head, leant to the left, a smile on her face. In the background, the grainy shape of a motorway sign. 'Another selfie. Lucy, what are you like?'

'Dad. You need to see.'

'See what?'

Lucy started swiping from left to right. A selection of photos with her, different expressions, positions and facial features.

'Lucy. They're all pictures of you. Just you. I know you love selfies. Most teenagers do, but I don't get it.'

'But, Dad. It's a game. We all play it.'

'Who? Who plays it?'

'Me and my friends. We capture cars as we pass them.'

Matt reached for the phone, looking at the picture of his daughter and a blurry background. He started to swipe the screen.

'See. We get selfies. Vehicles we pass. We send the best ones to each other. The people in the pictures never notice. That's the best thing. When you overtake someone, I click. I have loads. We share them.'

Matt continued swiping. There were so many photos. Families, drivers alone, people smoking, others with phones balancing on their shoulders or held in front of them. Passengers in the back, sleeping, children kneeling and looking out of the windows, others so blurry that Matt struggled to make anything out. He scanned, now curious himself. As he moved back to the last photos Lucy had taken, one picture stood out. Possibly the car he'd seen earlier. The driver was looking directly into the camera, but his face was blurry.

'How good are they?' Lucy asked. 'They don't even know, that's the great thing about the game.'

Matt stared at the picture. Something didn't feel right. 'Lucy. You shouldn't do this. It's an invasion of privacy, of people's lives. It's wrong.'

Lucy reached for the phone. 'We all do it, Dad. It's just a bit of fun. Can I have my phone back?'

Matt touched the screen. He pressed his thumb and forefinger against the glass, spreading the picture to make the image wider. The driver seemed to stare at the camera. Although his face was blurred, the background was visible. Matt moved his fingers, dragging the photo and tapping to enlarge it. Then he saw it. A woman sat slumped on the front passenger seat. Her face was bloody, as if she'd been attacked with a blunt instrument: Her body, limp, lifeless.

Matt turned. The car with the erratic driver was now parked at the front of the petrol station.

Possibly the same car captured in Lucy's Selfie.

2

Present Day.

Matt turned towards his daughter. 'Lucy, get in the Jeep, now.'

'Can I have my phone? You're not annoyed, are you?'

Matt passed the phone to his daughter. 'I'm not annoyed. The Jeep. Now.'

As they walked across the forecourt, Matt forced his eyes away from the car. It was still parked by the entrance of the petrol station. An alarming figure in his peripheral vision. His daughter was standing behind him. 'Lucy. The Jeep. Move.'

Matt opened the driver's door. A few seconds later, Lucy got into the back. He turned his head, looking at the air compressor and water machine. The pumps were all vacant. The car was stationary. A gap of maybe ten yards between the vehicles. Matt was too frightened to look at the driver. His only concern was getting away, protecting his daughter.

'So, it's a good game, isn't it?' Lucy asked.

As Matt pulled out onto the road, he heard the loud sound of a lorry's horn. He stamped on the brake, realising he hadn't looked. The driver passed Matt, giving him a repulsive hand sign. Matt waited a second, eyeing his reflection in the mirror. He looked stressed. His deep blue eyes were fearful. He pushed a hand through his black hair, rubbing the stubble on his face, composing himself. He darted his eyes to the right, making sure the road was clear. 'Lucy. Put your seatbelt on, please. The beeps will just get louder. I need you to keep the last few pictures.'

'I've deleted them.'

'What?'

'The last couple were blurry. There's no point. It will clog up my phone.'

Matt hammered his fist on the dashboard. He had no proof. He hadn't looked closely enough at the car to get the registration plate. What evidence was there now? Matt looked in the wing mirror to the left of his Jeep. He saw the vehicle stationary.

As he pulled out onto the motorway, Matt sighed with relief, then pressed the screen and called his wife. 'Hey, Nadia.'

'Matt. Are you guys there now?'

'No. Another while to go yet. How's your mum?' His voice was trembling, and his hands were tense on the steering wheel. He looked in the mirror and wiped the sweat from the side of his face; the lines under his eyes appeared more evident. He continually glanced behind. The inside lane was clear. There was no sign of the car.

'She's sleeping and still in a lot of pain. How are you both? Not bickering, I hope?'

Matt stayed silent. Nadia could hear the distraction through the phone as he began to talk.

'No. We're good. Lucy. Say hello.'

'Hi, Mum.'

'Hey, Lucy Lou. Are you behaving for your dad?'

'He won't let me play music. He's listening to a boring talk show.'

'Matt. Let her play Spotify.'

'I would if there was a decent song on her playlist. Most of the singers just talk.' Matt could hear his daughter and wife laughing. Another glance in the mirror showed the inside lane clear.

'So, look, I'm going to tidy here a little, call me later. Drive carefully, Matt, okay?'

'I will. Speak later. Oh, Nadia.'

'Yes.'

'I love you.'

'I Love you too, now go on. I'm busy.'

Matt ended the call. His mind was distracted. He wondered if he had seen someone in Lucy's selfie. Maybe as he'd flicked through the photos, a shadow, a thumbprint, some kind of glitch could have caused the appearance of a woman. But he knew what he saw. The guy was staring straight into the camera. His face was distorted and pixellated. But Matt could clearly see the dead body of a woman slumped next to him. He visualised her face, the way her body was strewn across the seat. The blood. His focus returned as he heard another click. Lucy was pressed against the Jeep door in the back, taking selfies as vehicles passed in the middle lane.

'Enough. Lucy, stop this instant.'

Lucy placed the phone on the seat. She fished her arm into the carrier bag and removed her sandwich. 'How long left?'

'Not long, honey. Are you alright?'

'Well, I'm excited. We can play cards in the bar tonight if...'

Matt saw the car. It was a hundred yards behind them, moving along the inside lane. His mind had stopped processing what Lucy was saying. His heart pumped faster; his hands gripped the steering wheel tight. He watched as the skin on his forearms changed colour. Matt pressed his right foot on the accelerator, the speedometer now tipping eighty miles an hour. The car was still behind, a safe distance between them. *Come on, Matt. Pull it together. This isn't happening. How could there be a dead woman on the passenger seat? Your mind is playing tricks. You're tired. Get a bloody grip. Listen to yourself. It's crazy.* He turned around. Lucy held a sandwich in her right hand, her phone resting between the fingers of her left hand, watching a video on Youtube, her eyes focused, her smile wide. He peered out of the back window. The vehicle was still in the first lane. Matt spun his body and looked to the fields on his left. They stretched for miles. As the dark clouds enveloped, pushing a foggy bleakness, he could just about see the blanket of green. The red blotches which had threatened traffic ahead had now disappeared. The Satnav promised a clear run to the hotel. Matt needed to gain control, to pull himself out of this. His daughter was in the back, and they were looking forward to the break. A welcome opportunity to spend quality time together. Nadia would join them tomorrow. They had much to look forward to. A night at the bar, a bite to eat and conversation with his daughter.

He jumped as the car appeared in the left side wing mirror. It was now less than fifty yards from Matt and Lucy. *Shit.* Matt swiped the steering wheel and nudged the Jeep into the second lane. A truck overtook them, the force of wind rocking their vehicle. The driver shook his head like a pissed off schoolteacher. The car behind was still following, getting closer. Now in the middle lane, tailing them. *What is it with this guy?* Matt jabbed the breaks, hoping the car would pull out and overtake. As he watched it slow down, Matt hammered his foot on the accelerator. He pushed his body forward, looking at the speedometer as it rose to eighty-five. Ninety-two. Now he was almost doing a hundred. The driver behind struggled to keep up. Matt could see the car moving faster, but it seemed the driver couldn't cope. Matt was now doing a hundred and six. He knew he was putting them in danger, driving like this, but the guy behind was psychotic. Lucy had captured a selfie, the driver peering at them while the possibility of a dead body lay on the passenger seat. It was real. Matt had seen it.

'Dad. Slow down. You know I get nervous.'

Matt forgot where he was for a moment as Lucy shouted from the backseat. He jabbed the brake, watching the car close the distance between them. A sign ahead showed the turnoff they needed to take. As the car gained, Matt slowed. Again, he wiped the sweat from his brow and pushed his body further along the seat. The vehicle behind was ten feet from them. Closing in. At the last second, Matt saw their turning to his left. The single lane leading towards the roundabout. Quickly, he glanced in the wing mirror, checking the inside lane, then spun the steering wheel hard anticlockwise. Lucy fell to the side of the Jeep and her sandwich spilt onto the floor. Matt struggled to gain control as the tyres rolled over the grass. It felt like a plane landing on the runway as the tyres surged along the road markings. The driver of the car had tried in vain to hit the brakes and take the turning. But he'd missed it.

'Yes. You bastard. Yes.' Matt drove to the roundabout, pushing out a deep breath.

'What's going on, Dad? Did you not see the turning? I hate the way you drive. My food has gone everywhere.'

Matt didn't answer. He'd just saved his daughter's life.

* * *

Matt pulled over, letting the stress seep from his body. He was unsure how long he'd sat in the layby. He could hear Lucy's voice, telling him to drive. He watched as their surroundings darkened. Eventually, he pulled out onto the road and drove, his mind picturing the woman in the passenger seat, as if her image was haunting him.

They'd driven in silence for the best part of ten minutes. Matt's thoughts were plagued with what had happened earlier. He tried to get it straight in his head. Lucy had taken a string of selfies. She hadn't noticed the picture. To her, they were an array of photographs. People going about their lives whom they'd never see again. Matt had to admit it was a clever idea. He pictured the woman slumped in the passenger seat. The vision now haunting his mind. He wanted to call the police, but what if he was wrong? Maybe she was asleep. It's possible his mind was playing tricks. A hallucination. He thought about the drive, the hotel they'd looked forward to, a weekend break. He'd had a coffee before leaving the house, nothing else. He'd had an early night, a couple of beers. He'd spoken to Nadia before going to sleep to make sure her mum was alright. He told his wife he loved her. *The dead woman in the passenger seat. You saw her, Matt. Lucy photographed her. The driver knows. He's coming for us.*

Lucy managed to salvage the last of her sandwich and had now opened a bag of crisps. She leant forward. 'How long, Dad?'

The Satnav indicated that the hotel was another twenty minutes' drive. Matt glanced at the screen. 'Not long. Are you tired?'

'Nay. I'm good. I'm looking forward to the break. Oh, you know Chloe in my form?'

'Chloe. Didn't she have a sleepover recently?'

'That's her. Well, she's not talking to me. She's jealous that I'm up for head girl. It's ridiculous that some people can act this way. Why can't she be pleased instead of behaving like a petulant child?'

'I'm sure she'll get over it.' Matt watched the road ahead. It was dark; the bleakness seemed to surround them like a blanket smothering the horizon. They hadn't seen another vehicle since they'd taken the slip road towards the Cotswolds. The full lights radiated the narrow road. Dark fields stretched out either side, adding to the seclusion that Matt was feeling.

'Do you think I'll make head girl? It would be amazing. I know it's a lot of responsibility but it would help with my confidence too.'

'Lucy, you can be anyone you want to be. Don't ever doubt yourself.'

Matt swerved as they reached a sharp bend in the road. Another car came pelting around the corner towards them. Matt hit the brakes, narrowly avoiding a ditch. 'Bloody arsehole. What is your problem?'

'Dad. Language.'

'Sorry, baby. There are so many idiots on the road. Don't ever drive.' Matt placed the Jeep in reverse, moving away from the edge of the road. He looked in the rear-view mirror. The car had stopped. He could see the backlights glistening towards him. Bright specks in the darkness. He turned around. 'Lucy. Are you alright?'

'Yeah. I'm still going to go for head girl. I don't care what Chloe thinks.'

'That's the spirit.' Matt moved the gearstick to drive and pulled away.

The car behind remained stationary.

Matt couldn't help worrying if the driver from earlier had turned off at the next junction and driven back. 'It has to be here somewhere.' Matt eyed the screen. The soft voice pushing through the Satnav declared they'd reached their destination a couple of minutes ago. 'Do you think we've missed a turning, Lucy?'

'Maybe.'

'Maybe doesn't help. Did we pass any roads on the left?'

'I don't think so.'

Matt listened to the music coming from his daughter's phone. She was jabbing her thumbs on the glass, enthralled by a game.

'Lucy. Help me here.'

'What, Dad?'

'I'm not sure whether we've passed the hotel. Christ, this place is secluded.' Matt drove slowly, pushing his face to the glass. He listened to the radio: a caller had come on air to challenge the presenter on his views about Brexit. Matt turned the volume down and touched the brakes. 'This is crazy. Where the bloody hell is this place? I'm getting out. Come on, Lucy.'

'Dad. What if a car comes?'

Matt opened the door and moved to the side of the road. Lucy joined him a second later.

'So, according to the dulcet tones of Oprah Winfrey on the Satnav, we should be here.'

'Who?'

'How have you never heard of Oprah?' Matt pointed behind him. 'That's where the hotel should be. I don't see anything. Do you?'

Lucy looked to where her father was pointing. 'Nothing. I see nothing.'

Matt faced the road ahead. It was pitch black. He contemplated turning around and driving back along the road.

'Dad. I see something. Lights. It must be back this way.'

Matt turned. He watched where his daughter pointed. He saw a light in the distance. A single glint in the solitude, unique in the bleakness of where they stood. It was spreading in the darkness, pushing through, moving towards them. Matt ordered his daughter back to the Jeep.

'Dad. It's back there. Come on. Let's go back.'

Matt had a bad feeling. He watched the lights as they gained, expanding faster, eating the gap and swallowing the distance between them. His mind threw images at him, plaguing his thoughts. He envisioned the driver with a hammer resting on the floor by his feet, picking it up, leaning on the front seat, holding it above his head, the leather dented from the shape of his knee. The woman, lifting her hands, begging him not to do it. Him, raining blows as she pleaded for her life. With each swipe, the spill of blood was heavier. Splatters over the dashboard, the steering wheel, the glass. As Matt opened the driver's door, he imagined the same thing happening to his daughter. He closed the door, forcefully ripping the seatbelt and pushing it into the clip. Lucy was lying on the back seat, phone in hand, pulling at her chewing gum and swirling it around her finger. Matt started the Jeep, watching the lights gain on them, getting closer. He started the vehicle, pushing the speed, tapping his right foot between the brake and accelerator, left and right, the lactic acid building in his calf muscle. Matt reached for the clip under the rear-view mirror to dim the full lights behind. He lifted his hands to shield his face. Bushes ripped against the passenger door as he pressed further on the pedal. His hands were pulling one way and then the other, trying to keep control of the steering wheel. The road resembled a conveyor belt, rolling under the Jeep. He needed to find the hotel. Matt struggled to rid the visions in his head. The woman on the seat. He had to lose this maniac.

The car was now behind them, a gap of no more than ten feet, gaining all the time.

'Dad. Slow down. I don't like you speeding. You know...'

Matt and Lucy jolted forward as the car behind rammed into the back of them.

'Son of a bitch!' Matt screamed.

Lucy didn't bother to criticise him. 'Dad. What the hell! You need to stop. Someone hit us.' Lucy undid her seatbelt and turned around. 'Dad, we need to stop.'

'Lucy, this guy is crazy. You need to sit still.'

'Just stop the car. They've hit us. Dad, please.'

Matt could hear the terror in her voice. 'Lucy. I'm a little preoccupied here.' He hit the accelerator. At the same time, the car behind gained speed. They jolted a second time as the car hammered into the back of them.

Lucy screamed. 'Dad. I'm scared.'

'I'm not going to let anything happen to you.' Matt could hear the loud beep filling the Jeep, alerting them that a seatbelt needed fastening. Louder, now aggressive in its tone.

'Lucy. Hold tight and put your seatbelt back on.'

Matt suddenly had a breakthrough. The driver behind had backed off, ready to charge again. Further along the road, he could see a tractor, waiting to pull out onto the main road, indicating right. Matt slowed down, flashing for it to come out of the turning. At the last second, Matt hit the accelerator and went around it, leaving the tractor in the middle of the road, now blocking the car behind.

As the horns played out, Matt pulled away.

* * *

A few minutes later, Matt saw a sign for the hotel. He pulled into the car park and told Lucy to wait. If the driver pulled in, Matt had to be ready. He kept low, hidden behind a bush with a large rock in his hand which he'd found on the ground. He'd use it if it meant protecting his daughter. He listened, the sound of the engine cutting into the silence. As the driver slowed, Matt saw him. A couple of seconds later, the driver pulled away. Matt stared ahead, stunned, his eyes unable to follow the driver who'd tried to kill them. His legs felt weak, and his face was flushed. He wiped the sweat from his forehead. He struggled with the feeling of nausea. Matt had to keep it together. He waited until the sound of the engine faded into the distance.

He stood in the cold as mist drenched his face, unable to comprehend what had happened.

It wasn't so much the incident that stunned him. People were capable of anything. He knew that.

But he'd seen the car for a brief moment as it slowly passed the hotel.

Matt was certain he recognised the driver.

3

One Month Earlier.
Brighton.
United Kingdom.

'Please. Don't do this. My husband can transfer money. However much you like. Oh God, no. Let me out of here.' The woman was kneeling, her hands cuffed to a railing above her head. A dim bulb hung on a thin wire which provided adequate lighting. Enough for her to see. She was alone, mumbling to herself. She eyed the white walls: the paint, patchy from years of neglect, flakes had gathered in one corner where damp had set in. She was cold, hungry, her head ached. The dull pain which had worked from the top of her head along her face was now throbbing. Every heartbeat caused the ache to intensify. She pulled her hands down in a sharp motion, feeling the burn on her wrists. She twisted her body, pulling ferociously, then screamed. Her voice bounced off the walls of the basement like a distant noise, muted, like a remote cry. The room was insulated. She knew as she called for help, her voice sounded peculiar. She may as well be in a coffin, six feet underground.

* * *

She recalled walking home through the town centre earlier that morning, taking in the sea air, the taste of salt strong on her lips. The sound of seagulls screeched above as they followed her along the path, searching for food. It was early, and she found it comforting. She gazed over the horizon; the sea was calm, a blanket of stillness, like a tranquil layer, spread out in the distance. The sun began to push through the clouds, and the warmth felt good on her tan skin. Adriana had taken a stroll to The Lanes; with its narrow cobbled streets, a mixture of shops, cafes and restaurants, it was her favourite place to visit. She purchased a loaf of bread and a box of doughnuts. After gazing in a few shop windows, Adriana walked back towards home.

She and her husband had been in Brighton for almost a week. They'd saved up, illegally entering the United Kingdom from Albania, packed in the back of a lorry. The journey was harrowing, but the promise of a better life was too good to pass up. They were staying in an area called Whitehawk, in a small house with other couples and single women with children. The conditions were poor, but they were told they'd find work. The men who'd shipped them over had contacts. Everything would work out. Adriana was willing to make a better life with her husband. This was the dream; all they'd talked about for so long.

Adriana spoke good English, and, before meeting her husband, she'd worked as a part-time model. The pay was appalling, and she'd been treated badly, but at least she saw parts of the world she'd never usually get the chance to visit. She'd done everything from modelling beachwear to the catwalks at small fashion shows. In her early twenties, she'd been offered large sums of money to pose for erotic magazines, but it wasn't what she wanted through fear of it biting her on the arse at a later date and causing embarrassment to her family. She was thirty-two, happily married and still completely breath-taking. Eventually, she'd left the modelling business. The sleazy men with their hands everywhere, treating her like a piece of meat was too much. She dreamed of moving to the UK and eventually having children. Now, she was going to live that dream.

As Adriana turned into the road, a few seconds from home, a van pulled up. Adriana ignored it at first. As she walked, she heard the sound of the window being opened, then a voice, rude, harsh. The driver asked for directions. The streets were empty, and, although she felt vulnerable, Adriana stopped. She turned towards the guy. He wore a leather jacket; his brown hair was short and receding at the sides. His face was round, almost swollen looking, and his skin was rugged. He had a light stubble shaped in the form of a goatee beard. It was like his eyes were hidden, buried under his fat cheeks. As she moved towards him, she noticed a scar along the left side of his face. The next sound was the side door sliding open. A man placed a cloth bag over her head and lifted her into the back of the van. She heard the screech of the tyres as her world sunk.

* * *

They were still in Brighton. Adriana was positive they'd driven no more than five or six minutes. The men remained silent. They were careful, stringent in their behaviour. They'd planned this carefully. A sting which took much organisation. As the van came to a halt, Adriana heard the side door opening. She remembered hearing a voice, the instructions clear as one of the men pressed a sharp blade into her back. She felt the point digging into her skin and almost piercing it.

The guy spoke in an English accent. 'One false move, just one, and we'll visit your home. We'd hate for something to happen to your husband.' As they stood outside, he repeated her address, the street and the door number. They knew everything. Adriana was led along a car park, a man on either side, their arms placed on her back and pushing her forward. She heard the sound of metal shutters opening. Adriana sensed she was standing in a large room, possibly a warehouse. She heard the buzz of a refrigerator, extractor fans and the whirring of machinery. Adriana struggled to breathe. The cloth hood stank of old socks. She tried vigorously to push it from her mouth with her tongue, the foul odour filling her lungs. She could feel the cold, salty tears running down her face, resting on her mouth. She ran her tongue over her top lip as a door opened, hands shoving her from behind. Adriana placed her arms in front, swiping the air like a swimmer trying to perform the front crawl in an empty pool. She felt sick. Her stomach was churning, and her skin seemed tight. She'd never felt more frightened. She could hear one of the men stepping in front of her, taking her hands, holding them tight. She stood, feeling appalled, her body tense as the man guided her.

'Mind the steps.'

Adriana lifted her leg, moving down, carefully feeling for the next step. She counted eight in total. Anything to occupy her mind from this nightmare. At the bottom, the man let go of her hands. Another door opened, and they shoved her into a room. She froze, biting hard on her lip. Her body was shaking, and she fought the feeling of claustrophobia which drenched her mind as she waited for the next instruction. Her body was tense, ready to fend off the blows, preparing herself. The cloth hood was removed from her head. The driver of the van was standing in front of her.

Another man stood by the door. He was taller, much skinnier and bald, except for the cluster of hair at the sides of his head. He kept watch, looking through the small square of glass towards the top of the wooden door.

The driver of the van forced Adriana onto her knees, cuffing her wrists and securing them to a large piece of iron which was around a foot long and had been bolted to the corner of the wall.

* * *

Now, Adriana was alone. 'Somebody help me. I need to get out. Hello? Can anyone hear me?' She tugged hard on the cuffs, desperately ripping her arms towards the floor. She urinated. It stung her thighs as the warm liquid seeped through her jeans, down her legs and onto the cold concrete. She pictured the sea, hearing the waves gently roll to the shore, caressing her feet. A stroll along the beach, her husband, placing his hand in hers, the warmth of the sun, uplifting, enhancing their energy. Adriana began counting, a distraction from the feelings that frightened her. An escape. She'd almost reached two hundred when the sound of a door handle interrupted her. She closed her eyes, screwing them hard and held her breath. Adriana listened as the footsteps came closer, fingers now touching her face, caressing her cheeks, moving further down towards her neck. She pushed out a breath, held it, more counting in her mind, waiting for whatever it was this person wanted. After a minute, the man brought his hand from her neck to her long black hair. He listened to her whimpers, the loud breaths while he stood close.

'This has taken a lot of organisation. We've been watching

you for months. We've planned everything meticulously. I must say, you're even more beautiful in the flesh. You're going to make us a lot of money. It's time. My brother and I have been waiting. The anticipation was painful, the days and weeks were quite a drag, but you're finally here. Please settle, make yourself at home. I'll be back later when we know the plan. Oh, one more thing. If you try to escape, we'll have no hesitation in killing you.'

    The footsteps became distant, and the door closed.
    Adriana was alone.

4

Present Day.

Matt stood by the entrance of the hotel, clutching the large piece of rock to defend himself and his daughter. The grounds at the front were well lit: spotlights provided enough for him to see. Matt turned and saw Lucy in the backseat of the Jeep, looking out of the window towards him. Her face was adorned with confusion, and she seemed to call out, mouthing words he couldn't hear. Matt waited; the sound of the vehicle had faded to silence. He sprinted towards the Jeep and opened the back door.

'Dad. Why don't you call the police? That person banged into our Jeep. They can't do that.'

'I will when we get inside. Lucy. I need you to be quick. Grab your bag, and let's go.' Matt moved to the back of the Jeep, assessing the damage. The bumper was cracked, and the metal dented. 'Come on. We need to hurry.'

Lucy got out of the back seat and followed her father as he moved away from the Jeep. Matt grabbed his phone and dialled Nadia's number. The screen displayed eleven digits and then crashed. 'Damn. The reception is dreadful.' Matt walked along the gravel footpath leading to the main entrance. 'Lucy. Stay close. Don't leave my side.'

'I'm fifteen, dad. Not five.'

'I need you to stay with me.' Matt listened to the huffs behind him. He glanced back towards the Jeep parked to the side of the entrance. The road was clear. As they walked towards the front door, another spotlight shone against the beautiful white building. Matt saw the bar to their left. A man was seated at a piano, and diners were conversing. He needed a drink now, more than ever.

To the right of the main building, he saw a spa. A list of treatments displayed on the window. The smaller building claimed to have a heated swimming pool. He'd choose a hot tub every time. The roof was thatched a light brown colour with a half door leading inside. He assumed it was locked for the night.

Matt and Lucy made their way inside Pembroke House. They instantly felt the warmth of the large space. Matt glanced at a rack towards the main desk filled with flyers, advertising day trips and tempting people with boat rides, local zoos and amusement parks. He made sure Lucy was close and moved towards a woman, tapping her manicured fingers on a laptop keypad; her nails were painted red and appeared to glow.

'Hi. My name is Matt Benson. This is Lucy, my daughter. We have a reservation.' Matt listened to the piano. A familiar jazz song filled the room, bringing a sudden calm over him.

'Benson, you say?' The woman had a high pitched voice, which resembled a squeak.

'That's correct. My wife will be joining us tomorrow morning.'

'Ah, yes. Here you are. Two nights. Three of you. Room twelve on the second floor. You can take the lift. When you come out, turn right, you'll find the room further along the hall to your left.'

Matt repeated the instructions out loud. He watched the woman smile at his daughter.

'Welcome. You'll find lots to do here. Let me know if there's anything you need. The restaurant is open until 10pm. The last sitting is 9.15pm. The bar is open all night.'

Matt glanced at his watch. It was just gone eight. 'Thank you,' he offered.

The lady passed two cards across the desk. 'Tap and go. Place the card in the slot when you enter the room. Enjoy your stay.'

'Do you have the WIFI password?' Matt asked.

'Oh, wait.' The woman grabbed a small piece of paper and scribbled the letters and numbers down. She passed it across the desk. 'I'm afraid it's not great. We've been having trouble with the reception the last couple of days.' She looked towards Lucy. 'Besides, there's too much to do here. Why spend it on the internet?' She smiled, and Lucy smiled back.

Matt moved to the lift, keeping his eyes on the front door.

He was watching for the driver.

* * *

Matt and his daughter were standing in the hallway on the second floor. He pressed the card against the security tab, and the door gave a loud, clunking sound. Matt pressed the large, silver door handle down and they walked into the room. It was adequately sized, with a king-size bed and a small foldaway one further along the floor. To the left was a bathroom, with a white toilet, bath and shower. All standard. Lucy raced across the room and dived onto the bed. Matt sat on the edge, his body jolted as his daughter bounced.

'Aren't you a little old for that?'

Lucy laughed and Matt was envious of her energy.

'I need to call your mum.' Matt pressed re-dial. Again, the eleven-digit number displayed. The screen froze. Matt turned the phone off, watching the screen become blank. A minute later, the white Apple symbol appeared. He dialled again. The same thing happened. 'For Christ sake. This is ridiculous.' Matt sat on the bed, staring at the phone. He tried Nadia's number once more, then placed the phone back in his pocket. 'Lucy, let's grab a bite to eat. Are you hungry?'

'Silly question, Dad. What's going to happen about the Jeep?'

'Lucy, I don't want you to worry.'

'But the driver hit us from behind. Twice. What if they come back? You hear these stories. Maniacs on the road. I'm scared.'

'Lucy. I'm here. I'm not going to let anything happen. Your old man can handle himself.' Matt smiled.

'I don't see you as being tough.' She smirked.

'How do you see me?'

'An old man who thinks he can handle himself but is nothing more than a big softy.'

'There's a compliment there somewhere.'

Matt walked to the window and looked towards the road. There was no sign of the car which had followed them earlier. Had he seen a woman in the passenger seat? He thought. Matt recalled the arrangement of photos on Lucy's phone. The guy, staring at the camera, his face a blur and fuzzed-out of the picture. He'd followed them to the hotel. Why? Did he know what Matt saw?

They left the room and turned out the lights.

Outside in the hallway, they walked side by side. Matt was anxious. He hated not being able to call Nadia. The receptionist had said the WIFI could be down all weekend. Matt would need to drive along the road until he found a signal. But the driver could be waiting.

Further along the hall, they heard the ping of the lift. The doors slid open; a rough clatter gave the impression it wasn't safe to use. Matt stopped. He removed the phone from his pocket, holding it in the air. The WIFI sign flickered and then faded on the screen. He stepped backwards, hoping it would rectify itself.

'Dad. I think someone's hiding behind the wall.'

Matt looked down at his daughter. She was staring ahead, watching towards the lift. 'What do you mean?' Matt asked.

'You heard the lift, right? I've been watching. No one got in or out. While you were trying to call mum, I saw someone, standing by the doors. They saw me looking and turned to the side. It's like they're waiting for us.'

Matt glared towards the lift. Lucy's fear was now playing off on him. 'Really, Lucy? Why would someone be hiding?'

'Dad. Someone is there.'

Matt looked to the screen of his phone one last time, then placed it in the back pocket of his jeans. He glared towards the lift. The rooms on either side were closed. The hallway was still, as if the place were deserted. As Matt began to walk, Lucy followed.

'Is anyone there?' Matt didn't expect an answer. 'Hello?' He had to prepare himself. If Lucy had seen someone, Matt would need to deal with it. Again, he called out. 'Hello?'

The lift door opened, the rolling sound caused them to jolt. Matt stopped, seeing the doors close a few feet from where they stood. The sign above the lift doors displayed the ground floor.

It was possible Lucy was correct.

* * *

Matt and Lucy were standing by the doors. Lucy pressed the button to her right and called the lift. They watched the digital display above, still on the ground floor. They waited, Matt, shuffling impatiently, moving from one leg to the other. He looked behind, watching the empty corridor. He felt uneasy as the lift began its climb to the second floor. As the display showed number two, Matt grabbed his daughter's hand and raced to the stairs.

'What's wrong, Dad?'

'I think this is a better option. I don't fancy getting stuck for hours.' He opened the door leading to the fire escape. Matt smiled to ease Lucy's tension. As they moved down the steps, Matt looked behind them; someone was standing by the lift doors, looking both ways along the corridor.

They reached the ground floor and walked into the main reception area.

The woman was still behind the desk, tapping away on the laptop. She glanced towards them, then looked back to the screen. Matt looked towards the front door. He wanted to go and check if the car was outside but didn't want to explain his thought process to Lucy. She'd worry. It wasn't fair. If the car had pulled into the hotel, the driver could be waiting. It wasn't safe. Matt jumped as a man in a smart suit approached.

'Are you dining with us tonight, Sir?'

Matt spun around. 'Yes. Two of us.'

'We have a table by the window if you'd like to follow me.'

Matt wanted to call the police, but he needed to make sure Lucy was safe. He couldn't chance her hearing the call or leaving her alone. He had no proof of what he saw. And besides, he didn't want her worrying.

As they entered the restaurant, they could smell the scent of garlic, fried chicken and onions. The waiter showed them to the seats. Matt sat down and watched him pull out a chair for Lucy. He returned a minute later and took their drinks orders. Lucy asked for a diet coke, and Matt had a beer.

Lucy watched her father. 'Dad. What's going on? Are we safe?'

The question stunned Matt. His face flushed, and he played with the edge of the tablecloth. 'Yes, Lucy. Why do you think we're not safe?'

Lucy poured her drink into a tall glass. She took a sip, then questioned her father. 'Dad. You're acting; I don't know, weird.'

Matt swigged his beer. 'What do you mean?'

'Someone hit our car as we arrived here. You didn't even get out to check the damage. Or get the driver's details. You've been on edge since we arrived.'

'Lucy, there's nothing wrong. I won't let anything happen to you. I didn't think it was safe to stop. You know what people are like. Anyway, it's just a little damage to the bumper. I can get it fixed.' Matt watched as Lucy dropped her head and began tapping on her phone.

'Let's enjoy tonight. Mum will be up in the morning. I don't want you to worry about anything, Lucy. I'll always have your back. You know that!'

Lucy looked up from her phone. 'Huh?'

'Oh, don't worry. It's just great to be here with you.'

'I know. Although I wish mum was here too.'

Matt smiled, feeling a little unappreciated.

* * *

The waiter returned and passed them both menus. As they chose the food, the piano player took his seat and began playing Van Morrison's *Moondance*. Matt glanced at his daughter, watching as she placed her phone on the table. 'So, what do you want to do tomorrow?' Matt asked.

'I'm going to get up early and swim.'

'How early?'

'Around eight. I'll wake you if you like.'

Matt noticed a couple sat at the next table. The man smiled as if to say, good luck with that one.

Matt returned the silent communication with an upwards glance, looking for pity. 'I'll see how I feel. It's a bit early, Lucy.'

'How is it early?'

'We're on holiday.' Matt checked his phone. The signal was blank. He needed to talk to Nadia. 'Lucy. Can you come with me for a second? I'm going to go outside and see if I can call mum.'

'Dad. It's cold.'

'Lucy. Please. We'll only be a minute.'

Matt stood and walked to the front door of the restaurant. Lucy followed. He informed the waiter that he needed to make a call.

As they stood outside, Matt held the phone in front of him, waving it in the air like he was taking part in a game of fencing.

'It's freezing. Can I go back inside?'

'Lucy, I want to let your mum know we got here safe. Can you be a little patient?' He heard her tutting. As Matt moved the phone around, he walked along the path towards the car park. The small lights planted along the ground illuminated the gravel footpath. 'Sod this. I'll ask at reception.' As Matt put the phone away, he noticed a car, parked close to where they stood. A BMW. The front bumper was damaged. Panic rose through his body. He turned, facing the front door of the hotel. The couple from the restaurant were leaving. As they passed, the woman smiled, and Matt returned the gesture. He could smell her perfume as they walked to their car. Matt glanced back, watching the BMW. He debated going over, taking a look. Matt edged from one leg to the other, watching the vehicle, twenty yards from where they stood. He couldn't let his daughter realise his fears. 'Lucy. Back inside. Let's go.'

'Thank God.'

They walked to the reception desk. The woman behind the counter had stopped tapping on the laptop and was now sorting out a filing cabinet. She walked towards Matt.

'Can I help you?'

'I need to use your phone. It's an emergency.' Matt insisted.

The lady looked around as if checking to make sure no one could see her.

'We're not supposed to do this. Make it quick.' She opened a small door at the end of the desk and let Matt and Lucy into the back office. Then she handed the phone to Matt and walked to the front desk.

Matt dialled his wife's number. He listened as it went to voicemail. 'Damn this.' He hung up, then dialled again. After the fourth attempt, he left a message. 'Hun, we're at the hotel. I need to talk to you. You can't call because there's no WIFI. We're fine. Lucy's fine. Everything is fine. I just need to speak to you. Call the hotel and ask for me. I'm not going to bed for a couple of hours. Love you.' Matt hung up.

He stared at the phone, contemplating calling the police. He couldn't. There was no proof. The BMW had hit them from behind. Twice. Matt had watched the driver as he slowly passed the hotel. How would it look if the police arrived and

Matt had wasted their time? He imagined them laughing, mocking him.

One for the boys back at the station. What's that? The guy was driving, with no attempt to hide the dead body in his car. Yeah, that's a good one, mate. Where's the proof? Oh, your daughter deleted the picture. How convenient. Have you been drinking tonight, Sir? Been on the old juice, have ya?

Lucy would freak out. She worried. Matt backed out of the office, thanking the woman at reception.

'Are we going to eat now? I'm starving.'

Matt looked towards the front door of the hotel. He wanted to grab Lucy, get in the Jeep and drive far away from here. Now, a BMW was parked outside, possibly the same car that hit them earlier. What could Matt say to his daughter? How could they leave? She'd been so excited about coming here.

Matt and Lucy returned to the restaurant. As they made their way to the table, the waiter moved towards them. He looked irritable.

'Are you ready for your food?' He glanced towards the clock. The piano player was finishing up for the night, gathering his music sheets and placing them inside a folder.

'Yes. Sorry, I had a bit of an emergency,' Matt instructed.

A few minutes later, the waiter returned with the food. A fillet steak cooked medium for Matt, and a cheeseburger for Lucy. The waiter placed the food on the table, then returned a minute later with a plate of chips.

'Enjoy.'

Matt watched him walk towards the kitchen. 'Well. Tuck in, Missy. It looks great.'

Lucy turned the bowl of chips on its side and spilt them onto her plate. 'So, I'm going swimming tomorrow. I'd love you to come, Dad. It might help you relax.'

'Not too early, though. Give me a shout at about eleven.'
Matt watched as Lucy frowned.

'What are you like?'

As Matt forked the steak into his mouth, he saw the door swing open. The lady behind the reception desk was walking towards them; her name badge bounced with every step.

Matt watched the slight concern on her face.

'Mr Benson.'

'Yes. Has my wife called?'

'No. Can I sit for a moment?'

Matt pointed to the seat. 'Of course. What's wrong?'

'I think you should know. A guy came to the desk a couple of minutes ago. As a family left for the evening, he slipped through the main doors and made his way to the lift. I called over to him as he seemed lost. He asked about you and your daughter.'

Matt hesitated for a second. 'What did he ask?'

The receptionist stared at the wall for a moment, then turned her eyes back to Matt. 'He wanted a key to your room.'

5

One Month Earlier.

It seemed like hours since Adriana had been taken off the street, a hood placed over her head, thrown in the back of a van and locked in the dingy basement. Her arms ached from being bound above her head. The rough concrete floor made her knees hot. Her jeans were damp, and she needed the toilet again. The smell of urine was becoming unbearable. Adriana moved her arms, twisting her body to try and get warm. She crouched, then pushed her body upwards. Adriana managed to hoist her body so far before the position of her arms stopped her. The pain was too much. She pulled hard, yanking her wrists away from the handcuffs, feeling sharp pains in her hands. She whimpered, calling out. 'You bastards. Let me go. I beg you, let me fucking go. I haven't done anything. Why are you doing this?' Slowly, she dropped to her knees, the strain becoming intolerable. She swung her head, feeling her black hair as it brushed her shoulders. She spat heavily on the ground as more bile filled her mouth.

Adriana went to wipe the drool from her full lips. For a moment, she'd forgotten her predicament. She knelt, her arms raised awkwardly, wondering if she'd die in this room. She recalled her journey to England from Albania. She and her husband had believed everything would be better. A better life for them. Her modelling days were over, money was scarce, and they were desperate. They'd lived in poverty. No bath or shower. No access to running water. They'd moved to temporary sheltered accommodation due to severe floods. The harsh winters and heavy snowfalls meant their village was isolated from main roads and stable food supplies. She remembered her husband walking through the door, the smile on his face, the belief in his eyes as he told them it was finally happening. Life was going to get better. Their bags had been packed for days, ready for this moment. The journey had been harrowing. They were loaded into a lorry, contained like animals and told not to speak. Thumps on the side of the truck, men laughing, the noise of the engine as they'd tried to sleep.

She'd heard others, whispers in the darkness.

Now, Adriana knelt, the stones cutting into her jeans, the damp, cold feeling around her groin. She turned her body slightly as the door handle jolted. A man walked towards her. She heard his calm breaths, like he was strolling along the beach on a warm day. He lifted a small glass to her lips, tilting it, watching the water flow into her mouth and the sound as drops hit the concrete floor. He looked into her deep brown eyes, her soft skin, her elegant cheekbones and full, shapely lips. Christ, she was breathtaking, he thought. He'd never seen a more beautiful woman in his life. He briefly contemplated dropping his jeans, pulling her into him, pushing himself inside her. He couldn't. If his younger brother saw, he'd kill him. He struggled to fight the stir building in his pants.

Once the glass was empty, Adriana spoke. 'Please. You have to let me go. I can't be here. I have a husband. He'll be worried sick. You can't do this to me. I'm begging you.' Adriana screamed.

The man watched her, like he'd watch a bird in a cage, intrigued, observing, understanding her mannerisms, her characteristics.

Suddenly, he grabbed her around the throat, his grip tightening, watching her face go red. It looked as if she'd explode at any moment. Then he moved away, edging towards the door.

Adriana listened as the door opened, and a moment later, he was gone.

* * *

At around 3am, Adriana heard the door to her room swing open. Although uncomfortable, kneeling on the floor in her own urine and petrified, she'd briefly slept. Her eyes opened, and she scanned the room. Adriana searched for her husband, confused for a moment. It took her a second to realise where she was.

She listened to the sound of footsteps approaching, the heavy, wheezing noise in her ear. Adriana eyed the man standing in front of her, wanting to spit in his face but fearing the consequences.

He reached into the back pocket of his grubby jeans. His shirt was tight around the waist, and the bottom half of his belly was on show. He coughed without covering his mouth, and Adriana could smell stale cigarettes and coffee from his mouth. He lacked patience as he fiddled with the lock of the cuffs, moving the key and groaning while he struggled to unlock her.

'Keep still,' he ordered. His accent was English, but Adriana hadn't been here long enough to distinguish where exactly it was from.

Once her hands were free from the cuffs, Adriana dropped her arms and felt the sudden rush of blood. She was lightheaded and fell forward, the palms of her hands now placed flat on the floor.

'Get up,' the man instructed.

Adriana pulled her body upwards and balanced on her knees. She felt his arm clutching her, pulling her to her feet.

'We're going to bring you upstairs. If you make a sound or call for help, we'll hurt you.'

Adriana needed to know why she was here. What they wanted with her. She had so many questions, but fear stemmed her mouth from forming the words. She stood and felt his hand push her, making her stumble forward. He was aggressive, destructive in his actions, and Adriana knew she'd have to follow the orders.

They stood in silence, waiting for the lift. Adriana glanced above without moving her head, watching the digital display as the lift approached. They stepped inside, and she looked at herself in the mirror. She was unrecognisable. Her reflection was like a different person. She noticed the dark circles under her eyes, the mascara, now a mass of smudge, like a child had coloured her face with a crayon. She looked tired with fear, worn out. She pulled her face away from the refection, and the doors closed. The man was silent as he faced away from her, staring at the floor. He was tall, skinny and menacing in his actions. The same man who earlier, sprung from the side of the van and placed the hood over her head.

A minute later, the lift opened. They walked along the dingy corridor until they reached the last room on the left.

The guy pressed a card to the lock, and it clicked loudly. He beckoned for Adriana to enter the room first. Wow, this guy is forever the gentleman, she thought.

Once inside, Adriana watched him standing at the entrance. He didn't enter the room, which indicated he might leave. A welcome relief.

'Get some sleep. Don't do anything stupid. Do you understand?'

Adriana nodded without answering.

The guy backed away.

Adriana stepped further into the room as the door closed behind her.

She fell onto the floor and wept.

* * *

Adriana woke with a jolt at just gone 7am. She'd slept after sobbing alone on the bed. She still wore her urine-stained jeans and a jumper, smudged with vomit, that she'd dressed in early yesterday morning when leaving the house. She lay on the bed covers and turned to the man standing in her room. She instantly saw the scar along his cheek: the driver of the van who had called out to her yesterday.

He waited a couple of seconds before starting to speak. 'A lot of planning has gone into this. It's taken months to find the right person. We've been watching you. Making life difficult for you and your husband back home. The man who entered your place at night, the home invasions, forcing you out. We've planned everything. We could have taken a local woman. Someone from Brighton, but imagine the press here, the coverage. We can't go through that again. It's easier this way. No one will miss you. You should feel honoured. I hope you're settling in okay. How is the stay so far?'

'Fuck off and leave me alone.' Adriana regretted the words as soon as they left her lips.

The man moved towards her, quickly removing the large belt holding his jeans up. He lifted the belt in the air and struck Adriana on the left side of her back, the buckle hitting against her skin. He lifted the belt and brought it down again.

Adriana writhed in agony. She crawled along the bed, pushing her hands over the edge and her body slowly dropped to the floor. She'd never felt pain like it.

'That's the last time you'll talk to me like that. If this disrespect occurs again, I'll kill you. Do I make myself clear?' Again, he lifted the belt above his head, ready to bring it down. He watched Adriana on the floor. She turned her head away, nodding.

'We have some very wealthy clients waiting for you. Businesspeople. Investors, lustful gentlemen who have sexual urges.' He grinned. 'You are going to make us a lot of money. This operation has been planned meticulously. No stone has been left unturned. We have no choice. It has to go this way. Once it all runs smoothly, there will be more joining you. That's the plan. You work for us now.'

Adriana pulled herself back onto the bed. She thought about the man her husband had talked about. The promise of a new life. Was this the outcome the trafficker had in mind for them all along? A trap?

'You will rest until you're called. We'll get you a selection of dresses, jewellery and shoes. We need you looking your best. Until then, get some sleep. The first client is expecting you at 7.30pm. You will not be late.'

Adriana watched as the man calmly walked out of the room.

* * *

Adriana spent the day like a caged animal. She paced back and forth, watching the front door, listening for any movement in the hallway outside. Earlier, she'd tried to open the windows. Black steel bars stopped her from reaching the glass. She'd tried desperately to push her hands between them and bang the window with her fists. It was pointless. Opposite, she saw the empty beach, the calm water and deserted horizon. She imagined summers here, families building sandcastles, standing on the water's edge as the sea caressed their skin, lapping their toes. She envisioned her and her husband, walking along the shore, the sound of the ocean as it pushed closer. They'd walk, further into the blue sea, water covering their bodies, reaching their waist. Later they'd go onto the pier and buy fresh doughnuts, candy floss, maybe get their fortune read and spend a few pounds in the arcade. They'd go to a restaurant, then finish the evening with a drink outside one of the trendy bars.

Now, as Adriana looked out of the window on the fourth floor, she saw a dull grey. She shivered at the thought of how lonely and bleak October was here. The sky was dark, a hideous overcast which drowned the light.

She paced along the concrete floor, muttering to herself. The room was dull, lacklustre.

She jumped as a phone rang from across the room. Adriana walked towards it and held the phone to her left ear. She recognised the voice instantly, the same man who came to her room this morning and had struck her with the belt. His fat face and piggy eyes, his frame, small, stout, the smell of his leather jacket as he beat her. His tone commanded respect as he spoke, slow and deliberate.

'Two men will come for you at exactly 5.45pm this evening. They will have clothes, shoes, perfume, makeup, everything you need. You will take a shower now and get dressed in your new clothes when they arrive. You will leave with them no later than 7pm, where they'll take you to a restaurant. You'll meet a top client of ours, a business investor, and you'll be friendly and courteous with him. You'll answer anything he asks, and you'll flirt. Whatever he wants to do, regardless of what he asks, whether he wants to swim in the ocean or to take photos while you stand on your head, you'll tend to his needs. You will spend the night together and again; nothing is off-limits. You'll wear a wire, and we'll hear everything you say. Do I make myself clear?'

Adriana stood, listening to his voice. She had to escape. She felt sick, vulnerable. Her chest suddenly became tight, and her cheeks flushed with the rush of blood. His instructions were sinister. Adriana could never go ahead with this.

Again, the caller asked the question. 'Do I make myself clear?'

'Yes,' she answered.

* * *

She stood in the bath, the phone call playing out in her head. Her shaking hand reached for the shower hose, and she immersed herself in the heat from the water. She washed, then wrapped a towel around her body. She used a smaller one to hold her hair in place.

At 5.45pm, she heard pounding on the door to her room. She checked the towel was tight enough not to drop and then let the men inside. She could feel their eyes scanning over her body. The tall, lanky one who had dragged her into the van held a small case. She hadn't seen the other man before. He was medium height, good looking and spoke with a Spanish accent. The tall guy with the case placed it on the floor, clicking the lock on each side and opened it out.

Adriana reached down, pulling out the clothes.

'There are enough to choose from here. Make sure you look good. You'll find something to fit,' the lanky guy instructed. His accomplice remained muted.

Once she'd dressed and applied makeup, the Spanish guy opened the front door. The other one pushed her from behind. They walked along the communal hall, keeping silent.

The lift brought them to the basement. They linked her arms, one each side of her and led her through the warehouse and out to the car park where a black van waited. Lanky man sat in the driver's seat and started the engine while the other man opened the side door.

Adriana kicked off her heels and raced barefoot through the gates and onto the road. She screamed,' Help me. Somebody, please help.' She glanced behind, watching the two men running towards her.

Adriana raced along the pavement and onto the road, swinging her arms frantically, bemused as drivers steered around her. She listened to the horns, desperately trying to stop vehicles. 'Help me. I've been kidnapped. Someone, please do something.'

A couple watched from the pavement. They waited for a second and then kept walking.

The men caught up with her. Lanky man gently placed his hands on her shoulders and waved his arms in the air. 'Sorry. She's our sister. She suffers from delusions.' He stated. No one was watching.

They calmly steered her back to the hotel car park and towards the lift.

They kept quiet. Adriana pulled her body sideways, tugging from their strong grip. As they reached the fourth floor, they steered her towards her room, opened the door and pushed her inside. Adriana fell onto the bed, crying. She screamed and then pounded the covers. A moment later, she heard the door close. As she turned, she realised the men had left.

* * *

It was gone 9.30pm. Just over two hours since her attempted escape.

Adriana lay on the bed; the blanket was pulled up to her face. Her whole body shook with fear. As she looked around the room, the front door opened. She pushed her body up and leaned against the headboard. She watched as the scar-faced man entered the room. He seemed to be the one in charge of this operation. This morning he'd beaten her with a belt. Earlier, he'd phoned with instructions. She doubted he was bringing room service.

'I want to show you something.' He made his way to the large flat-screen telly on the wall opposite where Adriana was lying. He grabbed the remote control from the dresser, fiddled with a couple of buttons and then a room appeared. The layout was identical to the room she was staying in.

Adriana watched, wide-eyed at the empty space. She kept silent. The guy sat on the end of her bed, and she listened to the whistling noise coming from his nose as he breathed. She was too frightened to ask what was happening. A minute later, she saw the front door open. For a moment, she thought it was her room as she looked around, then focused back on the screen. Lanky man was standing by the door. He waited, as if expecting someone to join him. Suddenly, another person appeared, moving into the room as Lanky man held the door open. Adriana leant forward on her bed, her mouth open. She watched as they started talking.

The other man was her husband. She could hear their conversation as her husband began to speak.

'I can't thank you enough. How did you find her?' he asked.

'She was wandering the streets earlier, dazed, confused. We got her into the car and brought her here. She's safe. A little confused, but she'll be fine.'

'Can I see her?'

'Of course. I'll get her now. Wait here.'

'Thank you so much. I've been worried sick. Thank you.'

'There's no need to thank us. Anyone would do the same.'

Adriana watched Lanky man leave the room. She heard the door close. Her husband was standing alone. As she observed the live recording, Adriana clutched her hair, hearing her husband repeat the words, over and over to himself as he paced the floor.

'Thank you, thank you. Oh, thank you.' He waited impatiently, shuffling from one foot to the other, biting his knuckles with anticipation. Suddenly the bathroom door towards the back of the room flung open and a large figure in a ski mask appeared. She watched her husband turn, confusion adorning his face as the person in the ski mask ran towards him.

As her husband fell backwards onto the floor, he shouted, 'No. Oh my God, no.'

The person was now standing over her husband. They produced a large machete from the back of their jeans and began stabbing her husband in the chest. A few minutes later, she saw the intruder, stood still, glaring at her husband's blood-soaked body. Adriana's husband had been butchered to death in front of her.

6

Present Day.

'A key to our room? What are you talking about?' Matt, Lucy and the receptionist were sat in the restaurant. 'That's what he asked me.'

Matt glanced past the woman and towards the reception desk. The foyer was empty. 'What did he look like?' Matt asked, concerned that Lucy could hear the conversation.

The woman leant back on her seat. She was dressed in a black jacket and skirt, a white blouse and flat, black shoes. He looked at her badge.

'Mary. Tell me what he looked like?'

'Erm, he was tall, taller than you, I think. He had glasses, black, thin-framed. He had greyish hair and about your age. That's all, I think.'

'What else did he say? Have you seen him before?'

'Nothing else, and no. I don't remember seeing him here.'

'Where is he now? Did he leave?' Matt asked.

'Yes. I told him I'd call the police. He walked out through the front door.'

'Okay. Thank you so much. I appreciate your help, Mary.'

As the woman walked away, Matt realised his fears.

Mary had described someone Matt knew well.

* * *

Matt sat in the restaurant, trying to figure out what to do. Lucy had just finished dinner.

'Who's looking for us, Dad?'

Matt pushed his plate to the middle of the table. 'No one, Lucy. I think she's confused.'

'Dad. What the hell is going on? Talk to me.'

'Lucy. Don't worry. Whoever was asking for a key must have us mixed up. It happens. Right. Shall we go to the room? You can watch telly for a while. I'll keep trying your mum.'

Matt and Lucy made their way out of the restaurant and stood by the lift.

'Wait a second, Lucy.' Matt walked over to the desk.

The receptionist looked up. 'Can I help?'

Matt leant across the desk. 'Are you on all night, Mary?'

'No. I'm leaving in ten minutes.'

'Who takes over?'

'No one. I leave at 11pm. That's it until tomorrow morning at 6am.'

'How can people come in and out?' Matt asked, pointing to the main doors.

The woman sighed at the barrage of questions. 'If someone is staying here, a guest, I mean, they can tap their key on a pad outside the front door. That will give them entry to the hotel. It's different during the day, but this system is in place at night.'

'Is that the only way?'

'Well, unless someone slips in the door with a guest. But it's quiet. Everyone has left the restaurant. I think the bar is empty too.'

'Thanks for your help.' Matt walked back to the lift. He pressed the button, and the doors opened a few seconds later. 'Wait. Stay there, Lucy. I need to check something.'

'Dad. What the heck?'

'I'll just be a second.' Matt ran to the front door, pushing it hard and then moved along the path. The BMW with the smashed bumper was still parked outside. He needed to check. As Matt walked towards the car, he heard his daughter's voice.

'I'm going up, Dad. I'm not waiting.'

Matt turned. 'Lucy. Give me a minute. Please.'

'I'm going.'

Matt stopped. He was a few feet from the BMW. Their Jeep was further towards the front of the car park. There was no one else around. He couldn't let Lucy go upstairs on her own. 'Wait. I'm coming.'

A minute later, they were stood by the lift. Lucy pressed the call button. As the doors opened, Matt watched the receptionist going out through the front doors. Suddenly, he felt alone. They stepped into the lift, and, as the doors closed, Matt watched over the empty foyer. A few seconds later, the lift stopped on the second floor. Matt stood out in the hallway, glancing along the bleak corridor. An automatic light sprung into action as they walked side by side. As they reached the room, Matt pressed the key to the lock, and he opened the door. 'Wait a second. I need to take a look.'

'Dad. You're frightening me.'

Matt turned to his daughter, placing his hand on her shoulder. 'Honey, I won't let anything happen to you. That's a promise. Just wait by the door.'

Matt moved forward. First, he checked the bathroom to their right. He walked in and pulled the shower curtain back, staring at the plain white tiles and the electric shower. There were no other hiding places. He stepped out backwards, walking further along the room. He checked each side of the beds, the cupboards, the small storeroom with the electric water heater, and finally pulled the curtains back, checking behind them. 'All clear,' he confirmed.

Lucy was staring at her phone. 'Dad. Look. The WIFI is back on.'

'No way. I'll call mum. Great news, although I don't know how long it will last.'

Matt listened as Lucy's phone began to ping. He watched her smile as she looked at her messages loading.

On his phone's display, he saw three missed calls from Nadia. Matt breathed a sigh of relief. He dialled her number, and she answered on the fourth ring.

'Wow. I've been worried sick,' Matt announced.

'Oh, Matt. You know I'm here. I tried to call. Mum's asleep, and I'm just about to go up myself. Is everything okay?'

'Yeah. We're good. Can't wait to see you.'

'How's Lucy Lou?'

'Hang on. I'll put it on loudspeaker. Lucy. Mum's on the phone.'

'Hi, Mum. See you tomorrow. I miss you.'

'Are you having a nice time?'

'Yeah. It's lovely here. Dad, tell mum about the weird man.'

Matt eyed his daughter, shaking his head. He didn't want Nadia worrying. 'Oh. It's nothing. I'll tell you tomorrow. Just a strange guy, acting a bit creepy, you know. Give your mum a kiss, and we'll see you tomorrow. Love ya, Nadia.'

'Love you both too. See ya.'

As Matt pressed the end call button, he saw a shadow under the front door. The automatic light would only come on if someone was in the corridor. He quickly looked towards Lucy, who was sat on her bed, texting on her phone. Matt stood and made his way across the room. The shadow was still there. He could see it moving under the gap. He waited a few minutes, then grabbed the door handle, thrusting it down and pulling the door open. He stepped out to the corridor. The light was off. Matt waited, listening. Then he closed the door and twisted the lock.

He moved back along the room, keeping his eyes on the front door. 'Lucy. Everything alright?'

'Yeah. I'm just talking to a friend. I'm telling her about the hotel.'

'Excellent.' Matt turned on the telly and flicked through the channels. He saw an old western with John Wayne, a horror film from the Scream franchise and a dating show. He placed the telly on mute. As Matt watched the front door, his mobile phone rang from a withheld number. Matt debated whether to answer. 'Hello?'

The voice was deep and chirpy. 'Hi. Mr Benson?'

'Yes, speaking.'

'It's one of the night staff at reception.'

Matt hesitated for a second, immediately feeling suspicious. 'What are you talking about, mate? Mary said the desk isn't staffed through the night.'

'Oh. That's strange that she'd say that. She's new, so maybe she got confused. Anyway, sorry to ring so late. We've had a small blip with the booking and the computer has crashed. It's just a health and safety procedure. How many of you are staying? I understand it's Mr and Mrs Benson and your daughter. Am I right?'

Matt answered impatiently. 'Just me and my daughter tonight. Look, I don't appreciate being called so late.'

'Okay. Thanks for clarifying that. Sorry to have bothered you. Sleep well.'

The phone went dead.

Matt lay on top of the bed. Something was bugging him about the phone call. Something didn't feel right. He glanced at his watch. It was gone half eleven. It was late. Too late for someone to call about a health and safety matter. He remembered the conversation with Mary earlier. She'd told him that no one worked at the desk overnight. Matt stood. 'Lucy. I'm going to take a look downstairs. Don't answer the door to anyone. Do you hear me?'

'Dad. Why would I answer the door?'

Matt walked over to Lucy and kissed her on the head. 'I'll be back in a few minutes.'

* * *

He walked along the communal hall. The automatic lights turned on. The doors on either side were closed. He approached the lift to his left and pressed the call button, deciding at the last second to take the stairs. He couldn't risk getting stuck or announcing he was coming. Matt pushed the bar and moved down the two flights of stairs. Once he reached the ground floor, he walked out to the foyer. The restaurant doors were closed, and the lights were off. He placed his hands against the glass of the doors, looking inside. Matt turned, facing the front desk. Slowly, he walked over. As he stood, watching the empty desk, he suddenly felt weak. He reached his hands forward, leaning against the counter.

The person who'd called a few minutes ago sounded as if they were putting on a voice. A disguise to put Matt off. What had he told them? He tried to remember the conversation. The person said the computer had crashed. Okay, nothing strange. He'd asked how many were staying in the room, something about health and safety. Matt had presumed it was in case of a fire. Why had he given this information? He was caught on the hop. *Just me and my daughter tonight.* That's what he'd said.

Matt began beating himself up inside. He should have put the phone down, asked to meet the guy face to face. Why had he answered the question without clarifying who the caller was?

As Matt walked over to the entrance and out along the path, he heard the screech of wheels. The black BMW was pulling out of the car park. Matt raced towards it and watched as the driver drove out onto the street. He stood, trying to figure out what was going on. Matt was certain he knew the driver. But surely it couldn't be him. His mind must be playing tricks, hallucinating.

Matt waited for five minutes, stood alone in the cold. Then he went back inside.

* * *

He opened the door to the room and saw Lucy texting.
'You okay? Sorry, I had to check something.'
'I'm fine. We still have WIFI.'
'Well, how good is that, Lucy? We're being totally spoiled on this break.'
Lucy laughed.
Matt opened Facebook and posted on his wife's timeline: *Can't wait to see you tomorrow, Nadia. I hope your mum is feeling better and it's not too cold in High Wycombe. Give her a kiss from me. Love you, Baby.*
He signed off with three kisses.

* * *

It was just gone midnight. Matt had drifted off to sleep. His phone rang from the bedside cabinet, and he reached to his left, pawing his hand on the table. Matt sat up and glanced at the screen. He saw the name, "Sean," written in large letters, one of his best friends since school. Matt pressed the answer button. 'Wow. 'I've been trying to call you. What's going on, Mate? Is everything okay?'

'No. We need to talk, Matt.' Sean's voice was loud and agitated.

'Okay. Can't it wait until the morning?' Matt went on to tell Sean about the BMW, what he may have seen on the passenger seat and how the driver followed them.

'Christ, Matt. Okay, I'm deadly serious. You need to listen. Sorry it's so late. I just saw your Facebook post. You need to take it off.'

'What's going on, Sean?'

'Take the post down. Now. Quickly,' Sean screamed.

Matt looked across at Lucy. Her sidelight was on, and she was talking; her voice was low.

Matt opened the Facebook app. His post had six likes. He also had a DM from Sean. He scrolled to the top of the post and pressed delete. 'Do you want to tell me what the hell this is about? I've called you numerous times over the last few weeks after the lad's weekend away in Brighton, and now you ring at God knows what time with some shit about a Facebook post.' Matt waited as Sean composed himself.

'Peter was here last night,' Sean announced.

'Peter Simpson?' Matt felt numb at the mention of his name. He pushed his body upwards and stepped out of bed, then moved into the bathroom. Peter Simpson was one of Matt and Sean's oldest friends. It was also Peter who Matt suspected was driving the car earlier with the dead body in the passenger seat.

'Where's Nadia?' Sean asked.

'We're away. Lucy and I. She's joining us tomorrow. Her mum's had a fall.'

'You don't know what happened in Brighton, do you?' Sean asked.

'Brighton. For the meet up a month ago? Yeah, I thought it strange how you all left without waiting. Then you don't answer your phones. I was beginning to feel a little paranoid.'

'Matt, listen to me. You need to go to Nadia. You need to leave now.'

'Why? What's wrong with Nadia?'

'Peter Simpson has gone off the rails. None of us are safe.'

7

One Month Earlier.

'Here's to old friends.' Matt was holding a glass in the air, beer spilling around the edges. One by one, his friends lifted theirs, and they clinked them together, followed by raucous screams.

Matt continued, his voice loud. 'Peter Simpson. Billy, the mechanic.' The guys laughed. 'Sean Carney, and of course, me. To old friends. And quantities of alcohol. Let's do this.'

They had gathered at The Blair Hotel in Brighton. A trip that was long overdue. They had decided to start early at the hotel bar, then spend some cash at the casino. The guys were all married now, apart from Sean who, when asked, jokingly claimed he was still testing the water with Mia. They'd lived together for seven years, and although serious, they hadn't moved on from the boyfriend, girlfriend stage. The guys came to the conclusion he was too tight to buy a ring. The four friends had been best mates since school.

'Where did you park that heap of a truck?' Matt directed the question to Billy.

'It's parked out the back. Why?'

'Aren't you embarrassed?' Matt responded jokingly.

'Not in the slightest.'

Matt looked at Billy's large hands. He'd never seen them without oil stains or cuts. Tonight was no different.

'How are things with you and Lydia? All going swimmingly?' Matt asked.

'Always, mate. That woman has tamed me.' Billy answered.

Matt rubbed Billy's head. 'Yeah. I doubt that.'

Peter and Sean were deep in conversation. Matt watched his friends who were sat opposite. Peter was more reserved nowadays. He'd worked hard, moved up the ranks and was now the boss of a car showroom or, as Matt liked to call him, Chief bullshitter. He was happily married to Anna, but Matt felt sorry for them. Peter often referred to Matt's relationship with Lucy and how he'd love to have the same bond with his daughter, Phoebe. Matt always thought he'd be a good father, but a wedge had been driven between Peter and his daughter in her late teens. Peter disliked the way her partner spoke, the way he treated her. When Peter confronted Phoebe, she packed her bags and left home. As far as Matt knew, he hadn't heard from her for a couple of years, but she'd recently been in touch to heal their broken relationship. Peter adored Matt's daughter, Lucy, and always gave her money when he visited. He and Matt spoke weekly.

Matt watched Sean, a gentleman, great company and a good listener. He cared, asked questions, and was always concerned with how Matt's family were doing. Matt considered Sean as his best friend. He watched him, remembering the early days and how he had envied him. He was taller than Matt, more sporty and oozed confidence. He still had thick brown hair, deep green eyes and looked much younger than his forty-three years. Matt recalled the first day Sean had arrived at Saint Teresa's. The start of the second year in infant school. While other kids had ignored him, Matt welcomed him with open arms, sharing his packed lunch with him on that first day. Sean still mentioned it, how Matt had looked out for him from the beginning.

Tonight was going to be amazing. The friends had looked forward to the get-together for so long.

Sean downed the remaining contents of his beer and reached for a whisky chaser. He lifted it, then threw the contents down his throat.

'Sean. It's a long night,' Matt reminded him.

'I intend on having a long queue of drinks too.' Sean lifted another small tumbler from the tray in front of them. He clicked glasses with Matt. 'Thanks for organising tonight. I've been looking forward to it for ages. I've missed you guys.'

'I've missed you too. How's the new house coming along?' Matt asked.

Sean and Mia had been renting a two-bedroom flat in Hammersmith, West London and managed to get enough together for a mortgage to buy their own place. They chose to remain in the area, and, although expensive, it was vibrant, exciting and boasted one of the biggest shopping centres in Europe.

'You need to visit again soon. It's been a couple of months. Hammersmith is where it's happening.'

'We will. Nadia and I will come for a night.' Matt stood up. 'Right. You all ready to spend some cash?' He watched the anticipation as his three friends stood.

***

The casino was bigger than they'd imagined: every gambling station you'd expect. As they entered the large room, a waitress approached with a tray of champagne. All four men grabbed a glass.

'Now this is the life,' Peter declared. He pushed the stylish Ace and Tate glasses further up his nose. 'You'll have to show me how to play roulette. I'm not a gambling man.'

'It's all a matter of luck, Peter,' Matt explained. 'Just place your chips down and hope for the best.' Matt looked towards the poker table. A woman stood behind a low counter, dealing cards to three men who were sat with stern faces, concentrating, peeling the end of each card to glimpse their hand. 'You ever play poker, Peter?'

'I'm afraid not. Snap is about where my card skills end. Although once, I did lose a game of snap to a guy who had a stutter.'

Matt looked at Peter, seeing the smile on his face, unsure whether to believe his story.

A few minutes later, they were seated on black stools, watching the roulette wheel. As the ball spun around, the croupier called, 'No more bets.' A few seconds later, she announced, 'Red, twenty-three.'

They watched as piles of chips were placed for the next round. One guy, dressed in a tuxedo, was covering as many squares as possible.

Billy leant forward. 'How the hell can he win money? He's placing more down than he could make.'

Matt watched. 'Maybe that's the point of this game? Cover as many options as possible.'

A minute later, the guy pounded the table with his fist and walked away.

'See. I told you. It's a long game.' Billy reached behind and grabbed another glass of champagne. He threw it back in one. Then, he leant forward and piled four chips on number fifteen.

'That's it? Just one number?' Matt asked.

'It's only one number that will win.'

They laughed as the croupier called out, 'Black, number four.'

Billy huffed loudly to vent his frustration and grabbed more chips. He began to spill them on the table one by one in front of him, then picked them up, repeating the action.

'What are you doing?'

Billy smirked at Matt. 'It's what you do, Matt. Look professional, my friend,

I've seen them on telly. It gives you an edge, makes you appear to look threatening, a professional.'

Matt laughed. 'I think you're talking about card games, Billy. A tactic to knock people off their game. You're not playing anyone at roulette. It's just you and the numbers. No competition, like the lottery.'

Billy dropped the chips. 'Oh I am. See, I get pissed off when I see someone walking away with winnings. It's me against every other person on this table. I love the challenge.'

'You haven't changed, have you?' Matt declared.

'Not me. I'm a winner, Matty boy. Always will be.' Billy tousled Matt's hair, then placed his arm around him and pulled him close. 'Love ya, Matty boy.'

Billy watched as a couple walked over to the table. He nudged Matt. 'Christ, would you look at that?'

Matt shot the couple a look. The guy was around six foot. He had grey hair, combed over to the left. His face was a contortion of lines, thick-set wrinkles with hollow cheeks, like he'd had the air sucked out of him and he'd deflated too much. The lady wore a bright red dress; her plunging neckline revealed ample cleavage. Her waist was slim, and her hips curved. Her dress was slashed to the waist, showing her long, toned legs. She didn't so much walk as glide, as if floating across the room. Her dress swept behind her and her high heels revealed red soles. Louboutin's. She had extravagant taste and oozed sophistication. As she turned, her shoulder-length black hair swung elegantly. She looked towards Billy, smiled and then stood at the table.

He smiled back, struggling to control his emotions. She was a vision, a fantasy that Billy would struggle to invent, and he wanted her, regardless of the consequences.

The couple stood side by side. As the gentleman placed a pile of chips on the table, covering a quarter of the numbers, she looked towards Billy, biting her top lip. She smiled, holding her gaze for a couple of seconds. Billy smiled back, trying to control his legs from collapsing and his body dropping to the floor.

Easy, Billy. You got this. Deep breaths. It's in the bag already. Slam dunk. Home run. Away we go. He turned to Matt. 'I have to talk to her.'

'Who?'

'Red dress lady. I've never seen anyone more beautiful.'

Matt laughed. 'Are you mad? The guy she's with looks like a proper gangster. For one, they're together. Look, he's holding her hand. They're an item.'

'Light work. How's that an obstacle?'

'Number two, you have a beautiful wife. Lydia. You can't do that to her,' Matt insisted.

Billy took a sip of his drink. 'What happens in Brighton.'

Matt finished the sentence. 'Stays. Yeah, I know. But not this. I've come to meet three of my oldest friends and get pissed. That's it.' Matt noticed how the woman stared across the table. Billy had always been extremely handsome with his smouldering brown eyes and chiselled jaw. He resembled Tom Hardy. He'd kept himself in shape, and Matt had been envious of his looks. He remembered when they first started going to pubs and clubs in their late teens and how women flocked around him. But he thought Billy had settled, that he was happy. Obviously not.

Sean had ordered more drinks, and Billy was putting them away. The more alcohol he consumed, the more he stared across the table. He was building the courage to go over and talk. The only problem was, how could he do it with her partner beside her?

The breakthrough came at just gone 11pm. Matt had got down to his last few chips. A woeful evening of gambling. Billy had broke even. He glanced across the table. Grey-haired gangster man lifted his hands and announced he'd had enough.

Billy watched as he gently took the lady's hand. *Shit. That's it. The chance is gone. I don't know what you see in him. He must have a massive...* Billy's thoughts were interrupted as the woman in the red dress pulled her hand away. The guy was shouting, dragging her by the arm. He grabbed her left wrist, but she ripped her hand away. Gangster man turned towards the table, adjusting his tie and walked out. Billy waited a few minutes. The roulette wheel spun, he listened to the ball as it bounced, the cheers ringing out around the table as people leant forward, taking their chips, the clink of glasses in celebration. His friends behind him were talking about leaving. For Billy, he hoped the night had just begun.

* * *

Billy and red dress lady were deep in conversation. His friends had gone over and tried to coax him back to the hotel bar, but he refused. He'd never been so captivated in his life. He had one thing on his mind, and nothing was going to deter it from happening.

It was almost midnight. Red dress lady stood. 'So, are you going to invite me back for a coffee?'

Billy stood, and they left together.

His hotel room was on the ground floor. Billy had a key to the back door. He knew if he walked through the bar, he'd never live it down. He had to avoid his friends. They stood in the cold as he opened the door and let the woman through first. Billy went to the mini-bar, and, as he turned to ask what she wanted to drink, she'd already slipped out of the dress and stood in her bra and knickers. Billy paused, taking in her body. He'd drank so much that she became blurry. He staggered as he moved towards her. As he got closer, he could see her. The object of every desire he'd fantasised about, stood in his bedroom, wanting him. He pulled her close and kissed her hard on the lips. She reached forward, tucked her hands inside his shirt and ripped it apart, listening to the sound of buttons as they hopped on the floor. She reached down, undoing his trousers and slid them down his legs. Billy was kissing the side of her face, pulling her closer. He pushed his body against hers, kissing her hard on the lips, the warmth radiating from every pore as they fell onto the bed. As Billy kissed her neck, gently sucking on her skin with his lips, she slapped him hard around the face. He stopped, feeling the burning sensation, his face numb with pain. He hadn't had anyone act like this before.

She whispered, 'Be fucking rough.'

As Billy placed his hand on her shoulders and entered her, she slapped him again. Harder this time. He pulled out, struggling to find the courage and ask her to stop. As she lay on the bed, she grabbed Billy's strong hands and wrapped them around her neck.

'I want to feel your power. My desires come from strength.'

Billy got on top of her and entered her once more. She

placed her hands on Billy's as he gripped her neck, squeezing as hard as she could. She thrust her body against Billy's, panting. 'That's what I like. I want to feel helpless, worthless. I want you to stop me breathing, stem the airflow as you fuck me. Do it.'

Billy squeezed harder. He felt pressure, uncomfortable with her demands. Her hands were placed on his, like a vice as he pushed himself deeper inside her.

'Harder. Crush the airflow. Squeeze your hands harder around my throat.'

She threw her head from one side to the other like a possessed animal. Billy felt her hands grip his, tight, tighter as he crushed her neck, pressing as firmly as he could. Suddenly, she stopped moving. The room swirled, his eyes, unfocused and blurry. He stopped and pulled out. As he leant forward to see if the woman was alright, he saw her eyes were rolled back. Billy forced his fingers against her skin, pressing deep, searching for a pulse, anything to show she was breathing. She lay motionless, limp. Her body, still.

Billy's world became blurred. He rubbed his eyes, trying to focus, hoping it wasn't real. He turned on the bed and faced the door, sensing his life coming to a halt. It felt like the room was closing in on him, ready to break him at any moment. He charged towards the bathroom, turned on the light and held his head over the toilet. As he vomited, he felt a migraine work from the top of his head and begin to spread across his face. He stood up, glancing at his reflection. Panic raced through his body. Billy turned on the tap at the sink and splashed cold water on his face. He composed himself, glancing again in the mirror, then made his way back to the bed. He stared at the body, his head aching like never before, his eyes stinging from the mixture of water and sweat.

Billy had killed her.

* * *

Matt, Peter and Sean were sat in the bar of The Blair Hotel in Brighton. It was open all night, and they intended to make the most of it.

Sean signalled to the barmaid for another round of drinks. They'd moved to pints of lager and double shots.

'Sorry, Sean. I haven't had the chance to speak properly this evening. It's been chaos. How are you and Mia? Any wedding bells or babies on the horizon?' Matt asked.

'Well, you know me. I don't make decisions in haste. I need time to contemplate. To make sure she's the right woman. As for babies, I don't know. They scare me. But joking aside, Mia's great. She started a new job, four days a week. A law firm, assistant to one of the hot-shot solicitors. She enjoys it. The money helps too. What about you, Matt? Still the second-best electrician in London?'

Matt laughed. 'Who's the first?'

'You're looking at him,' Sean smirked.

The barmaid appeared at the table with another tray of drinks. She placed them in the middle and moved back to the bar.

'How's your lot doing?' Sean asked.

'Good. I told you that Nadia lost her father, didn't I?'

'Yes. Bless her. How is she coping?'

'Well, it's her mum that's suffering more. She's on her own.'

'Sorry to hear that. How's Lucy?' Sean saw Matt's eyes light up at the mention of his daughter.

'Lucy's amazing. An old head on young shoulders. That little lady will break my heart. She's into netball at the moment, and she's made the school team.'

'Isn't that like basketball, but you can't move? How the

hell does that work?' Sean laughed. 'Wow. Good on her. That's great news.'

Matt reached forward and swallowed the drink in one go. He was tired. The excitement of the evening had caught up with him, and the room began to spin. He'd drunk too much, and although it pained him to leave, he needed sleep. 'Guys, sorry, old lightweight here is calling it a night. I have to go. Let's have breakfast tomorrow. Around 8am?'

Matt listened to his friends' pleas to stay as he walked towards the door and made his way to the room.

Sean and Peter finished the drinks and ordered more. They were in it for the long haul.

Sean looked at Peter. 'So how did you fare at the roulette table?'

'You know, I think I broke even...'

The men turned towards the door. Billy was standing at the front of the bar. The look of horror on his face was undeniable.

Sean stood. 'Are you joining us for a drink?'

Billy didn't answer. He stared past his friends, his mind preoccupied and unable to process what had happened.

'Billy. Come and join us,' Peter shouted.

Billy walked slowly towards the table. His mouth was open, his eyes lifeless. As he reached the table, he grabbed a small tumbler, downing it in one. Then he grabbed another and repeated the action.

'Slow down, son. It's a long night,' Peter stated.

'You have to help me.'

Peter and Sean looked at each other; confusion adorned their faces.

'Has she pegged you out already?' Peter asked.

Billy eyed his friends. 'I need your fucking help.' He spat the words out, which made his sentence more effective.

'What's going on, mate?' Sean asked.

'You have to come. Now. Where's Matt?'

'He's gone to bed. Should we wake him?' Peter asked.

'There isn't time. Oh, Christ. Hurry.' Billy was panicking as he moved from the table.

Peter and Sean stood, the chair legs screeching against the floor, and they followed Billy to the door. The three of them walked towards Billy's room in silence, along the dark corridor, past the toilets and stood outside his room.

Peter broke the silence. 'Listen. I'm not into any kinky shit, so if you want us to watch, that's not happening.'

Sean laughed. But the tension in the air was unnerving. Billy removed the card from the back pocket of his trousers and tapped it against the reader. The door clicked. The three men stepped into the darkness as the door closed.

'I'm so sorry.' Billy pawed for the light, and the guys stood together, looking towards the bed.

The woman had a blanket placed over the lower part of her body to cover her modesty. Her neck was awkwardly twisted to her left side.

Peter was the first to realise. He jumped onto the bed, feeling for a pulse. Then, he placed his hands underneath and lifted her up. 'She's dead. She's fucking dead.' He turned to Billy. 'What the hell happened here?'

'I don't know. I'm not into it. She was one of those kinky kinds. She started slapping me and things.'

Sean moved around the bed. He sat on top of the duvet and placed his head in his hands.

Billy continued. 'We were having sex. She wanted it rough. I was uncomfortable. I stopped. Then, she pulled me close. As we carried on, she grabbed my hands and placed them around her neck. Something about asphyxiation making her orgasm more intense. I've read about it. She squeezed her hands around mine, tight around her throat. She wanted me to crush her. She threw her head one way and then the other. I didn't mean for this to happen.'

'We need to go to the front desk. Tell them what has happened.' Sean moved towards the door and opened it.

'Sean. Shut the door now. Shut it. We need to think,' Peter ordered.

Billy stood alone towards the back door. 'I can't go down for this. I can't. I have a baby on the way. Lydia's pregnant.'

Peter turned towards his friend. 'Congratulations. However, I can think of better circumstances to tell us. Billy, I'm sorry. We have to call the police. It's the right thing to do. You'll say it was an accident. That you didn't mean for it to happen.'

'I didn't,' Billy sniped.

'I know. Come clean. Dial 999,' Peter insisted.

'I'm not doing it. I can't go to prison.' Billy began pacing the room.

'Billy. You are,' Peter ordered. 'You do it or I will.'

Billy paused; he scanned the room, looking at the shocked faces glaring back. He was desperately trying to get through to Sean and Peter. 'I'll deny it. I swear to God. I'll say it was all of us.'

Peter jumped off the bed. 'You bastard.' He punched Billy hard in the face, and the two men grappled, then fell onto the floor. Sean pulled them apart.

Billy tucked his shirt back into his trousers. 'You're all here. The place is covered with your DNA. I promise, if I go down for this, you're all coming with me.'

Peter realised that Billy was serious. It was his word against theirs. Peter had jumped on the bed and felt for a pulse. He was part of it now. 'You son of a bitch. You've always been the same. You can't keep it in your fucking pants. You've always been a self-centred bastard, taking what you want without a fucking thought for others or the consequences.'

'I'll do it. I swear. If anyone calls the police, I'll bring you all down.' He was sobbing, his tear-soaked eyes focused on the dead woman in his bed.

'What was that?' Sean asked. They all peered towards the door.

'I didn't hear anything?' Peter moved across the room, dropped to his knees and listened. The sound of a door slammed in the distance. Sean went to talk, and Peter silenced him. 'Wait. I can hear voices. Keep quiet for a second. What if a member of staff opens the door, or someone has heard us?' Peter thought back to the scene on the floor, moments ago, him and Billy fighting. The voices in the hallway were closer, becoming more apparent. Peter turned. 'We need to move fast. I think someone is coming.' Silence fell over the room as someone passed the door. The footsteps stopped outside the room. Peter pushed his body against the door to prevent it from being opened. 'We need to do something. We're going to be caught.'

'Should we bring her out to the car park?' Billy asked. 'I'll load her in the car, and we can dump her body.'

'Have you completely lost your mind? Carry her out to the front of the hotel for everyone to see? We have no choice. It has to be the garden. There's no other way.'

Sean opened the back door.

'Where are you going?' Billy asked.

'To find a shovel.'

* * *

Peter and Billy pulled the woman off the bed. Her legs slammed on the floor, and they dragged her across the room and outside.

Sean had found a bin shed with gardening equipment. He grabbed a pick and a couple of shovels.

The three men now looked across the garden at the back of the hotel. There were no security cameras, no spotlights and the curtains were drawn in the other rooms.

Peter pleaded with Billy and Sean. 'Guys, you can't do this. It's inhumane. Think about what you're all doing.'

'Grab her legs, Sean'. Billy placed his hands under the woman's shoulders, and they carried her across the grass.

Peter watched from the back door as the horror unfolded. The woman was slumped on the cold ground, her dignity crushed. Billy was digging, swapping every few minutes with Sean. Once they'd dug a deep enough hole, Peter joined them, and the three men turned the woman on her side and dropped her into it.

Half an hour later, her dead body was buried under the soil.

* * *

The following morning, Matt ate alone in the restaurant. He'd rang the others and decided to leave them to sleep when they didn't answer. He sat at a table next to the window, looking out at a side street, sipping a latte and biting into a crusty bacon roll with lashings of brown sauce, unaware of what had happened after he went to bed. When he'd finished, he called his three friends once more, then decided to leave.

An hour later, Billy, Peter and Sean met in the car park, their shame forcing them to remain silent. They'd skipped breakfast. Food was the last thing on their minds.

Peter broke the ice. 'We need to talk. People will be looking for her. Someone is going to find out what you've done.'

Billy placed his hands on Peter's shoulders. 'I'd have done the same for any of you.'

Peter felt numb. He wanted to kick the shit out of his friend for what he'd brought to the night.

The three men got in their vehicles. Billy followed behind Peter and Sean. Billy stopped suddenly, realising he'd lost his phone. He reversed into a parking space, watching as his friends pulled out onto the road, the cars going in different directions. Billy stepped out of his small truck and made his way around the back of the hotel. He hadn't seen any other guests. A couple of cleaners were wheeling trollies, walking together. They smiled as Billy edged past them. As he made his way to the back of the hotel and looked to the mound where they'd buried the woman, he saw someone standing where they'd dug the hole.

* * *

Billy remained silent. It had been almost three weeks since that fateful night, and he'd heard nothing from his friends. He'd watched the news obsessively, every breaking story, every headline. There was nothing about the dead woman in Brighton. Billy managed to put it to the back of his mind. He watched his wife, Lydia, as she blossomed, her bump enlarging, the beautiful baby growing inside her. They'd been together for almost two years. Matt, Peter and Sean knew Billy was a player and swore he'd never settle down. Billy had been on a golfing weekend in Portugal with a close friend, Carl, who lived in the North of England. They'd played a round of golf and then finished the day off with a couple of drinks in the local bar.

As they sat, sipping ice cold beers, a group of women came in and ordered Margaritas. A couple of drinks later, Billy summoned up the courage and joined them, coaxing his friend over a few minutes later. Billy was captivated by Lydia. They hit it off immediately. He was even more enthralled when he found out Lydia was also from London, and they too were on a golfing weekend. They spent the evening chatting, flirting, eye contact and laughing together. As the evening drew to a close, Billy asked her back to his room for a coffee with sex as his aim. She refused, making him wait a month before he could share her bed. Although her rejection perturbed Billy, deep down he knew Lydia was a keeper.

Now, he listened as Lydia came down the stairs. She was sore this morning. Her frame was arched back, and she struggled to walk. Billy pulled out a chair, sitting his wife down at the table. He walked to the kettle, filled it with water and turned on the switch. He watched her, seeing her rosy cheeks, her beautiful skin, her eyes, a deep green.

'Did you sleep alright?'

'No. I was tossing and turning all night. How about you?' Her phone rang before Billy could answer. She looked down, 'No Caller ID,' written across the screen. 'Hello? Who's speaking? Sorry? No. It's not Billy's number. I'm his wife. Who is this? I said I'm his wife. How can I help you?'

Billy reached forward.

Lydia passed him the phone. 'He wants to talk to you.'

Billy placed the phone to his ear. 'How can I help?'

The voice was deep and calm. 'You need to take this outside.'

Billy stood, his face flushed as he thought back to that night.

'I can't hear him. I'll go to the front door.' He leaned forward, kissing his wife on the head.

Billy opened the front door and stepped outside. 'Who is this?'

There was a pause. 'I know what you did. Hang up, and

it's over. You'll go away for a very long time. I have the proof. Footage showing what you have done.'

Billy felt the blood drain from his body. He turned around; his heart felt like it had accelerated to treble the speed. His legs dropped slightly, and he placed his hand on the wall to stabilise himself. Billy opened his mouth to speak, but the words refused to spill out.

'I'll be in touch.'

The phone went dead.

8

Twelve Hours Before Lucy Took The Selfie.

Peter stood on the street. The boot of his BMW 8 series was open. Again, he screamed as he stared at the dead body of his wife. He'd let this happen. He should have taken the threat more seriously. It had been one month since the terrible incident in Brighton. Peter had tried to cope; he'd kept what had happened from Anna. He'd braved it out. When his wife had asked him about the weekend away, he'd given short, blunt answers. He recalled the questions.

'So, how was it? You must have some stories to tell, at least? How was Matt? I love him. Did Sean get pissed? I hope Billy behaved himself? I know what he's like when he's had a drink.'

Billy. Peter scrunched the paper in his hands. He reread the note while staring at his wife's dead body.

You should have done as I asked.

'No. No. No. This can't be happening.' Peter stood on the

street, looking across at the closed curtains opposite, boiler flues pushing steam from the side entrances, houses warming as the central heating came to life, showers spilling warm water over tired bodies. Clouds rising into the cold air. He dropped to his knees on the dirty ground. The pain was a brief release.

Peter knelt, holding his head in his hands, pulling at his face. He stayed in the same position for what felt like hours. Finally, he stood, composing himself. He wiped the dirt stains from his trousers, brushed himself down and tried to work out what to do. He knew calling the police was out of the question. A half-hour ago, he'd had breakfast with his wife. A ritual they'd performed every weekday morning. A coffee together, conversation, he'd walk to the front door and place the scarf around his neck, push his arms into his jacket and return to the kitchen. Anna would ask him what time he'd be home. She'd pour a bowl of cornflakes; he'd kiss her gently on the head, grab his neatly packed sandwiches and then walk to the front door. As he'd close it, he'd shout that he loved her. Peter would wait for her reply before closing the front door and heading towards his car. He was always the first of the residents up and out.

Now, he realised he'd never share breakfast with Anna again. He'd never laugh with her, hold her, discuss their interests or lie in each other's arms. He wiped the tears from his eyes, recalling the first phone call he'd had on his way to work.

One Week Ago.

He'd driven through the dark streets of London, LBC radio on in the background. It was a morning much like any other, a typical journey to work, muggy, wet and as tedious as hell. Occasionally he liked to listen to music. His playlist compiled mostly of jazz and old school funk. Today, the topic of conversation was Brexit. Peter was a Remainer. It felt like he'd cast his vote so long ago. Nothing had moved forward. As he drove, he saw the lights of the shops and cafe's gleaming in his side vision. He heard the sound of shutters being open as he sat at traffic lights; he watched the piles of newspapers loosely strapped outside shops and placed on top of each other. The radio show had gone to a break. Peter often wondered what they did as adverts played. A nip to the loo, an off-air chat with friends, a quick call home to make sure the kids were up and ready for school. As the presenter welcomed listeners back and went through the schedule for the next hour, Peter's phone rang. He glanced at the screen. "No caller ID," displayed along the top. Peter hated answering these calls. It usually meant one of two things. A sales call. No, too early for that, surely? Or a wrong number. He watched, listening to the loud ringing tone as it played out over the car. Peter glared at the traffic lights. Amber, red. He jabbed the brakes. The phone stopped. *Go on. Go and bother someone else. I'm one of probably two hundred calls that you'll make today. How's that for a start?* He smirked to himself. The phone rang again. Peter tensed his hands, curling his fingers around the steering wheel. They rarely call back. He jabbed his finger on the screen. The answer button disappeared; only the end call button was displayed. Peter watched as the lights went from amber to green.

'Hello?' He pulled away from the lights, listening as the automatic gears adjusted to the speed he was going. The BMW 8 series was beautiful to handle. After a brief pause, he heard a deep, gruff voice. He could hear the twenty cigarettes a day and the effects of strong alcohol tarnishing the voice.

'Peter Simpson?'

How do they do it? Okay, my interest is piqued. First base, you're good, I'll give you that. A name is a great start, it gives you an edge. Their first catch of the day, Peter thought. 'Speaking.'

'How did you enjoy Brighton?'

Peter suddenly felt sick. The world around him began to spin. The last thing he recalled about the weekend away was pulling out of the car park. Billy, Sean and Peter had avoided each other since. What happens in Brighton. Even murder. 'Who is this?'

'I'm going to tell you a little about the way this will play out. See, I love to gamble. I think you do too. That casino was quite something, wouldn't you agree? It's the buzz. There's nothing quite like it. Let's examine it for a second. The first move towards the goal, the first rush is to take the wallet from your trousers; maybe you start with a couple of notes. You remove them, listening to the crisp snap as the corners flap against the leather. The anticipation as you walk towards the cashier, hand the money over and in exchange, they hand you your chips. You'll often see a seasoned gambler caressing the chips, clunking them together. Some roll them along their fingers with all manner of impressive tricks. I must admit, that's not me, but some do. I know you like to gamble, Peter. You like the odd flutter. To take a chance when the odds are stacked against you.'

Peter felt numb. He'd listened to the man talking for the last couple of minutes. He tried to speak, but the words were jammed in his throat.

'I, I'm...'

The caller continued. 'I watched you all at the casino, the buzz as the four of you walked towards the roulette wheel. Personally, I would have played differently, but that's me. Your friend took a gamble, wouldn't you say? The spin of a coin. Fuck or duck, I call it. He should have chosen the latter. We wouldn't be in this predicament. Our paths would never have crossed, I wouldn't be calling you, and we'd all be getting on with our lives. How happy we would all be? So, I have a bet for you, Peter. Let's play a game, a challenge. I have the recording, the evidence of what you and your friends have done. You have two options as I see it. You are going to replace Adriana. Christ, we had it all planned. She was simply wonderful. Now, she's gone. So, a substitute is required. Your friend left his phone by Adriana's dead body. How careless, dumping her in the garden. Tutt, Tutt. We managed to hack it, not complicated. We've accessed your Facebook account, and I must say, your friend's wife is an ideal replacement. His name is Matt. His wife is Nadia. She reminds me of Adriana. Then there's Mia. The girlfriend of your mate, Sean Carney. There's a photo of her on the beach, wearing a blue swimsuit, taken a few months ago during a summer vacation. You're lucky; you have choices. Billy's wife, Lydia, another stunner. But pregnant. Oh, the drawback with her. It's a shame. We did look up your wife. Anna. Not the best looking apple on the tree, if you don't mind me saying. That's why I've contacted you, Peter. So hey, it's either Mia or Nadia. Pick one. You know what you have to do. There. I've said it. I feel so much better now. Let me assure you we are watching. We've placed a tracker on your car. We'll know if you remove it. You, and only you, will take the blame if anything goes wrong. You have one week from today. I'm giving you a choice. You bring one of them to us. If you don't, then I'll kill your wife.'

The guy ended the call.

* * *

After the phone call a week ago, Peter had pulled over to the side of the road. He watched the streets as people began their commute to work. The bleakness which hung in the air had been replaced with light. The radio was off, and he sat in silence. Peter considered calling Matt. He'd been one of his closest friends. He picked up the phone, which rested on the passenger seat and searched for Matt's number. It had been a couple of weeks since they'd spoken. Anyway, what did he say?

Hey, Matt. Sorry for the lack of contact. It's been a while. I just wanted to thank you for the fabulous weekend. It was a scream, wasn't it? Oh, you didn't hear, did you? Silly Billy and what happened, murdering a woman in his room, but hey, such is life. Oh, by the way, do you mind if I pop over some time? There's something I need to do. It won't take long, Matty boy. Just a little task I've been set. I need to kidnap your wife.

Peter had a thought. If this guy had managed to get his number, it was possible the others have been set the same task. He looked in the mirror, adjusting it to see his face. It seemed he'd aged twenty years in the last ten minutes. Peter stared at his reflection. The lines under his dark green eyes were more profound; beads of sweat rolled from his brow, dropping onto his glasses. His face looked gaunter. He dialled Anna's number, pleading for her to pick up. Three rings. Four. *No. Pick up. Come on, Anna.*

'Hello.'

'Oh, thank God. 'It's me.'

'I know it's you. Is something wrong?'

'I. I don't feel well. I'm going to come home.'

'Oh, hun, that's not like you.'

As Peter listened to her voice, he realised how much he loved her. He wouldn't let anything come between them.

'Yeah. It must have been something I ate. I'm going to turn around and come back.'

'Okay. Drive carefully. See you in a short while.' Anna hung up.

Peter balanced the phone on the palm of his hand. Again, he searched for Matt's number, contemplating calling him. Then he placed the phone on the passenger seat and carried out a U-Turn.

Peter got out of his car and looked towards the house he and Anna had shared for almost ten years. As he stared, peering at the large white bricks, the balcony above the top bedroom, the small fir trees planted in the front lawn, he recalled the parties they'd had, the summer barbecues, long evenings dining together in the garden. He thought about the phone call. Did it happen? Did the guy really just ring him? The caller knew everything. The woman in Billy's room and what they'd done to conceal the body. Burying her in a fit of panic.

Peter walked up the steps, placed his key in the door and went inside the house. He stood for a moment, peering along the hallway towards the kitchen. The house was silent, tranquil. He reached behind, closing the door gently.

He called out softly, his voice low. 'Anna.'

'Up here. I'll be down in a minute.'

Relief washed over him. Peter had worried for the briefest of moments that his wife was gone. He pushed the thought from his head as he made his way towards the kitchen and sat at the breakfast bar. The phone call played out in his head. The conversation he'd had earlier.

You have one week from today. I'm giving you a choice: you bring one of them to us. If you don't, then I'll kill your wife.

He heard a voice at the kitchen door. Peter spun around; his wife stood with a dressing gown on, the belt tied around her waist.

'Did you not hear me calling you?' she asked.

Peter smiled. 'Sorry. I was lost for a moment.'

'How are you feeling?'

He remembered the excuse he'd given earlier. 'I don't feel great. I think I may need a lie-down. It's probably something I've eaten.'

'Well, we had the fish supper last night, but I'm okay. Go on, take yourself to bed. You'll feel better after a nap.'

As Peter stood, he grabbed his wife around the waist, pulling her close, planting kisses on her cheek like a desperate lover, knowing he may have placed her in severe danger.

'What's got into you?' Anna asked, her face beaming.

'I love you so much,' Peter answered. 'I don't know what I'd ever do without you.'

'Me either. But you're sick. Go and rest. I have to do some work on the laptop. Go on. Up you go.'

Peter struggled to let go as his wife pulled away.

He lay in bed, his mind plagued with thoughts. When he'd slept, his dreams conjured up stories, terrifying nightmares. He was back at the hotel. Billy and Sean were standing over the mound. As Peter walked towards them, he saw a hand pushing out of the earth, the veins a dark blue colour, fingers spread. The soil opened out as if it were being pushed from underneath. Red dress lady was now walking towards them.

He opened his eyes; the bed sheets were damp with his sweat, his eyes were sticky, and his head ached. Peter turned on his side, pulling the blanket further up his body, his head now submerged under the cool material. He glimpsed the alarm clock. 2.20pm. How had he slept so long?

He lay still. The sinister voice from earlier, playing in his mind.

Peter gently pushed the blanket off his warm body and moved towards the upstairs hallway. Comfort replaced the fear as he heard his wife singing in the kitchen to a Madonna song: *Papa Don't Preach.* Maybe Anna should have listened to her own father. She wouldn't be in this situation. Guilt had taken the place of comfort for the briefest of seconds. How had this happened? A weekend away, ending in such tragedy. If Peter had someone to talk to, anyone, maybe the offence would be easier to deal with, to absorb. He moved down the stairs. The loud music eased his tension.

Anna was piling the dirty dishes from this morning into the dishwasher. 'Hey, sleepyhead. How are you feeling?'

Peter smiled. 'Better. Thank you.' He moved towards his wife and kissed her cheek; then, he helped her. He had to take his mind off the phone call.

Later that evening, they decided to eat out. Anna had wanted to cook pasta, but Peter needed a night with his wife. He needed the security of people, noise, a romantic candlelit Italian restaurant, pizza washed down with a couple of beers.

They sat at a round table, opposite each other. Tonight, Peter couldn't draw his eyes away from Anna. The waiter startled him.

'Here are the specials, Sir.'

Anna noticed the tension in her husband's behaviour. She listened as the waiter reeled off a menu she wasn't interested in sampling. Once the waiter had given them a few minutes to decide, she reached across the table, holding her husband's hand.

'You're jumpy tonight. I can feel the anxiety. Is everything okay?'

The front door opened, like a fridge, the sound of a balloon deflating.

Peter flicked his eyes to the front. A woman stood, looking across the room. She was tall, elegant looking and wore a stunning red dress. Peter gripped the tablecloth, scrunching one end with his right hand.

'Peter. Relax. What is it?'

The woman moved across the floor. Chic and sophisticated. Peter eyed her, then looked down at the table. He heard shouting, the voice of an older lady. 'Marie. You look stunning. Happy birthday!'

Peter looked up, seeing the woman join a large table of people who had started singing happy birthday. The older lady grabbed the woman's cheeks and then kissed her forehead.

Peter pursed his lips together, inhaling and then blowing a deep breath hard enough to inflate a tyre in one go. 'I'm sorry. It's just stress. Work is hard at the moment, and some of the staff are not meeting their targets.'

'Well, have a night off. I'm sure it will all work out.'

Peter thought to himself if only she knew.

The waiter returned a few minutes later. 'Are you ready to order drinks?'

He handed the list to Anna and removed a small pad from his apron.

Peter was staring through the gap between the waiter and Anna. He saw something on the floor. He pushed his legs, digging them into the ground and his chair slid away from the table. A woman was crawling, making her way towards where they sat. Her arm was held out in front of her, decorated with thick blue veins. Her fingers were long, her nails sodden with mud. She was mouthing something to him. Peter leant forward, trying to hear what she was saying. He watched her dark, purple lips, like she'd been strangled, thumb marks now visible on her neck. Her head was turned to the side in an awkward position. As Peter stared, she began talking.

'Let me out. Let me out of the hole.'

Anna spun around as Peter's chair collapsed. 'Oh, my goodness. Peter. Are you okay?'

'I need to go. Please. I have to go,' He shouted.

* * *

Peter and Anna stood outside the restaurant. They watched through the window. Guests were standing around their tables; others had moved towards the front bar to see what had happened. Peter held his wife's face as they stood in the cold.

'I'm sorry. I don't know what happened.'

Anna held her husband's hands. She pulled them to her face and kissed his fingertips. 'Peter. I've never seen you like this. Is something on your mind?'

He stepped back to let a couple pass. Peter watched the excitement on their faces as they opened the door of the restaurant. He felt envious. Peter had wanted to go back inside, relax, converse. His head was too loaded with fear. It had driven him to hallucinate. Something he'd never suffered with before.

'Peter. I'm talking to you.'

He turned towards his wife. 'Sorry. What did you say?'

'Shall we get a takeaway and have a drink at home?'

'Sounds great.'

As they walked, Peter opened an app on his phone and ordered a Chinese. They stopped at an off-license and grabbed two bottles of red wine.

As they reached home, Peter noticed a glow of light towards the side entrance.

'Where are you going? Come on. It's cold.'

'Hang on. The security light is on. Someone is in the garden.'

'Peter. For heaven's sake. This is ridiculous.'

'I'll just be a minute. Go inside. I'll be there in a second.'

As he made his way around the side of the house, he listened as Anna placed the key in the lock. The door closed.

He stood, gazing into the back garden. He could see the

large lawn, the fence towards the back. 'Hello? Is someone there?' Peter waited. He moved forward, taking light steps. 'Hello?' Silence. The light went off. Peter leant against the side wall; the stone chippings cut into his back. He could hear his breaths getting heavier. Again, the phone call from earlier played on his mind. Over and over, repeating as he stood in the darkness. Could he really kidnap Nadia? Or Mia? Would this lunatic follow through with the threat he'd made? What the hell would happen if he went to the police? The guy had a recording, evidence. Peter stood, waiting for another sign to determine if someone was there. *The security light had come on. It happens: cats, foxes. It's probably nothing,* he thought. Peter stayed for a couple of minutes. *This is crazy. Go inside, make the madness of this evening up to Anna. Get a grip of yourself, man.*

He backed away, keeping his eyes fixed on the back garden. His phone pinged, a WhatsApp message. As Peter reached the front of the house, he removed his phone from his pocket. It was a photo, taken inside his house. It showed his wife, sat on the sofa, a glass of wine in her right hand, a magazine on her lap.

Peter ran towards the front door, seeing it marginally open. He felt nausea flood through his body as he pushed the front door back. 'Anna. Anna. Where the hell are you?'

He could hear her voice from the living room. 'For Christ's sake, Peter. Where do you think?'

Peter charged around the house, checking every room, top and bottom.

As he returned to the living room, he saw his wife, sat on the sofa, a glass of wine in her hand and a home magazine resting on her lap, identical to the picture he'd just been sent.

9

Sean and Mia.
The night before Peter Simpson finds his wife's dead body.

Sean Carney seemed to suffer the most. The weekend to Brighton nearly a month ago had played on his mind over and over. He'd suffered panic attacks, he'd lost his spirit, the hunger for life, his sex drive was non-existent, and he'd lost over a stone in weight. When he'd slept at night, visions of what they had done flooded his mind.

Sean's partner, Mia, was growing more concerned. Frustrated that her boyfriend had become withdrawn. On a number of occasions, she'd spoken with him, trying to draw it from him, to understand how he felt and work it out together. It was pointless. The more Mia reached out, the more reserved he'd become. She was certain he'd taken a lover and had started going through his phone. She'd search his pockets while his clothes lay in the wash basket. Mia had found nothing to prove her partner's infidelity. She watched him now, sat up in the bed. He was staring towards the wall opposite, unaware that his wife was awake. Mia grabbed a couple of pillows from the floor and propped them behind her back.

'Morning,' she said.

Sean looked at his partner. He eyed her brown negligee, her blonde hair which had dropped over her face. He looked at her full lips, her perfect skin. She was beautiful. Mia turned towards him, placing her left hand on his chest and bringing it further down his body towards his groin.

'I'm sorry. I don't feel like it,' Sean announced. He stood up, grabbing his jeans and stepping into them. Then he placed a jumper over his head.

'Sean. Talk to me. What's happened between us?'

She watched as he left the room without answering, then she turned into the pillow and sobbed.

* * *

Sean was sat in the kitchen on his second cup of coffee. He'd contemplated calling his friends so many times since the weekend away. As he sipped his drink, he recalled the early days. He'd spent the first six years of his life in Ireland. His parents had struggled to find work, and money was tight. He could still remember standing at the port in Dublin, his grandparents holding him close, tears flooding down his nan's face. He hadn't realised at the time that he'd never see her again. She died three years later. His grandfather had died a few years after her.

They'd moved to London, and Sean's first memory was the excitement at seeing so many cars on the street. It was so different from the life he was used to living. His first day at school had been something of a let-down. He'd expected the other pupils to flock around him and make a fuss. At lunch, he'd sat on his own, glaring at the strange faces as people laughed. Then, a tall skinny guy walked over. He pulled out a seat and introduced himself.

'Hi. You're the new kid?' he'd said.

Sean looked towards him, pushing his hand up to greet the high five offered to him.

'I'm Matt. We'll be best buddies from now on. I'll show you the ropes.'

Sean listened as Matt continued to tell him the hiding places, the mean teachers and the classes which he'd enjoy. Their friendship blossomed, and Peter and Billy sealed the fab four.

Now, Sean placed his coffee cup on the table in front of him. He jumped as his phone rang. Sean picked it up, his heart racing as he saw the name. Peter. Part of him wanted to decline, to block the number and never speak to him again. Almost a month since that weekend away. His life would never be the same again. Sean moved to the hallway; his wife was still in bed. He pressed the answer button and waited for the voice.

'Sean. How are you? It's been a while?'

It's been a while. Yeah, why's that, Peter? Why would you think it's been a while? he thought. Sean held his breath for a moment. 'Peter. Wow. It's good to hear from you. How have you been?'

Peter's voice was loud, enthusiastic. 'I've been good. Yeah. You?'

'Yeah. Good too. How can I help?' Sean realised how abrupt his last comment had been. He didn't care.

'I'm working in the area. Fancy a beer?' Peter asked.

Sean had wanted to say no. He'd pleaded with himself as his lips pursed together, forcing the word from his throat, pushing it out. *Tell him, Sean. Tell him.* 'Yeah. I'm about this evening. It would be great for a catch-up.' Bang. The shit from the past is about to resurface.

'Great,' Peter replied. 'The Ship? Around eight?'

'That's good for me.' Sean ended the call. He wanted to slam the phone against the ground, stamp it into a hundred pieces. He brushed his hands against the stubble on his face, feeling his warm skin. *Why the hell did I say yes?*

* * *

At seven forty, Sean came down the stairs. He'd showered and dressed. As he walked into the living room, Mia was sat in front of the telly. The room was dark, and he felt the heat from the open fire.

'Wow. Now that's the Sean I know and love. You look great.' She eyed his white, pressed shirt, his tight jeans. A waft of aftershave suddenly filled the room.

'I'll be an hour, tops.'

Mia stood and moved towards her partner. He reached to her, pulling her close. He fought the lump in his throat, the tears which threatened to spill down his face. After a minute, he backed off.

'I love you, Mia.'

'I love you too.'

* * *

Sean opened the front door. Outside, a murky grey hung in the air. He moved down the steps and out onto the street. He wanted more than ever to take the phone from his back pocket, call Peter and tell him something had come up. He was ill, or there was an emergency job he had to attend, a power cut, far away from here, and the memories of that hideous weekend which he'd be forced to confront. Sean knew he couldn't do that. Peter had made an effort. He'd called Sean and asked to meet for a beer. Maybe it would finally bring some closure to that terrifying night.

At just gone 8pm, Sean opened the door of The Ship public house on Fulham Broadway. He looked towards the back of the pub, seeing a man sat on his own with a drink. As Sean walked towards him, the two men made eye contact.

* * *

As soon as Sean left, Mia got off the sofa. She made her way to the kitchen and reached to the cupboard, grabbing the bottle of Jack Daniels whisky, which they'd saved for special occasions. Tonight, she needed to feel the warm liquid on her tongue, the burn deep in her throat. She wrestled with the cap, twisting hard, realising she had to peel the label. She acted like a desperate alcoholic, impatient and needing the fix. Once the cap had been removed, Mia grabbed a glass, turned the bottle on its side and poured. She filled the glass to the top. Then, in one go, she downed it.

Mia placed her hand on the side of the sink; the hit was more powerful than she'd imagined. She was building the courage to speak with Sean. All attempts so far had failed. Tonight, she was going to get plastered. Then make him tell her exactly what was going on in his life. She stood for a moment, wallowing in the stupor. She tilted the bottle again, filling the glass to the brim. Suddenly, the doorbell rang. Mia felt dizzy; the room began to spin. She moved towards the hallway. Through the glass at the front door, she could see her friend, a neighbour she'd become close with over the last couple of years. The letterbox opened, and Mia heard her voice.

'Open the frigging door. I'm bloody freezing.'

Mia smiled, feeling the rush of enthusiasm work through

her body. Sean was out, she was already on the way to being uncontrollably pissed, and her friend was at the door to share the experience.

Mia opened the door. Her friend hugged her, instantly smelling the alcohol. 'Look at you, girl. It's a little early, isn't it?'

'Come on. I'll get you a glass.'

Mia poured another for herself, the same measure as before. As she poured Kate's drink, her friend held her hand up, signalling for her to stop.

'That will do. I told Paul I'd be home in an hour. He'll have the right hump if I'm out all night. Where's Sean?'

Mia emptied the glass. As she grabbed the bottle, half its contents already gone, her friend grimaced.

'He's out with a mate.'

'Did you manage to speak with him?'

Mia shook her head. 'What am I going to do? I think there's someone else. I can't prove it. I haven't found anything yet, but he's so distant and cold towards me, Kate.'

'Talk to him, Mia. It's the only way.'

'I try. I try so hard. He's closed up on me. Since the weekend in Brighton, he's a different person. God knows I've done everything to get through to him. He keeps saying that nothing has happened. He's fine. To stop going on at him. Well, I have needs. I miss him. I miss him so bloody much. It's not just the sex.'

Kate laughed. Mia realised the line of thought her friend had taken.

'Are you saying you haven't slept together since the weekend he went away?'

'Yes. It's not just that. He doesn't hold me anymore. The warmth is gone.'

The women jumped as a car alarm went off outside. The

lights blinked through the glass of the front door. After a minute, it stopped.

'So. Tell me?' Mia asked. 'What's happening with you...?'

'I think that's Sean's car. Hang on a second.' Mia walked to the front door. The noise was deafening. Neighbours were peering through the curtains opposite, and a couple of people had opened their front doors. Mia saw the lights blinking from their Volkswagen Polo. She grabbed the keys and pressed the fob. The alarm stopped. As she stood by the front door, she saw the large, gaping hole in the window of the driver's door; the glass was all over the pavement. She moved down the steps, seeing the damage. It looked like someone had used a brick to cause as much destruction as possible. Mia walked over to the car, then along the road, searching for the thugs who had done this. Suddenly, she realised she might not be safe. She turned and walked back along the road again, pausing by the car. Mia wanted to call her partner. But It wasn't fair. The only night he'd had out for a while. She couldn't do it. He'd leave the pub and it would put him in a bad mood for the whole night. He needed the time with Peter.

Mia stepped away from the car and returned to the house. 'Kids. They're doing it all the time.' She walked along the hallway to the kitchen. Kate was lying on the floor. Her head was facing away. Mia panicked. She screamed as she turned her over. *How had she fallen? She hadn't drank that much,* Mia thought. 'Are you okay? What happened?' As Mia rolled her body over, she saw the knife wound, blood pumping like a petrol hose.

Her friend was dead.

* * *

Sean had made his way towards the gentleman sat at the back of the pub. As he approached, he noticed it wasn't Peter. They shared an embarrassing smile, and Sean moved to the bar. 'A Guinness, please. And a packet of dry roasted peanuts.'

The barman reached above his head and removed a clean glass from the shelf. He pulled on the pump, stopping three-quarters of the way to let the drink settle. Then he proceeded with the top-up.

Sean sat at the bar. He glanced at the clock on the wall. 8.15pm. He turned, eyeing the front door as it opened. An elderly couple came in; the lady took a seat at the front while her partner used the toilet before returning to order drinks.

Sean looked at his glass. The clock showed 8.25pm. He ordered another drink and waited.

At 9.10pm, he dialled Peter's number, listening to the phone go straight to voicemail. He dialled again, the same thing. Like the phone had been turned off. *Why was he not answering? Something was wrong,* Sean thought.

At just gone 9.20pm, he received a distressed call from his partner, Mia. Their neighbour had been murdered in the house.

Mia was alone.

* * *

Peter watched from his car while Sean had made his way down the steps and along the street. He'd waited. His car parked a few feet from the house. Once Sean was out of sight, he bricked the window. He'd raced around the side of the house, listening to the loud screech of the alarm. When it stopped, Peter worried that Sean's partner would ignore it. It happened. When you hear an alarm on the street, how many people bother to check? It's always someone else's house or another vehicle. The alarm sounded again. Then stopped. Silence. Finally, he heard the front door open. He watched as the woman made her way down the steps. He walked into the hallway and hid in the living room at the front of the house. Peter gave it a couple of minutes. He didn't know someone else had been in the house. While he'd waited in the car, he'd been checking his phone and had missed the neighbour going inside. The alarm was loud, and he needed to be quick.

As he rushed along the downstairs hallway, he removed the knife from his jacket pocket, intent on kidnapping Mia. His confusion quickly turned to horror as the woman fought back. A woman who Peter didn't recognise. In sheer desperation, Peter drove the knife into the woman's chest.

He watched her drop, clutching her jumper, her eyes became still. Peter wanted to vomit as he witnessed the horror unfold in front of him. As he raced along the hallway, he saw the front door open. He stopped, then moved into the living room.

He'd killed a woman who was caught in the crossfire.

Peter was still in the house.

He had to find Mia.

10

The night before Peter Simpson finds his wife's dead body.

The lights went out. Mia was standing in the kitchen. Her best friend was dead, lying on the floor by her feet.

She screamed out. 'Leave me alone. I beg you, don't do this.' Mia listened in the darkness. She was struggling to breathe as she groped for the breakfast bar to get her bearings. Her hands slid along the table, tapping the rough wood, feeling the knots and searching for her phone. She crept slowly, squinting her eyes as she held her hands out and moved towards the back door. Her breathing was erratic as she looked behind, peering along the dark hallway, a mass of bleakness ahead. She touched the glass and moved her hand down towards the door handle. Mia yanked it hard, but it was stiff. She jerked it, pulling and lifting, desperately trying to open the back door. She pawed for the key, feeling only the barrel of the lock. Mia screamed again, banging against the glass and then moved towards the kitchen sink, looking along the dark hallway towards the front of the house. She placed her arms in front, reaching out, opening and closing her hands as if clasping the obscurity ahead. She stepped forward, aware that any noise could draw the killer to where she stood. She removed her shoes. The cold tiles below her feet sent welcome energy surging through her veins.

As Mia reached the hallway, she heard a noise coming from the living room. Like someone was standing on a floorboard. She listened hard as she balanced on one leg. Another creak could determine the person was moving. Mia waited. Five seconds. Ten. Indecisive about which direction she should take. Another creak. She heard the living room door fling open. Mia yelled and fell to the floor by the stairs. She reached upwards, forcing her body to the bottom step, crawling awkwardly. She felt for the stairs leading to the first floor. She could feel the person standing over her as she stood. Quickly, she spun around, jabbing at the darkness, then she scrambled up the stairs crawling on her hands and knees. As Mia reached the top step, she heard someone pounding up behind her. Again, she called out. 'Leave me alone. What do you want?' She stood up, forcing her legs to stabilise, to hold her weight as her body trembled. They were going to fold underneath her, collapse and drop her body to the ground. She could hear the deep breaths behind, a few inches from where she stood. Mia forced her hand against the wall, patting it, dragging her palm as she ran. She reached the bathroom door and stepped inside, pushing her body against it and desperately searching for the lock. The sound of footsteps was moving towards her. He was outside. Mia felt the presence as a hand touched against the door. At the same time, she twisted the lock, hearing the click. She stepped back, watching the bleakness and listening for his next move.

'Mia. It's Peter. Open the door.'

She recognised his voice instantly. Mia moved her hand to the lock. 'Peter? What are you doing? Have you lost your mind?'

As Peter barged against the wood, he heard the front door open.

'Mia. Are you okay? Where are you?'

Peter listened as Sean moved along the downstairs hallway. He heard the sound of doors opening, his shoes on the wooden floor. Sean was talking to himself, asking why the lights were off. Peter heard him at the foot of the stairs, calling for Mia. He saw the light, which he presumed was Sean's phone, shining close to where he was hiding. For a moment, Peter thought he'd been seen. Sean called for Mia again as he made his way slowly up the stairs. Peter backed away and used the wall behind him to work his way in the darkness. Just as Sean reached the top step, Peter slid into one of the bedrooms. He listened as Mia realised Sean was home. Sean tried the handle of the bathroom door first, then began knocking it.

Peter remained hidden.

'Mia. What's going on?' Sean waited in the darkness. He tried the handle again. Then he called a second time. 'Mia.'

The lock gave a clunking sound as Mia pulled it towards her. 'Sean.'

He listened as she sobbed hysterically. Sean placed his arms in front of him, and they held each other tight. After a minute, he asked her what had happened.

She started to talk, but her emotions stemmed the flow of her words.

'Mia. Take your time. Deep breaths.'

'Peter was here.'

His body suddenly ached as a pain jabbed at his chest. 'Peter. Are you sure?'

'Yes. He tried to kill me.'

'What are you talking about?'

Mia ordered her partner to close the door. She locked it behind him. The two of them stood in the bathroom, his arms resting on her shoulders. They remained in darkness.

Sean listened as his partner struggled to catch her breath.

'After you left, Kate called over. I had a couple of drinks, and she joined me. Your alarm sounded. As I went to take a look, someone had bricked the car.'

'Bricked the car? Did you call the police?'

'I didn't have a chance. I waited outside, then walked back into the house. Kate was lying on the floor of the kitchen. She was lying there, Sean. Dead. It was horrible.' As her body shook, Sean pulled her close, holding her. They waited in silence as minutes passed, lost in the embrace, magnetised, entranced by each other's spirit, like an invisible force which gave them strength.

Finally, Sean spoke. 'I'm going to take a look.'

'No. Wait here. I think he's still in the house.'

'Where's your phone?' Sean asked.

'Downstairs, on the kitchen table.'

'Okay. Take mine. If anything happens, lock this door and call the police.'

'Sean. Wait here. Why don't we call the police now?'

Sean thought back to the weekend in Brighton. The last thing he wanted was a spotlight on him. If there was a dead body, they'd have to call the police. Sean didn't need this now. He thought about what Mia had said. Peter was here. Why the hell would Peter come after Mia? It didn't make sense.

'Mia. If someone is in the house, I need to deal with it. Lock the door. I need to see what the hell is going on.'

'Sean. You can't go out there.' He felt his partner's hand brush his face.

'Just lock the door behind me.' Sean pulled the handle and

found it jammed. 'What the hell?' He turned to Mia. 'It won't open.'

'Here, let me try.' Mia pawed in the bleakness, reaching for the handle. She forcefully moved it up and down. 'He's pressed something against the lock.'

Sean panicked, now ripping the handle hard, moving it with force. Twenty minutes later, the sweat dripping from Sean's face, he finally heard something crashing to the floor. He opened the door and stood in the upstairs hall. Sean knelt, feeling on the ground for the object. The intruder had used the loft bar to hold the door handle in place, pressed against the frame. He heard the click, Mia securing herself in the bathroom. Sean used the wall to manoeuvre himself along the hallway. As he reached the top step, he looked down. Sean slowly moved along the stairs, one step at a time. He listened for a sound, anything to suggest that Peter was still inside. Mia's mobile phone was on the kitchen table. He could use the torch to find the fuse board.

He was standing in the hallway, halfway between the front door and the kitchen. He felt a breeze, a chill that hit him hard. Possibly an open door. Sean turned and faced the kitchen. It was dark, and it took him a couple of minutes to work his way around. Once he'd found Mia's phone, he tapped the four-digit PIN and summoned the light, pointing it towards the front of the house and creeping gently along the floor. The living room door was closed. He held his breath and slowly turned the doorknob. Sean scanned the torch towards the sofa, the fireplace where the flames had long burned out and then to the cupboard under the window. He walked into the room, swirling the torch, gliding the light through the darkness. A shadow appeared in the corner of his left eye, tall, still. Sean turned, steering the torch towards it. As he stared, he laughed to himself. A new lamp stand Mia had bought last week from Amazon. Once he was sure the room was empty, he crouched by the cupboard. The main switch had tripped. Sean reached his hand forward and pushed the switch upwards. He heard the satisfying clunk, the house drenched in light.

Mia was stood in the bathroom. The door was locked, and she gasped as the bathroom light came on. She'd gone through the worst trauma in her life this evening. She moved to the toilet and sat down. Her stomach was dancing like a moth around a lightbulb. She stamped her feet and wrapped her arms around herself. As visions played in her mind, her best friend lying slumped on the kitchen floor, she stood and vomited in the toilet. Mia gripped the side of the bath, pulling herself upwards and moved to the door. She pushed her ear against the cold wood and listened. The house was still. She wanted Sean to come back and to remain hidden together forever. She moved back to the toilet, then flushed it, aware the sound would draw attention to her. Mia ran the tap and washed her mouth, then patted her face with a towel. She moved back to the door and slowly un-clicked the lock. 'Sean. Where are you?' Mia listened for a reply. 'Sean?' Mia moved to the top of the stairs. Her partner was standing by the kitchen.

'You better come down.'

Mia walked towards her partner. As she reached the bottom step, she peered to the floor where Sean was pointing.

The blood had been wiped, and the floor was empty.

Kate's body had gone.

11

The night before Peter Simpson finds his wife's dead body.

The decoy was perfect. Peter had called Sean and arranged to meet him in the pub. Then, he waited outside the house. His plan to smash the window and draw Mia out of the house worked flawlessly. Everything was set up. He slid in through the front door, then murdered someone. This was deep. He'd fucked up on an astronomical scale.

He was certain once he'd turned off the lights that Mia would be easy to kidnap. She was fast. When he'd grabbed her legs on the stairs, she'd kicked out, catching him in the face. He hid upstairs when the front door had opened, and the forty minutes Sean and Mia spent in the bathroom gave Peter the time to clean up the mess. His footsteps along the upstairs hallway and the loft bar, which he'd found in the airing cupboard being placed against the lock, had been muted with Mia's sobs.

Downstairs in the cupboard under the sink, Peter found a cloth, a bottle of germ remover and went to work. He'd brought a torch and set it up by the kitchen door. Once everything had been wiped clean, he placed a bag over the dead woman's face and tied it with a piece of rope. How could he let this happen? He lifted the dead body, then slumped her over his shoulders, careful not to spill any blood.

Now, Peter drove, the dead woman in the boot of his BMW. He began slamming his fists on the steering wheel. The stress was too much. Peter contemplated driving the car into a wall or hitting the accelerator at the edge of a cliff. He didn't have the guts. He pictured the woman lying in the boot. The sack over her face. How the hell had he got in this situation? How did he allow himself to be drawn into this sick game?

As Peter drove, the phone rang. He stared at the screen. "No caller ID," was displayed. He knew who it was. 'Hello?'

'Quite the mistake. I'm disappointed.'

Peter hit the brakes, and he stopped the car in the middle of a side street.

They were watching him. 'I tried to do as you asked. It wasn't my fault she died.' Peter glanced behind him, looking for the caller, wondering if he was close. 'Leave me the fuck alone.'

'I'm afraid it doesn't work that way. I feel cheated.'

Peter listened to the deep, sinister voice. 'Cheated. You need to remember the culprit in all this. I didn't kill the woman in the hotel room.'

'But you were there. You helped to cover it all up. You assisted in burying her. You and your friends. You're all a part of it now. That's how I see it.'

Peter wanted to end the call. It would only make matters worse. 'I've taken part in your sick game. Now I'm done.'

The guy spoke, his voice authoritative. 'It's only the beginning.'

Peter listened, processing the last comment.

The guy continued to speak. 'You're playing a game of darts. You need double eighteen to finish. You hit double twelve. Do you win the game?'

Peter hesitated before answering. 'You're sick.'

The guy continued. 'It's 8.45am, Monday morning. Drop off time, but you realise you've taken a wrong turn and end up outside a school you don't recognise. Do you say sod it? This will do? Or drop your child at the correct place? My point being, you haven't done as I asked.'

Peter held his head in his hands; he moved down the seat and bit on the knuckle of his forefinger. 'Please. I'm begging you. Don't do this.'

'It's too late.'

The phone went dead.

* * *

Peter stared at the blank screen on the dashboard. The words resonated in his head. It's too late. The last words he'd heard as the guy ended the call. He sat in the car, parked in the middle of a side street. A dead woman lying slumped in the boot of his car. He had to get rid of the body. But how? Where was he going to hide her? Peter drove, eyeing the bins on either side of the road. It was too conspicuous. The containers weren't big enough. He imagined dumping her, pulling away, her head on display, the bin lid slightly open. He could drive to The Thames, place her by the shore and hope the tide would take her out. Or drop her off a bank and hope the spot he'd chosen would be deep enough. Again, he risked being seen.

Peter had to bring her home. There was no other choice.

Twenty minutes later, he pulled up outside his house. The lights were off; the curtains were open. Peter eyed the darkness on the top floor. He stepped out of the car and slowly walked to the front door. As he walked into the hallway, he listened for a sign that his wife was awake. The kitchen was empty, as was the living room. Peter could suddenly smell blood. He looked down, seeing the stains on his jacket. There were more on his jumper and jeans. He removed his clothes, then walked along the hall and into the kitchen. Peter placed the clothes into the washing machine and pushed a tablet underneath them. Then he pressed the start button.

He walked up the stairs, glancing along the hallway and stepped into the bedroom. The radio was on, a book open and faced down on the cabinet. Anna was asleep, lying on her back, her eyes closed, and her face directed towards the ceiling. He backed up and out of the bedroom. Then quietly made his way outside, wearing only his underpants.

Peter struggled to remove the dead body from the car. The bag was covered in bloodstains, as was the boot. He dragged her out, placing his hands under her arms. Her legs pounded against the road. Peter looked around, then lifted her, first crouching, then springing upwards. As half her body rested over his shoulders, he fell back, moving his legs to stabilise himself. He jerked forward, balancing like a ropewalker. Once he felt steady, Peter walked up the steps and made his way around the side entrance.

The shed door was closed, and with his left hand, Peter pulled the door. The damp weather had caused the door to expand, and it sprung back. The noise was harsh. Peter waited a second. He felt a pulse in his chest as his heart started pumping overtime, pushing the blood so quickly he felt dizzy. Peter placed his hand against the rough wall, edging the door back open with his foot. The weight of the dead woman was becoming too much. He fell forward, his head banging against the wall. He leaned back, his legs now spread on the path, then looked towards the house. The lights were still off, but any second, Anna would hear something. She'd come down.

Peter turned sideways, forcing his body through the gap. Once inside the shed, he placed the body on the worktop. The smell of oil was overbearing, which could soon be replaced by rotting flesh. As he stood, watching the body laid out, Peter burst into tears. This wasn't him. It wasn't in his nature. But the guy had so much on him already. A recording of the weekend away. What Billy had done. Christ, they were all a part of it.

They'd get life in prison.

A jury would conclude that they'd all killed her.

They'd all been there.

They were all responsible.

Peter hid the body in the freezer and walked out of the shed. He just hoped that Anna didn't need to come in here.

* * *

Twelve hours before Lucy took the selfie.

The following morning, Peter left the house. He'd acted as normal as possible. As he walked towards his car, he'd found the note.

Look In The Boot.

He'd expected to see the body, taken out of the freezer and dumped in the back. As Peter made his way inside the house, calling his wife's name, panic washed over him. He fought the pulse which had started throbbing along the side of his face, a stroke-like sensation. It worked through his body as he searched the house, calling his wife's name.

He'd found Anna's body, twisted, almost folded and broken. Her head had been hit so hard he couldn't recognise her. As Peter dropped to his knees, unaware of his surroundings and his mind temporarily paralysed with shock, he screamed. Peter expected his throat to open, his insides to spill on the street. He heard the sound of his mobile. Peter looked around, now focused. His forehead was drenched with sweat, his eyes wet. He grabbed the phone and held it to his ear.

'You have one last chance. Get rid of your wife. We can't risk her being seen. Hide her body in the house and then drive. You're going to do it properly this time. No mistakes. I don't want to tell you what happens if you disobey the command. Look at the WhatsApp picture I'm about to send you.'

As the guy hung up, Peter watched the blank screen. A picture came through a moment later: a woman stood by her front door. Peter zoomed in, fighting the terror which saturated his body.

The picture was of Phoebe.

His daughter.
Taken from the street.
From outside her house.

* * *

Peter saw a post on Matt's Facebook page.
"Looking forward to our weekend in the Cotswolds. Much needed R & R. Do not disturb."

Peter had one last chance. That's what the caller had told him. No more mistakes. Mia had heard him calling her name at the bathroom door last night. It was a disproportionate blunder. It couldn't happen again. How long would it be before Sean called him, asking what the heck was going on? He had to get to Nadia, Matt's wife, or they'd kill his daughter, and he'd be next. There was no other way. They'd already murdered his wife, Anna. He was terrified of dying. Thanatophobia. A fear he'd had since being a child. Peter drove, unsure how to carry out the instructions which the caller relayed. He knew there could be a backlash, but Peter needed his wife beside him. It wasn't an option for him to hide Anna in the house. He couldn't bear to be without her. Maybe it was PTSD, the shock of finding her body in the boot of his car. Whatever the cause, Peter needed Anna beside him. He was sure once he'd taken Nadia, the caller would see past this mistake and let him go.

As he drove, he turned, looking at his beautiful wife in the passenger seat, then hammered his fists on the steering wheel. Sweat had started running down his forehead, building on the tip of his nose. He was petrified. He'd already killed an innocent woman last night and hid her in the shed. He hoped the freezer would delay her body from causing a stench and drawing attention. He hadn't expected her to fight back. When she'd seen him, they had grappled. He had no choice.

He kept seeing the knife plunge into her chest, her body dropping and all the blood. Thankfully, he'd managed to get her out to the car and clear up the mess in time. He thought about her body, lying in the freezer at home. How the hell would he get rid of her? He looked at Anna. The bastards had killed his wife. Now, he stared at her broken body. The blood which covered her face had dried. Her nose had been broken, her eyes bruised and battered. He could see into her mouth, the smashed teeth, her face a bloody mess. He screamed, crying hysterically. How the hell could he get out of this? There was no possible way. He wanted to call Phoebe. Tell her he loved her. But he couldn't. The men were somehow monitoring him.

He had to kidnap Nadia.

Peter drove over to Matt's house and pulled up at the end of the street. He carried out a U-turn and parked close to the curb. He waited, his eyes focused on Matt's Jeep. As Peter sat, it dawned on him that Anna was on show. He swung his head towards her, the sudden realisation that people could see her. How had he not thought about it? Was it a subconscious decision that somehow exposing her made Anna seem alive? Peter opened the car door and grabbed his jacket from the backseat, draping it over his wife, covering her face. He got back in the front seat, moving next to her. 'There. That's better. I'll put the heaters on. You must be cold.'

Peter turned on the car engine, spinning the control knob on the dash to full. 'I'm waiting for Nadia, Anna. You know how bad I feel, don't you? Christ, these men are beyond wicked, aren't they? Did they hurt you? I guess they did.' Peter realised his wife was motionless. He knew he was snapping in and out of reality, a confused state which seemed to overtake his mind due to stress.

Peter waited for hours, the car running, Anna on the seat next to him.

He rehearsed over and over, how he'd take Nadia. First, he'd planned on knocking at the house, using a hammer or other tool to hit Matt and place Nadia in the boot. No good. Matt was strong; he'd overpower him with ease. Then he thought about calling Matt, disguising his voice and pretending he had a problem with his electrics. He was useless at voices, and besides, Matt could know it was him. Peter would wait; he'd follow the Jeep and bide his time. There would certainly be ample chances to spring on Nadia. Surely Matt would take his eye off her at some stage?

* * *

He was bored, the waiting was tedious, and his eyes were heavy. Peter drifted to sleep. When he woke, he checked his watch: just gone 6pm. The last time he'd checked, it was 5.23pm.

The Jeep was gone.

As Peter drove, he peeked under the jacket making sure Anna was comfortable. He watched his wife's face, then back to the busy streets, the pedestrians, Friday night revellers sat in beer gardens with trays of drinks in front of them.

'Anna. Are you okay?' A police car passed him on the other side of the street. The sirens were off, and the vehicle was going slow. He looked in the rear-view mirror, watching it disappear behind him. He wondered if the driver would turn around. Follow him. Peter imagined the conversation.

Yeah. A regular serial killer here. How many more have you hidden, Richard? Or Dick. Whatever they call you. A proper nasty bastard we have here, Sarge. Lock him up and throw away the key. That's the only way to deal with these sickos. I'm saying there's at least two. The one in the front seat, for starters. You've done a proper job on her. The freezer in his back yard. Oh, great hiding place, Dick. Well thought out. What's that? Another in the garden of The Blair Hotel. You'll do time for this, my friend. Lots and lots of it.

Peter drove, mopping the sweat from his brow with the back of his hand. He wanted to steer the car into an oncoming truck. He visualised it, ploughing headfirst through the windscreen. All this would be over in a second. If only he had the courage. Death. That word again. Those five letters that put the fear of God into him. To Peter, each letter began with a phobia of his, coinciding with his anxiety. Dead. Earth. Ash. Tomb. Hearse.

He tapped the accelerator, keeping to the speed limit, visions of his wife's face flashing in front of him. He was dazed. A mass of confusion swamped him.

As Peter drove, it seemed he was restrained in a capsule. He watched the signs for Oxford, mopping the sweat from his forehead, passing the same cars, mopping, passing, over and over, stuck in a virtual world that he'd never escape from. As he moved into the middle lane, he watched the passengers on the inside. Vehicles with families going away for a weekend break, commuters on their way home. Faces looking out of the window. Roof-racks, suitcases, football scarves trapped in windows and blowing in the wind.

It was getting dark. Peter pressed hard on the accelerator, needing to find Nadia.

Twenty minutes later, Peter had the breakthrough he needed. He spotted the Jeep further up, cruising in the middle lane. He recognised the number plate as he approached. He suddenly lost control; his foot jammed on the pedal. He drove erratically, swerving from one lane to the other. He tried to control his body, but it was like he'd become possessed. The steering wheel swirled uncontrollably, and his right foot was stuck. He watched Matt as he passed on the inside lane. Peter saw the empty passenger seat. His daughter, Lucy, was sat in the back on her phone.

He couldn't see Nadia in the car.

Peter slowed up, not wanting to take the chance of Matt seeing him.

He followed the Jeep into the petrol station, still unsure if Nadia was with them.

By the time he'd reached the hotel, Peter knew. Matt and his daughter were alone. He'd waited outside, hoping Nadia would turn up. He'd braved it out, calling Matt from a withheld number. Although the thought petrified him, Peter put on a voice and was sure he'd got away with it, pretending to be a member of staff.

Now, Peter was heading to Nadia.

12

Present Day.

Matt had just come off the phone to Sean. He'd told him everything that had happened at The Blair Hotel after Matt had gone to bed. Billy, bringing a woman back to his room and killing her by mistake. Billy, Peter and Sean, burying her body on the hotel grounds. Matt stared at his phone in disbelief. How the hell could this happen? Why hadn't they told him? He had so many questions. Matt was certain the guy who'd followed them earlier was Peter. This couldn't be happening. Matt considered what Sean had just said. Peter had called to their house, Mia had found him inside, then locked herself in the bathroom. Their neighbour, missing. Mia was convinced she'd seen her dead body lying on the kitchen floor.

Matt had to call Nadia. He looked towards Lucy, who was

still tapping on her phone. 'Lucy. I'm sorry, but we need to leave.'

'What do you mean?'

Matt had to think of something. 'Mum's not well. That was her calling. We need to go, baby. Can you get your things ready? We need to be quick.'

Lucy placed the phone on the bed and gathered her clothes into the small holdall.

Matt reached his arms out, and Lucy walked over. He hugged her tight, kissing her on top of her head. 'I love you so much. We'll make it up to you. I promise. We need to get to mum now, okay?'

'Okay. What's wrong with her?'

'I'm not sure. She's sick; that's all I know at the moment.'

Matt stood and filled his bag with the folded clothes he'd placed in the wardrobe; then, he grabbed the toiletries. He struggled to stem the overwhelming panic which began to rise through his body. The room became hazy for a second, and he steadied himself. After a couple of minutes, Matt grabbed the phone and dialled Nadia's number. It was late, but this was an emergency. He listened for the ringtone, waiting, then glanced at the screen. Matt pressed the end call button and re-dialled.

'Dad. The WIFI is down again.'

'Oh, for Christ's sake. This bloody place. I'll be glad to see the back of it. Are you ready, Lucy?'

'Dad. Watch your language.'

'Sorry. I'm just stressed at the moment. I'll put extra in the swear box when we get home.' He listened to Lucy tutting.

'Yeah, sure you will.'

'I will. Right, ready?'

Lucy grabbed the holdall, and they left the room.

* * *

They drove out of the hotel car park. Lucy was in the backseat. Matt was talking, and when Lucy didn't answer, he looked in the rear-view mirror. She was asleep. He watched her beautiful face, how she slept, her innocence. Christ, he loved her so much. Nadia had never been the type to want children. Matt had asked her many times, and she'd fobbed him off. She wanted to get settled, have a career, live a little. Matt was the opposite. He'd have a football team if it weren't so expensive. They'd go shopping, and Matt would nudge his wife, pointing to a cute baby in a pushchair. Nadia would turn, laughing and eye up a dress on display in a window. Nadia ran her own cosmetics company online. She'd built a huge client base and distributed worldwide. Matt was an electrician and worked for himself. Between them, they'd built an enviable customer base.

Nadia was two years older than Matt, and when he hit thirty, he thought having a child would never happen. He recalled Nadia coming home from a client meeting. One of the other women had brought her newborn in to show off. Something clicked with Nadia, and their world changed forever.

Now, as Matt watched his daughter, he wondered where the years had gone. Nadia and Lucy were his life, and he'd do anything to protect them.

Matt glanced at his phone on the passenger seat. The signal bar was empty. He watched the darkness surrounding him and the full lights radiating the road ahead. Shadows swept past on his left side, dull in the headlights, a mass of bleakness, faint shapes in his peripheral vision.

Matt checked his phone again. The bar was still empty. He searched for a light in the distance, hoping someone could help him.

He glanced at the clock on the dashboard, almost 1am. He drove, thinking about the weekend, a get-together, drinks, laughs, a chance to catch up with friends he'd known all his life. Billy, Peter, Sean. What the hell had they done? How could this happen?

Matt reached the main road and turned right. Lucy was still asleep. Again, he looked at the phone, two bars displayed, the third one began flickering. 'Yes.' He turned into a small lay-by and got out of the Jeep.

Matt dialled Nadia's number. He stood in the cold, stamping his legs on the ground to keep warm. A backdraft caused him to turn away as a heavy goods truck passed, blowing wind in his face. Matt brought the phone to his ear, hearing the dialling tone. Nadia answered on the fourth ring.

'Nadia. Thank God. Sorry it's so late.'

Her voice was quirky, alive; she hadn't been sleeping.

'Did I wake you?' Matt asked.

'No. Peter is at the door. You'll have to give me a minute. Mum's asleep, and I don't want him to come in. He'll wake her. He seems in a state. I think he's had a row with Anna. Give me a minute.'

'No. Don't go to the door. Nadia. Don't go to the fucking door.' Matt listened. Nadia hadn't heard him. He could hear the voices, faint, distant. Nadia was consoling him, telling him it would all work out. Matt could hear Peter asking where he was. He knew. He knew where Matt was. More talking, more sympathising.

'Nadia. Shut the door. Can you hear me? Shut the front door.' He waited for a reply. Matt continued shouting. 'Shut the door, Nadia. Do you hear me?'

Suddenly, Nadia screamed. Matt heard footsteps, getting louder. Then the phone went dead.

Matt stood in the lay-by. He moved to the Jeep to check on his daughter. She was still asleep. He dialled Nadia's number, walking away from the Jeep in case Lucy woke. The phone was dead. A voice recording played, Nadia, apologising that she couldn't get to the phone. Matt screamed and dialled again. The same message. His head started to pound, his temples ached, his face hot. He dialled Peter's number, shocked that it started ringing. After a few seconds, he answered.

'I know what you're doing. Lucy captured a selfie. I saw the body on the passenger seat. Peter, I'm begging you. We can work this out. Let Nadia go. Please. Let her go.'

'I'm sorry, Matt. I have to do this. These people know what we've done. We'll all go down for this.'

'You bastard. How could you do this? Let Nadia go now. Do you hear me? Let her fucking go.'

'Matt. We buried someone. They have the proof, the footage. We'll go to prison for a very long time.'

'Listen to yourself, Peter. I spoke to Sean. He told me what happened, how you broke into the house, how you tried to kidnap Mia. What the hell is wrong with you? We can talk. Tell me where you are, and we'll talk.'

'It's too late, Matt. They made me do this. It's their revenge.'

'Who? Who made you do this? I'm not following?' Matt listened to the large sigh coming down the phone.

'They murdered Anna. Phoebe will be next.'

'Anna's dead? Peter, what happened?' Matt pictured the haunting image of the body in the passenger seat. He realised what Peter must be going through.

'These men are criminals. They're dangerous. We've crossed them, and now I have to save Phoebe and myself. I have to take Nadia to them. It's what they've instructed. I'm sorry, Matt. I didn't mean for this to happen. If I hear one police siren, I'll kill her. That's a promise, and I'll tell them where you live.'

The phone went dead.

Matt dropped to his knees. He pulled his hair and then pounded the stony ground with the palm of his hands. A car passed, and the driver blew his horn, making Matt jump. He remained on his knees as the minutes passed, thinking what to do. He had to call Sean. He'd help. He stood and pressed the screen of his mobile, then dialled Sean's number. It went to voicemail. He dialled another couple of times, then placed the phone in his jeans pocket.

Matt set the Satnav to Greta's address, Nadia's mother. She lived just past High Wycombe. About an hour from where he and Lucy were. Peter had been there a few times with his wife Anna when Nadia had invited them for dinner.

As Matt drove, he dialled Peter's number. The phone went to voicemail. Nadia's was the same. He tried Sean numerous times and then threw the phone on the seat.

* * *

Matt steered the Jeep onto Greta's drive. Lucy was still asleep. He couldn't wake her. The travelling had made her tired. He stepped out of the Jeep and walked around the side of the house. Greta always left a spare key under a rock. He lifted it slightly, pushing his fingers underneath. The key was there, and Matt pushed a breath of relief from his mouth. He glanced towards the Jeep, then across the road to the other semi-detached houses. The street where Greta lived was quiet, the houses were large, and there was plenty of parking. Matt turned, eyeing the front door. He reached forward and applied the key in the lock.

'Greta. It's Matt. I'm here with Lucy. Are you awake?' He listened, remembering that Nadia said she'd gone to bed early this evening due to her accident. The house was silent. Matt stood in the hallway, waiting. He had to check if Nadia was here. She may have put up a struggle, ran to one of the rooms and locked herself inside. 'Greta. It's Matt.' He peered towards the Jeep to make sure Lucy was safe, then moved along the downstairs hallway. 'Greta. Are you here?'

He heard a faint cry coming from the living room. Matt opened the door and saw Greta lying on her side. He turned on the light and moved over towards her. Greta turned her head.

'Matt. What are you doing here?' Her eyes were wild, and for a moment, she looked disorientated. Her thin grey hair was standing up, and she had a small bruise under her right eye from the fall. 'I thought you were away. Where's Nadia?'

Matt placed his hand on Greta's arm. 'Was Peter here?'

'Peter? I don't think so. I've been asleep. Mind you, a herd of elephants could run through this living room, and I wouldn't wake.'

Matt smiled. 'Look. Can I have a check around the house? Something may have happened.'

'Look around. What for? Is everything okay?'

Matt left the living room and checked the house. He prayed that Nadia had got away. This wasn't Peter. He was gentle, caring, compassionate. What had these men turned him into? But his wife had been killed. At this moment, Peter was dangerous. He'd do anything to avoid prison. They all would. He remembered the words Peter had said. They were all involved. If he went down, they all would. Matt had been there too. Although he'd gone to bed earlier than the others, records of him at the hotel would be easy to find. They were in this together.

Once Matt had checked over the house, he returned to Greta. She was sat up, staring towards the living room door.

'Greta. I got a call earlier. You need to stay calm. I think Nadia has gone with Peter.' Matt didn't want to say too much.

'She's never liked Peter in that way. She wouldn't. She loves you.'

'Okay. Do you want to come with us? I need to find her.'

'No. I can't move. Look, do what you have to do to get her back. I have a neighbour coming here in the morning. I'll be fine. I can't believe she'd run off with Peter, of all people. Wonders never cease.'

Matt leant forward and kissed Greta on the cheek. 'I'll call in the morning.'

As Matt reached the front door, he kicked something on the floor. He looked down and saw Nadia's bracelet.

It confirmed Peter had taken her.

13

One year ago.

John Blair stood at the main entrance of his hotel. It was August. The peak of the holiday season. Although it was just gone 10am, he could feel today was going to be another scorcher. The sky was a beautiful light blue, clear, and the sun glistened like an exotic diamond overhead.

He stood, immersing in the warmth. Already the streets were packed. He watched families strolling along the pavement, kids with ice creams melting, spilling down the cones, candy floss, people in wetsuits crossing the road and heading to the beach. He glimpsed towards the sea, so calm and still. Perfect conditions for a morning swim. John was energised with the smell of coffee, sugar, the fresh air gently blowing on his face. He loved Brighton.

It was days like this that made it all worth it. He stood on the step, listening to the sound of a familiar nursery rhyme as an ice cream van pulled out onto the street, kids' laughter, excitement, this was the reason he opened The Blair Hotel all those years ago. He turned to the front window on his right; his mood dropped as he peered the vacant sign, the word "Open," flashed through the glass, its neon lights reverberating.

John Blair stepped back into the lobby and walked over to the desk. Fred, one of his longest-serving staff members, was tidying the counter.

'How are we looking?'

Fred tapped a couple of buttons, bringing up a diary on the computer screen. He swivelled it tenderly towards his boss.

John leaned into the screen, squinting his eyes to eradicate the blur. Almost every room on the ground floor was empty. Floors one, two and three were almost identical. The fourth floor had been closed off for refurbishment. John had invested almost every penny of his savings to modernising his hotel. He wanted a little elegance, luxury. Why not? He worked around the clock. His customers were his life, and he wanted to pay them back for their loyalty. As John watched his money haemorrhaging, the builders finding more problems, he had to face the fact that he may go bankrupt. The hotel was losing money. As he stood at the desk, glaring desperately at the empty rooms on the monitor, John recalled the morning the builders pulled off-site. John begged them, asking for more time, pleading with them to finish with all manner of promises that he'd pay. He owed them money, and they'd had enough.

John backed away from the desk, thanking Fred. He moved towards the restaurant. The breakfast area would normally be thriving, the staff rushing back and forward with pots of tea and coffee, asking the guests their plans for the day, chefs singing in the kitchen, the radio playing.

He saw the tables empty, the juice machine full, untouched, and a chef in the kitchen tapping on his phone. John moved away, out to the foyer and walked over to the staffroom beside the desk.

He pushed the door, locking it behind him, then opened his laptop and Googled, The Blair Hotel, Brighton, peering at the recent stories. In the last couple of months, three women had gone missing. Not too unusual, as Brighton has its fair share of crime. But they'd all stayed here at the hotel, weeks apart, never heard of again. The reason whispers had started about his hotel, the reason locals had turned against him.

John had helped with the police investigation; he was a pillar of the community, well respected and close friends with the local detective Inspector. John wanted to help in any way he could. The Blair Hotel had been host to numerous events and significant evenings: small award ceremonies, local council meetings, and the recently elected Mayor of Brighton, Charles Tomlinson, was a regular who visited every couple of months with his wife and three children. John and Mayor Tomlinson had become extremely close over recent years, and he even promised to help get the hotel back on its feet.

He remembered the last time he visited. John sat at the bar with Mayor Tomlinson and his wife, Cheryl. She was beautiful, polite and interested in everything her husband stood for. Their young children were captivated by the fruit machine, watching the stream of lights, the glowing words with a chance to win the jackpot. He listened as the older boy, no more than eight, explained what three of a kind meant to his sisters. John opened the box at the bottom of the machine, watching the excitement on their faces as he handed them money to play. He let them behind the bar, teaching them how to serve the perfect pint.

Mayor Tomlinson knew of the rumours, but he promised

John he'd do everything in his power to help him. That night, just over a month ago, was the last time he'd heard from the family.

John had called him numerous times. His secretary answered, announcing Mayor Tomlinson was in a meeting, out of the office or at lunch. Maybe it was for the best. The more functions and notorious guests at The Blair Hotel, the more the rumours were circulated. Needless to say, the locals had a field day.

He scanned through reports online. Articles which pointed the finger at him, his hotel, one headline lead with, The Mare Hotel. John scanned through the comments.

I'll never stay there again. The place is hideous. Declan Bourne.

Yeah, I stayed there once. The rooms are ghastly, and the food was dreadful. My wife had the steak and was ill for days. Mona C.

Yes, Mona. The staff are rude. I wouldn't be surprised if the missing girls were served at the restaurant with a drop of chianti. Lol. Becky O'Connell.

He recalled the times recently when he'd stood at the main entrance, greeting the familiar faces, smiling, raising his hand, watching the blank expressions as people hurried past the front door as if the place was dirty, tarnished. The locals looked at him differently. Shame in their eyes, steered towards John and his hotel. He tried everything, walking down the steps, approaching people, handing out fliers, guests he'd remembered who visited time and again, now turning away or crossing the street. He'd saw the rumour mill expanding on social media as the locals scrutinised him, whispers that he was responsible for running a sinister organisation or a crime syndicate. People stopped coming; they refused to acknowledge him as he stood at the main entrance, day after day. John Blair was as straight as they came. He'd bend over backwards to make his guests' experience as memorable as possible. He'd give half-price rooms to people if he heard a sob story. He'd turn away from guests at the buffet filling their plates three, four times. Visitors who came into the bar with their own drinks. John let it all go. As long as the hotel was busy and people had smiles on their faces, he was thrilled. It meant they'd recommend this place to others.

It was true the hotel had started to look shabby. The money he'd spent renovating the fourth floor meant the other rooms were neglected. Now, the builders had walked, and he feared his time running the hotel had come to an end.

John struggled to stem the fear as he sat in his office, realising where it had all gone wrong. He regretted the decision he'd made. But now, it was too late.

John's two sons had returned from Switzerland after a phone call. He'd told them he wanted to close The Blair Hotel and retire. John had lost his wife the previous year, and he was tired. At the time of the phone call, just a couple of months ago, the hotel was booming. They had bookings weeks in advance, and the restaurant was busy seven nights a week. He'd had the fourth floor completely gutted, investing everything into remodelling the place. John didn't care about the cost. He knew he'd get it back. The Blair Hotel was a goldmine.

He told his sons he would hand the hotel over to them if they wanted it, and he'd show them the ropes. John could hear the eagerness in their voices. Two days later, he picked them up from the airport. The first thing he noticed as he waited at the terminal entrance was their odd behaviour. His younger son, Marty, had a scar along his left cheek. He continually spoke about a man who had taken them in and looked after them. John had challenged his sons as to why they were in Switzerland, but they were closed, answering his questions with only smiles or nods of their heads. His older son, Vincent, looked spaced out as they drove to Brighton, smirking, laughing to himself and curling his tall frame into a ball on the back seat.

John went through everything with them. From early morning, the staff meetings, cleaning duties, booking guests in, the different menus that cater to every food allergy, the bar, the front desk, customer etiquette, and room service. He taught them everything about running a successful business.

A week later, the first hotel guest went missing.

John had seen her around the hotel. She was short, with long black hair and was painfully shy. She dressed casually, in jeans and a tee-shirt mostly. The odd time he spoke to her, once at breakfast and once in the hallway near her room on the first floor, she blushed. She was severely awkward with conversation. Not in a rude way, but engagement seemed to trouble her. John knew how to deal with it. Make it less uncomfortable. Just smile and don't ask questions. He'd passed her later that evening as she made her way to the restaurant, holding the door open and simply wishing her a pleasant evening. She'd booked her room for the week, arriving Monday afternoon and went missing on Tuesday evening. John had taken a phone call from her father on the Thursday. The man had said he'd not been able to contact his daughter since Wednesday morning, and he was worried. He gave John permission to enter her room. He'd found her suitcase open on the floor, her bed had been made, and her makeup was placed on the bathroom sink. The woman's father came to the hotel later that evening, staying in his daughter's room. He'd made fliers which he'd handed out and informed the police. They'd called over to speak with John, take a look in the room and assured the women's father they'd keep an eye out. Because she wasn't a minor, they assumed she may have just met someone in Brighton and was letting her hair down.

Over the space of two months, two more women went missing in Brighton. Both in suspicious circumstances, and both had stayed at The Blair Hotel. They were seen by police on the security cameras leaving through the main entrance and never returning. Detective Inspector Ryan Bartlett, a close friend of John's, assured him he wasn't being investigated and that most likely, the women had met friends and decided to travel on to someplace else. Again, John had taken phone calls from the frantic families, and the police had been called to investigate.

Now, John closed the laptop.

A couple of nights ago, he'd gone to the fourth floor, surveying what he needed to do to modernise the place. He'd run out of money, the builders had walked, and the hotel was in freefall. He had paced up and down the hallway, panicking. The place he loved and worked so hard to make a success was sliding through his fingers. As he walked to the end of the hall, he viewed the many symbols drawn on the walls and doors. The topic seemed to be grape related. John placed his hand on the drawings, fascinated as to how they got there. One was a picture of a bunch of grapes hoovering in the air over a chalice. Another had a cross with an arrow at one end, sticking out of a bunch of grapes. There were stencil pictures of a figure riding a leopard and the same figure in a chariot drawn by panthers. Below every symbol, the word Dionysus was written in black capital letters.

John placed his ear to the last door on the left, listening. He could hear voices. They became noisy, people were singing, and music played. He heard screaming, becoming louder, weird chanting, like a late-night ritual. His sons were different since they'd returned from Switzerland. He'd read about cults, brainwashing, ceremonies and the likes. Surely

John was wrong? Marty, his younger son, started calling the name Dionysus, over and over, his voice louder each time he said the word. John backed away as his son began chanting about the God of ecstasy and revenge.

He raced along the hallway, the symbols seeming like they were coming away from the wall.

Downstairs, John moved across the foyer and into his office near the front desk. He Googled Dionysus, scanning through the pictures, finding many of the symbols he'd seen on the fourth floor. He read on, searching for more information.

As the God of ritual insanity, Dionysius has the ability to make people go insane at will. He makes people go into a trance where they lose all awareness. He uses this skill for both good and bad reasons. The Maenads, also known as the Bacchantes, are sent into a state of joyful delirium through performing rituals in honour of Dionysius. This ecstasy is a good way in which insanity is associated with Dionysius. However, it is mostly used as a form of punishment for those who disobey Dionysius or deny his cult.

John read more articles.

The best example of both ecstasy and retribution regarding Dionysius is the myth of Pentheus. Dionysius' mother Semele was killed when Zeus, Dionysius' father, revealed himself to her in his true form and accidentally burnt her alive with a thunderbolt. Semele's sisters spread rumours that she was killed by Zeus as a punishment for lying about Zeus being the father of her unborn child. One of the sisters was named Agave and it is her son Pentheus who became the King of Thebes. He banned the cult of Dionysius, believing it was unlawful, dangerous and promiscuous.

John read another short piece.

Dionysius, or the God of wine, insists that his worshippers are drunk and therefore outside of themselves when they worship him. His rituals happen at night, in the hillsides, with a hunt staged.

Was this how the women had gone missing? His sons,

worshipping the God of ecstasy and revenge? Had they crossed paths with the women? Had something happened that drove his sons to act in an unruly manner? Had they taken the women as an act of revenge? Now, people were pointing the finger at him. He was almost bankrupt; his hotel brought to its knees. All this, because of a cult. A cult his sons believed in. A cult where his sons believed in the act of revenge.

* * *

Now, John glared at the closed laptop. He wanted to read more, to research what he'd started a couple of nights ago after what he'd heard coming from a room on the fourth floor. Dionysius, the God of ecstasy and revenge. Who were his sons? Did he know them anymore? What the hell were they capable of doing? John had just read the headline online, a recent report. The Mare Hotel. A cruel take on Blair. People were speculating, turning against him.

John moved out of the office and rode the lift to the fourth floor. He walked down the hallway, entered one of the rooms, locking the door behind him, and moved to the window at the far end. John stood on a ladder, left by the builders and gently removed the curtain from its pole. Then he removed the wire and placed it over the curtain pole. As John looked out over Brighton with sadness in his heart, he placed the wire around his neck and shimmied the ladder away. His body jerked, twisted and then became limp.

14

Present Day.

Marty sat in one of the rooms on the fourth floor of the hotel. It was late, and he'd been watching the recording on a large screen. He couldn't help himself. A month had passed since that night. They'd worked so hard to get Adriana into the country. She was the start of their ticket out. A better life of luxury, riches. Wealthy businesspeople were prepared to pay large amounts of money for a woman like her. She was the test run, the trial. The hotel was losing so much money. Others were cheaper, with better food, service, etiquette. In the short time the brothers had taken over from their father, they'd run it into the ground. Marty had to do something to save face. He wasn't going to fail like his dad, whom Marty blamed. He was too nice. He cared for people. He let these peasants walk over him. Marty had found him hanging from a curtain rail on the fourth-floor months ago. He was disturbed. Astounded that his father had let these people get to him. Christ, Marty regarded them as inferior. He couldn't care less about the people staying in his hotel or their requirements. He'd learn from his father's mistakes. Marty had watched his father slogging, often at the hotel sixteen hours a day. Always courteous, respectful, he spoke with the guests and made them welcome. But it wasn't enough. He'd hear their promises over and over; we'll be back next year, we'll bring the whole family. We love this place. He'd see them on the streets; his father had a knack for remembering faces; he loved people. They'd come back to Brighton and stay at a hotel down the road. Maybe the place offered live music, exotic cocktails, room service, a better minibar. They weren't loyal to him. They killed him. Marty would learn from his father's mishaps.

* * *

He pressed rewind on the remote control. Adriana, entering the room with a man. Marty watched the screen, clutching his fists. The guy moved to the minibar. Marty watched her drop her dress. Christ, she was beautiful. One of the most incredible women he had ever seen. His eyes were glued to the screen. Her, stood in a red bra and knickers. He watched them kiss, pressing their bodies against each other. Making love on the bed, him, grabbing her throat, her, losing control. Then he watched her die, her body, drained of life. She lay still, static in the bed.

Now, as he sat in a room on the fourth floor, he watched the friends together, trying to figure out what to do. A security camera on the wall at the back of the hotel captured them, carrying Adriana out, lifting her to a quiet corner of the garden. They were loaded with shovels, a spade. They slumped her body on the wet grass and started digging. Once they'd buried her, they went back to their rooms. Marty managed to load footage from the two cameras onto a file. The first one capturing the murder, the second one showed them burying Adriana. Marty had everything he needed. The following morning, he stood over the mound. He walked in circles, his mind racing, anger raging through his body. Then he saw something in the grass. A phone. One of the guys had dropped it while burying Adriana.

He'd get it unlocked and make them pay.

One by one.

* * *

Marty heard his phone beep. A text message. The screen lit up. He glanced down, seeing the word, "Here."

He grabbed the remote control and turned the telly to standby.

Marty opened the door to the room and walked along the dark corridor towards the lift. He pressed the button marked B, then glanced in the mirror as the doors closed. The text message excited him. A new venture. His father had always told him to have his fingers in many pies. He recalled his school days; Marty was hellbent on learning one subject: Spanish, a second language that was spoken all over the world. But it wasn't good enough. His father had told him to take up French and German too. Nothing like an education. When he was picked to play for the local football team, he dreamed of a career as a forward, scoring goals, his name in the local papers. His father wanted him to take up rugby and tennis as well. He bought him rackets, balls and insisted he played every Saturday morning. Anything Marty did, his father wanted more from him until he had to give everything up from sheer exhaustion.

He'd watched his father's dream crumble, the lack of guests, the empty restaurant. It wasn't going to happen to him.

Marty stepped out of the lift and pushed the door that led outside. It was dark, except for a small spotlight on the wall facing the car park. He looked towards the gate, watching it close. The van pulled up along the side wall.

Marty stood by the metal shutters outside the warehouse at the back of The Blair Hotel. It was quiet and secure. No cameras on this side of the building.

The driver got out, waving to him. He opened the back door, and a woman stepped out of the van with Marty's older brother, Vincent. She was small, skinny, with a hood over her head. She was mumbling something, but the hood made it difficult to hear what she was saying. The two men led her to the warehouse. Marty joined them as they walked to the lift and up to the fourth floor.

As they stepped out of the lift, the driver waited, taking payment.

'That's all for now,' Marty said. 'Are there more?'

'Yeah. The truck came in a couple of hours ago. We have them secure. Let me know when you want the next one. They're all refugees. Easy money.'

Marty knew this was the way forward. After the spotlight of recent months being shone more on his hotel, he had to be careful. Marty had to keep his head low for a while. He saw this as a way of revenge: retaliation for people trying to enter the country illegally.

Marty patted the driver on the back and watched the lift doors close.

As they walked along the hall, joining his brother, he watched the hooded woman taking small steps, her head frantically moving to try and free herself. They could hear the fear in her voice, and Marty was getting frustrated.

He fished a door card from his trouser pocket and opened the last door on the left. As he walked into the room, he saw the dustsheets covering the carpet. A guy was standing in the far corner, dressed in white overalls. He wore glasses, his hair was a mass of curls, and he smiled towards the brothers.

Marty removed the hood from the woman's head.

She looked mid-twenties, possibly Filipino. She seemed fit, healthy. Her eyes were dark, wild and filled with terror. Marty brought her over to the bench. He looked at the tools which the man had bought with him: scalpels, knives, an array of sharp implements.

They placed her on the bench, and she kicked out violently as they strapped her down. A second later, the guy pressed an injection into her body, a general anaesthetic, and she was unconscious.

'How long does it take?' Marty asked.

'The kidney? Three, four hours tops.'

Marty smiled, and the brothers left the room.

* * *

The surgeon turned the woman on her side. He cut roughly ten inches long just below her ribs. He carefully cut the fat and tissue. Then he cut the tube, which carries urine to the bladder. After cutting the blood vessels, he gently removed the kidney. Once it was out, he stitched her back up.

He stood back, admiring his work, excited about the new business venture.

They were going to make a lot of money.

Thousands of people around the world were on a waiting list for a transplant. He saw his work as simply helping others and reducing that list.

15

Present Day.

Matt drove, fighting nausea which began to weaken his body.

He'd just left Greta's house, finding Nadia's bracelet by the front door. Although the heater was on, he could feel a cold sweat rise through his body. His hands were clammy, and his face was flushed. He had to get a grip of himself and be strong for Nadia. He glanced at Lucy and saw she was still asleep. He listened to her light breaths coming from the back seat. He needed her to stay this way. Guilt began to push through his body. He knew the dangers ahead, what had happened in Brighton, Peter acting like a madman. He watched Lucy in the rear-view mirror, wishing he'd left her with Greta. Peter had been there. What was stopping him from returning to the house? Now he feared for Greta. Alone, vulnerable. Matt had no choice. He had to bring Lucy with him. It was too dangerous to leave her behind. Although he felt terrified for his daughter, Matt had to keep her close. Greta had a neighbour who was calling over in the morning. If Peter had wanted to, he'd have killed Greta. This was about Nadia.

Matt tried to digest the conversation with Sean earlier. Matt knew Billy had met a woman at the casino. Sean explained that Billy had gone back with her; they'd had rough sex, resulting in a terrible accident. Sean said the woman's neck had snapped. Billy panicked and ran to the bar for the others. Matt had already gone to bed at that stage. After deliberation, they buried her in the grounds of the hotel. Peter seemed to have lost it. Whatever had happened between then and now, he'd gone off the rails. He'd called over to Sean's house, possibly attacked the neighbour, then went after Mia. Now, he had Nadia.

Matt watched the signs for London and exited onto the M40. The road was quiet. He drove, his eyes staring at the bright specs separating each lane. He pushed his foot on the accelerator, watching the speedometer reach eighty-five miles an hour. Visions of his beautiful wife swept through his mind. The first time he'd met her. He'd been with the others too, Sean, Peter and Billy, a local pub in Camden Town. At the time, Matt rented a room. He'd left home at twenty-one, wanting to see the world. He'd ended up in North London due to a lack of work. The money he made during the week was mostly spent on a Friday and Saturday night. When Monday morning came around, he hardly had enough for a coffee on the way to work. He was young, enjoying himself, and it didn't matter. He was loving life. He recalled how they were playing pool one evening; Billy thought he was a bit of a hustler. Matt potted the black ball while six of Billy's colours remained on the table. Billy was sulking even more when the guys made him buy the next round. Matt looked over: a group of women were sat at a table in the corner. A bottle of red wine in the middle and a barman bringing another one over on a tray. He spotted a woman sat facing him; she was clapping her hands lightly together at his performance. Matt blushed and grabbed the chalk, wiping it over the cue. He'd had a couple of drinks and felt brave, so he signed for her to have a game with him. He watched with surprise as she got off her stool and joined him. Matt watched the shocked looks on his mate's faces. She was beautiful. Her hair was short but full, wavy, with layers chopped and dropping over her face. She wore a bright red jumper, skin-tight jeans and brown boots. Her eyes were the darkest brown, and her cheekbones seemed chiselled into her face. As they played, Matt struggled to hold the cue, his arms were shaking, and he was captivated by the aroma of perfume. She smelt of vanilla and sweet cherry. He watched as she potted ball after ball. As he played, he may as well have held a broom. His mates were making faces in the background, which added to the pressure. After the game was finished, Matt asked the woman her name.

'Nadia. Nice to beat you,' she replied.

'Oh. Very good. I like that. Beat you. Yeah, I'll give you that. Well, Nadia. Can I get you a drink?'

'I'm in a round, but I'd love a gin and tonic.'

Matt walked to the bar, pleased to see Nadia join him.

They spoke for the rest of the evening, and when it was time to leave, they exchanged numbers. Matt and Nadia soon became a couple, and their relationship quickly progressed. They moved in together six months later.

Now, as Matt drove, eyeing the rear-view mirror, watching Lucy sleep, he knew he'd do anything for his wife and daughter.

* * *

They reached home at just gone 4am. Matt got out of the Jeep and woke Lucy. She jumped as he leant over the seat. He watched her eyes as they struggled to focus; her face was marked from where she slept on the seat. She shivered, struggling to find her bearings.

'We're home. Where's Mum?'

Matt had to keep it from Lucy. He knew she'd freak out. 'She's still at Nana's. She'll be home later. Are you okay, baby? You slept all the way home.' Matt had to change the subject.

'Yeah. I'm cold. Can I stay up for a bit?' Lucy followed her father to the front door.

'Half an hour. That's it. Wow, you take advantage of your father, don't you?'

'Mum says I have you wrapped around my little finger.'

'Yeah. She'd be right.' Matt could see his breath as he stood on the drive.

As he placed the key in the front door lock, he could feel the emptiness. A sense of despair as if the house knew something was missing. Lucy walked into the living room and turned on the telly.

Matt moved to the kitchen, grabbed the mobile phone from his pocket and dialled Peter's number. When it went to voicemail, he slammed it down on the breakfast bar. He cried silently, tears streaming down his face. He struggled to cope. How could he tell Lucy her mother had been taken by one of his oldest friends? How could he tell her what had happened? He wanted to call the police, but Matt knew he'd be signing a death warrant. Peter would kill Nadia. Matt was certain. He'd also expose the crime his friends had done. He had to find Nadia himself and get her back.

Once he'd composed himself, he fired up the laptop and started searching.

First, he typed in The Blair Hotel, Brighton. He waited a

moment for the page to load. He saw a picture of the hotel from the front. A tall, four-storey building, elegant, sophisticated. A large name badge hung above the arched entrance. The picture was taken in black and white. A man dressed in a suit was standing by the front door. Journalists were crouching, taking photos. A couple of old-style cars were parked by the pavement out the front, a Ford Cortina and a Hillman Hunter.

Another picture showed the same well-dressed man cutting a ribbon. Matt could see people cheering, hands in the air, smiles. He read a small part of the article from The Argus, a local newspaper serving Brighton and Hove.

The Blair Hotel. Brighton's latest offering for fine dining and a luxury break.

Brighton welcomes John Blair and his wife, Irene, who officially open The Blair Hotel today on the seafront. John is finally accomplishing his dream and tells us he's always wanted to bring something to the people of Brighton.

'I've had this urge for a long time now. My wife thinks I'm crazy. She says I'm too ambitious. But I'll make it work. We have so many friends here. The community is amazing. Where better to open a hotel and bring people to our wonderful coast? Brighton has it all. It's growing in stature. More and more people are coming every summer. My hotel boasts over eighty rooms, all en-suite, ample parking and an elegant restaurant. Thank you to everyone who has given us this opportunity. My wife and I are looking forward to you visiting our hotel.'

Matt typed, Death at The Blair Hotel. There had to be something. Billy had killed a woman in his room on the ground floor. Peter and Sean had helped cover it up. They'd buried her in the grounds. The only report was that of Blair Adams, a thirty-one-year-old Canadian resident who was found dead in a parking lot in Knoxville, Tennessee, USA. Matt hovered his finger over a related link. He'd found something. He clicked the article, which was dated almost a year ago.

John Blair, hotel proprietor of The Blair Hotel, found hanged.

Matt felt a shiver down his back as he read the story.

John Blair, owner of The Blair Hotel, found dead.

Matt scanned the article and read more of the report.

John Blair was found by his youngest son, Marty, early this morning in one of the rooms of The Blair Hotel. It's unknown at this stage why the ambitious businessman took his own life. It is reported that the hotel was losing customers, and it's thought that John was struggling with debt. Irene Blair, John's wife, sadly lost her battle to cancer last year. The couple opened the hotel almost fifty years ago with an ambition to give something back to this bustling English coastal town. The family have asked to be left alone in their time of mourning.

Another story reported three women who had gone missing in Brighton and had all stayed at The Blair Hotel. Matt read the story, the reports speculating what had happened and an appeal for their safe return. He scrolled down the page then returned to the search bar. Matt typed, *Woman killed at The Blair Hotel*. He found nothing.

How is this not reported? There has to be a story somewhere, Matt thought. He tried rephrasing his words in the search engine.

Brighton hotel. Woman killed. Blair Hotel.

Nothing.

Matt closed the laptop. He thought about Nadia. He grabbed his mobile, his index finger hovering over the nine button. He wanted to call the police, tell them his wife had been kidnapped. Peter had warned him. He said he'd kill Nadia at the first sign of a siren. Matt believed him. Peter had lost it; Sean's call earlier showed that Peter was capable of murder. He envisioned Peter, driving with the body of his dead wife in the passenger seat, Nadia tied up in the back. Sean and Mia's neighbour missing. Peter, driving into a tree or over a cliff.

Matt had to stop him. He had to get to Peter. He dialled the number again.

The same answer message.

Matt stood. His body ached with tension. The lack of sleep was catching up, drowning his body with fatigue. He stretched his back, pushing his body upwards, feeling a bone crack under his lungs. His neck felt stiff, like his head was too heavy, and he just wanted to sleep. He thought of Nadia. He had to keep going.

* * *

It was almost five in the morning. Matt walked into the living room. He was surprised to see Lucy was still up.
'Hey, Lucy. Why are you still awake?'

'I'm playing Fortnite.'

'I call it Two Weeks. That's what the oldies name it.'

'I don't get it.'

'Oh, never mind. Lucy, I need to talk with you.' He watched her turn the telly off.

'Are you okay, Dad?'

'Me? Yes, I'm fine. Look, something has happened.' Matt had to come clean. He couldn't hide it from Lucy. They'd be too many questions. He'd have to make it less severe than it seemed for his daughter's sake.

'We called over to nana's earlier this evening. I wanted it to be a surprise.'

'Oh. Why didn't you wake me?'

'Well, this is the thing. Mum wasn't there.'

'Why?'

'Lucy, mum has gone missing. I'm not sure where she is.

But we'll find her. I promise.' Matt struggled with the tears that threatened to pour from his eyes. He fought the lump in his throat, swallowing hard to control his emotions. He couldn't break down in front of his daughter.

'What the hell, Dad? Why the heck didn't you tell me? For Christ's sake. Do you mean she's left us? Like, met someone else? She'd never leave. I know she wouldn't. What's happened, Dad?' Lucy broke down, her eyes filled with tears and she closed her fists in frustration.

Matt crouched beside his daughter. 'Lucy, our love for you is unconditional. You'll never know the things we'd do to keep you safe. Your mother and I will always be there for you. We love you more than anything in this world.'

'So why did she leave? Have you had a row?'

Matt thought for a second about how to word the explanation. 'Sometimes, in a relationship, people need their own space. It gets too much for that person to cope. Maybe they need a couple of nights away to get their head clear, or they just need time out. Okay, so, what's the one thing you love to do?'

'Netball,' Lucy answered.

'Right. Netball. So, you're playing Netball and maybe you're tired. Your body aches. Maybe you've turned on your ankle. The coach sees this although you want to play on, keep going for the team, give your all but in the end, you have to come off, or your body will give up.'

'I wouldn't come off.'

'Lucy, what I'm saying is, sometimes we have to do what's right for ourselves. We have to take a break, so when we come back, we're better than ever.'

'You're not making sense. If you've had an argument, just say. You'll work it out. Is that what's happened?'

Matt watched the irritation in his daughter's face, wondering if she was buying what he had said. 'In a way, yes.'

'So, let's bloody find her.'

Matt knew his next answer would erase everything he'd just said. He wanted to burst into tears, hearing his daughter and how brave she was. 'She's in Brighton. She's gone with Peter.'

The words spilt uncontrollably from Matt's lips. Although he'd smoothed over the harrowing truth of the situation, he felt he'd said enough for alarm bells to ring. Matt couldn't let Lucy know her mother had been kidnapped and possibly murdered. He struggled with his emotions, feeling he was losing his mind. He had to keep it together for his daughter's sake.

Lucy stood. 'This is madness, Dad. None of this makes sense. You're saying she's run off with Peter? It's crazy. I wish you'd stop trying to protect me and be truthful. Why are we sat here? Let's go already.'

* * *

Matt pulled up outside Peter's house. It was almost 6am. Lucy was sat in the back.

'Wait here a minute. I'll leave the engine running so you can keep warm. Lock the doors; I'll keep a watch from across the street. I need you to stay in the Jeep, Lucy.' He watched her nod her head.

Matt opened the Jeep door and slowly walked across the road towards the empty drive. The lights were off inside, and the curtains were open; the front living room was on display. Matt looked behind him towards the Jeep. Lucy watched from the backseat. His heart was racing; he fought to stem the trembling ache which rushed through his body. As he walked up the driveway, he took deep breaths, in through his nose and slowly out. He looked behind; there was no sign of

Peter's car on the road. Maybe he'd parked on another street, knowing someone may call at the house.

Matt checked the windows at the front. All locked. He walked around the side of the house and into the garden. A spotlight came on, which made him jump. Matt leaned against the wall, pressing his body to the cold brick. He waited for a minute, then moved to the sliding door of the kitchen. He reached for the handle and pulled. The door was solid. Suddenly, Matt heard something behind him. He turned, glancing towards the shed. Matt ducked. He watched a figure standing in the shadows. Matt was unsure whether the person was looking towards him or turned the other way. He struggled to see a face. He waited, crouching by the back door. The light came on in the shed, and Matt dropped to the cold ground lying on his chest. He saw a man, not Peter. This person was younger, possibly mid-thirties, now facing a large container. He hadn't seen Matt. The guy leant forward, lifting the heavy lid. He reached inside, and Matt watched a frosty plume of condensation rise into the room. He was lifting something, struggling to pull it out of the container. Matt realised it was a freezer. The guy was holding a body. He placed it on the floor as Matt looked on in horror. He saw the guy turn, grabbing a large saw from the worktop. He started cutting into it.

Matt gasped, quickly covering his mouth. Suddenly, the man walked to the door and stepped out into the garden. Matt watched as he pulled out a handgun from the inside of his jacket, moving it around in the air.

'Is someone there?'

Matt slowly got to his feet and backed away to the side entrance. As he moved towards the front of the house, the spotlight came on. Matt spun around. He could hear footsteps moving towards him.

'Who's there? Show your face.'

Matt had seconds before the guy came around the corner from the back garden. He charged along the side entrance to the front of the house. As Matt raced along the drive, he turned and saw the guy running towards him. Matt tried the driver's door, feeling it locked. He shouted, desperation in his voice. 'Lucy, open the doors. Quickly. Open the doors.'

Lucy leant into the front seat unlocking the door, hearing the loud clunking sound. As Matt pulled the door towards him, they watched the guy racing down the drive. Matt put the Jeep in gear and pressed his foot on the accelerator as the guy jumped onto the road. He was stood in front of them. His arm was extended, aiming the gun towards them.

Matt screamed, 'Lucy. Get down.' As he drove, he saw the man, about to pull the trigger. Matt pressed harder on the accelerator, and at the last second, the guy jumped out of the way.

It was too loud to fire a gun in a suburban area.

Matt watched in the rear-view mirror as the guy stood on the road, watching them escape.

* * *

As Matt drove, he tried to piece the puzzle together. Lucy was shouting from the back seat but nothing registered. Matt's head was too busy. He remembered Sean saying something about their neighbour calling over. Mia had seen her, lying on the kitchen floor. They believed Peter had been to the house and possibly murdered her. Although Sean hadn't seen the body, Mia was adamant Peter killed her and then chased Mia up to the bathroom. When Sean looked in the kitchen, the body and Peter had both gone. Was it possible the body in the freezer was Sean and Mia's neighbour? Could Peter really have done it? If he had, it was evident someone was forcing him to carry out these wicked deeds. Matt had seen Lucy's selfie. A woman, lying battered on the passenger seat of Peter's car. Had they done this as a way to show Peter they were serious? Was it Peter's wife that Matt had seen?

Matt recalled the article he'd read earlier on The Blair Hotel. Three women had gone missing recently, all within a couple of months of each other, never seen again. They'd all stayed at the hotel. Were they hidden somewhere in one of the rooms? Billy killed a woman in a sex act that went horribly wrong. Billy, Sean and Peter had buried her in the back garden of the hotel. So why had a body never been found? Why did no one come forward and report her missing? The more Matt thought about it, the more it pointed to The Blair Hotel. A few minutes ago, Matt had seen someone in Peter's shed, about to start cutting. Someone knew what Peter had done. They'd come to the house to get rid of the body. Something wicked was happening. Something evil.

Nadia was missing, and Matt knew he had to go back to The Blair Hotel.

16

The Same Morning.

Sean's phone rang at just gone 6am. He sat up and reached to the bedside cabinet, removing the charger. The curtains were open, and Sean glared at the bleakness outside. He summoned the torch on his phone, steering it across the dark space and shivered with the coldness of the room. Mia was still asleep. He pushed the covers away from his body and stood on the wooden floor. "No caller ID," displayed across the screen of his mobile. As Sean stepped into his jeans and placed a clean tee-shirt over his body, the phone rang off. He stared at the screen, waiting to see if the caller had left a message. After a minute, he moved from the bedroom, along the upstairs hallway, and stopped outside the bathroom. Sean leaned his hand against the door, thinking about the events two nights ago. Peter being in their house. Their neighbour, Kate, calling over. Mia had said she'd seen her body lying on the kitchen floor. Had Peter killed her by mistake? Cleaned up and removed the body? How the hell would he explain it to Geoff, Kate's husband? He'd already rang, asking if Kate had been there. Sean had managed to hold Mia off from calling the police, insisting she wait to see how it played out. If Peter had been here, murdered their neighbour, they could be blamed or accused of being involved. The longer it drew out, the more trouble Sean and Mia could bring to their door.

Sean moved down the stairs and sat in the kitchen. He placed his mobile on the table and contemplated their predicament. He jumped as the phone rang. Again, "no caller ID," displayed across the screen. Sean picked the phone up, struggling to control his shaking hands.

'Hello?' He didn't want to announce his name.

'I know what happened. Hang up, and I'll kill you.'

Sean listened to the deep voice. The caller was well-spoken with a clear, English accent.

Sean whispered, 'Who is this? What the hell do you want?'

'I know all about the trip. I know what you and your friends have done. How you covered up the death of that woman.'

Sean felt a hot flush rise through his body. His neck was itchy, his hands trembled, and he suddenly felt nauseous. The room became blurry.

The caller continued. 'So, here's what's going to happen. You'll wake your partner, maybe bring her a cup of tea, toast is always a nice touch. You'll insist that she packs a bag. You'll pack one too. Tell her you have a surprise booked, a sporadic last-minute decision, off the cuff. Then, you and your girlfriend will drive to Brighton. I hear it's a fantastic place to visit. You should know. Once you get there, you'll check into The Blair Hotel. Are you writing this down?'

'You're crazy. I have work, clients booked in who are waiting for me. What's my partner going to think? I can't just...'

The caller's voice became louder, more authoritative. 'Once you check into the hotel, await my instructions. Let me remind you, I have the recording. I'd hate for it to get into the wrong hands.'

Sean heard the guy ending the call.

He dropped the phone on the table and placed his head in his hands.

A tap on the glass of the front door jerked Sean out of his rumination. He peered along the downstairs hallway and saw a large figure facing towards him. Sean felt his heart race as he pushed the chair back and stood. He wanted to run, get away from the house, charge along the street and keep running. A couple of seconds later, the person tapped the glass again. Sean stood, watching the shadow at the front door. He crept along the hall and reached his left arm forward, unlocking the chain and the snib, then pulled the front door towards him. A large, overweight man in his mid-forties greeted him with a grin.

'Geoff.' Sean exaggerated the glance at his wristwatch. 'It's early.'

'Sorry. I've been up all night. Kate's still missing. I'm going up the bloody wall. Something's happened. I know it has.'

Sean purposely used his frame to block the entrance and let Geoff know he wasn't coming into the house.

'Oh no. Have you had an argument?' Sean could feel his face flush. He struggled to gain composure.

'No. Nothing like that. She left two nights ago. Her car's in the drive so she must have gone local. Mia is her only friend on the street. She told me she was popping out for a while and she'd be back in an hour. I assumed she came here.'

Sean turned away, unable to make eye contact. 'She definitely wasn't here. Have you called the police?'

'I'm about to again. I reported her disappearance yesterday morning. They went through all the options. The protocol. You know how it is, Sean. She's not missing until she's missing.'

'Well, I'll keep an eye out.' Sean realised the stupidity of his statement as he went to close the door.

'Are you certain she wasn't here?'

'How do you mean?'

'Maybe she called over when you were out. Sean, I'm grasping at straws here, mate. I'm desperate. Anything you can tell me. Were you out a couple of nights ago? Maybe she came over, and you didn't know. Can I speak with Mia?'

'Geoff. I was here all evening. Mia and I watched a film. I'd know if she was here.' Sean stepped back, hoping the lie didn't show on his face. 'I'm sure she'll turn up.' He went to push the door.

Geoff placed his hand on the glass. 'I swear I saw you pass the house around half seven on Thursday night. It certainly looked like you.'

'Sorry, Geoff. Not me, my friend. Look. I have to go but keep me updated. I'm sure she'll turn up.' Sean watched Geoff's hand drop from the glass, and he closed the front door.

Sean sat alone in the kitchen. The phone call a few minutes previously played on his mind. He and Mia going to Brighton. The Blair Hotel, where they'd stayed, where Billy had entertained the woman he'd met at the casino. *Entertained,* Sean thought. Billy had acted selfishly. A married man with a baby on the way fucking a girl while his pregnant wife suffered at home. He'd revelled in a kinky sex game resulting in her death. Sean had deliberated calling him many times;

he'd dialled his number, tapping in the last few digits, their awkward conversation running through his mind.

Hey, just checking in after our weekend away. It was great catching up. Alcohol, laughs, a flutter at the roulette table. Oh, do you remember the woman you killed by mistake? Yeah, sure you do. You were in a state at the time. We buried her in the garden out back. That's one to tell the grandkids for sure. Anyway, what's happening with you, Billy Boy?

Sean had tried many times, but he couldn't make the call. He glanced at his watch, unsure of how long he'd been sat in the same spot. 7.32am. How was the morning going so quickly? He stood and made his way to the kettle, removing the lid and holding it under the cold tap. He filled it halfway, replaced the lid and pressed the button down. As he listened to the slow boil, he heard another tap on the glass of the front door.

No, no, no, Geoff. I can't deal with this, he thought. Sean stood by the kitchen door, his body pressed against the wall, waiting. A few seconds later, another tap, like the knuckle of a person conscience of the time. Sean wiped the sweat from his face, feeling his hot, clammy skin. Any second now, Mia would wake. They'd had a conversation two nights ago when Peter had left. Mia had begged Sean to call the police. She'd pleaded with him. He'd managed to persuade Mia to wait with the promise he'd call Peter first and find out what the hell was going on. Reluctantly, she agreed. Now, Sean had to tell her the truth.

The letterbox opened, and Sean heard his name being called. He peeked his head discreetly around the corner and heard the voice calling again.

'It's Matt. Open the door.'

Sean blew a hard breath from his lips. He felt his heart slow as the tension began to filter from his body. He walked along the hallway and opened the front door. 'Christ, Matt. You frightened the shit out of me.'

Matt stood, his arms wrapped around his body like a naughty teenager coming home at some ungodly hour of the morning after a night out. He wore jeans, a loud jumper and a thin jacket. He stamped his feet on the step. 'Peter has taken Nadia.'

Sean peered past his friend and saw Lucy sat in the back seat of the Jeep. She waved wildly with a large grin on her face; then she went back to her phone.

'What are you talking about?'

'Sorry it's so early. I wanted to call, but it's a conversation that we needed face to face. I've been waiting out in the Jeep for ages.'

Sean looked behind, making sure Mia was upstairs. 'Keep your voice down. What's happened?'

Matt went on to explain Lucy taking the selfie, the car which had followed them to the hotel, the dead body in the passenger seat, the guy asking for a room key at the hotel, the phone call with Nadia and her screaming, finishing with Matt and Lucy calling over to Greta's place and finding the bracelet.

'Christ, Matt. I'm so sorry. I don't know what the hell is going on with Peter. It's like he's lost his mind,' Sean said.

'The weekend away. The girl that...' Matt couldn't finish.

'Do you think it's something to do with it?' The colour seemed to drop from Sean's face.

Matt turned, checking on his daughter. 'It's the only logical explanation. I think someone is forcing him to do it. Whatever the fuck is happening, I think Peter is being blackmailed. I have to find him, Sean. He'll kill Nadia if I don't get to him first.'

'Have you called to his house?'

Matt took a deep breath and explained how he'd seen a man pulling a body from the freezer at Peter's house.

'I've had a call,' Sean announced.

Matt stared into his friend's eyes. He watched the sullen look on his face, the dour expression. 'What do you mean?'

'I was woken at six this morning. A phone call. The person said he knows what happened. He knows about the weekend, Matt. He gave me clear instructions.'

'What? What instructions?'

'I have to return to Brighton. I have to go back to The Blair Hotel, with Mia.'

'This is crazy. Why? Why does the caller want you to go back? It doesn't make sense.'

Sean waited a second. 'I think he wants revenge.'

'I'm coming too. Me and Lucy.' Matt walked back to the Jeep. Lucy was still glaring at her phone screen on the backseat.

'Are you mad? It's not safe.' Whatever this guy has planned, I'm going to have to deal with it.'

Matt turned, facing Sean at the front gate. 'Sean. You're putting your life in grave danger. You don't know what this person has planned. I'm coming, Lucy and me. I think it's where Peter is taking Nadia. It makes sense. He's going on their instructions. I have to go with you.'

Sean smiled at the door. 'Okay. If that's where you think she is, then let's go and sort this shit out. Wait there; I have a small task that could go one of two ways. I need to tell Mia what happened the weekend we went away.'

* * *

Sean climbed the stairs and walked along the hallway. He pushed the door open and saw Mia stirring in the bed. She turned on her side, facing Sean. Mia frantically scanned the room, remembering Peter's visit. She smiled at her partner as he walked towards her.

Sean sat on the edge of the bed. 'Morning, baby. I need to talk to you.'

Mia sat up; she rubbed her hands over her eyes to focus. 'Are you okay, Sean? What's up, hun?'

'I need to tell you what happened in Brighton. Please, just hear me out before judging or flying off the handle.'

'Okay. I knew there was something. Go on.'

Sean took a deep breath; he felt his arms tremble and fought the anxiety which began rising through his body. 'Billy met a woman at a casino.'

'Oh no, Sean.'

'That's not the worst part. He took her back to his room. Whatever happened, it went horribly wrong.'

Mia stared at her partner, anticipating his next part of the story. 'In what way? Did he get her pregnant?'

'Mia. He killed her. She's dead.'

Mia brought her hand to her mouth. Sean watched the colour drain from her face. She went to talk but couldn't find the words for a moment. She stared at the wall opposite, processing everything her partner had said.

Sean continued. 'Mia, Billy lost it. He was terrified. You can imagine the state he was in, can't you? He brought us to the room and showed us the body. Peter and I. Matt had gone to bed. Mia, it was horrible. She was lying on the bed, naked; her neck had snapped. Billy threatened us. We insisted on calling the police, getting help, but Billy swore he'd blame all of us. He'd testify that we were all involved, like a kinky sex game we were a part of. We were in the room, looking at this dead woman. Our fingerprints, DNA were everywhere.'

Mia watched her partner as he spoke, the tears rolling down his face. The fear in his eyes. 'What did you do?' she asked.

'We had no choice. We had to hide the body.'

'Oh, Sean. Wait, has it got something to do with Peter being here the other night?'

Sean nodded. 'Someone knows what we've done, Mia.'

'Can we call the police?'

'They have the recording, evidence. We'll all go down for this.' Sean braced himself. 'I've had a call.'

'From who?'

'The same person who's pulling the strings. Peter kidnapped Nadia. I think he's heading to Brighton. He may be there already. Mia, we have to go. The caller has said we have to leave today. I'm so sorry. I'll get us out of this. I promise.' Sean broke down as Mia reached forward, pulling him into her arms.

* * *

A black BMW 8 series waited at the gates around the back of The Blair Hotel. A woman was bound and gagged on the backseat. She'd been wailing through the gag for most of the journey.

Peter was in the driver's seat. His head ached with pressure. He thought the world of Nadia. They'd been friends for a long time. When the call had come through and the instructions delivered, to kidnap Nadia, take her to the hotel, he had no choice. They'd murdered his wife; he'd killed a woman by mistake. They knew he assisted in hiding the body of the woman from the casino. Peter was up shit creek without a paddle. Whatever that meant.

He thought back to his childhood, his nana. She always had a solution for everything. He'd had trouble at school; she told him to rise above the jealousy and ignore the hate, if you react, you fuel their actions. He remembered visiting her, sat on her old sofa, the stuffing pushing out over the edge. He used to pick it, and she'd laugh. The tea and iced cakes she'd bring out from the kitchen, always on a round, silver plate. She'd whisper to him not to tell his mother. They'd sit and talk for hours, Peter pouring out his problems. He remembered his nan would get up and switch the control volume down to its lowest setting on the telly. She'd sit on that old green armchair, the delight on her face. How she loved it when he visited. He'd tell her embarrassing problems, stuff he'd never mention to anyone else. It was so easy talking to her. How he wished he could speak with her now. Ask her for advice. If only for five minutes.

He recalled mentioning a girl he liked in his form at school. His nan had said to talk to her. Be himself. Don't try too hard; it will work out.

Peter took the advice on board, even though he thought the girl had no interest in him. She was out of his league, or so he thought.

They became inseparable.

Her name was Anna, his wife. The woman lying dead on the passenger seat.

❦ 17 ❦

Peter waited in the driver's seat, sat in the car park. The engine was running, and heat bellowed from the grills. Nadia was lying in the back. Every so often, she'd kick the seat. His head ached; the stress of the last week had caught up with him. A migraine had developed. It was happening more frequently. The ache started at the top of his head and worked down, paralysing his face. He blinked his eyes rapidly, trying to focus. As he sat, he watched the rear of the hotel. A small building in front of him which Peter assumed was a warehouse. The shutters were down. Behind him, the gate was closed. When he'd arrived a few minutes ago, a security camera faced towards him and he'd watched as the heavy black gates slowly opened. He'd listened to the creak, like a rollercoaster slowly ascending into the air. The same anticipation he was feeling at this moment. For a brief second, Peter thought about reaching to the back seat, untying Nadia and the two of them racing along the road. They'd hide until all this was over.

He jolted as the phone rang from the dashboard. Peter

reached forward, watching the no caller ID appear on the screen. He pressed the answer button.

'Do you have her?'

'Yes. I can't tell you how this is affecting...'

'Shut your fucking mouth. I don't want to hear anything from you. A guy will be down in a minute.' The call ended.

Peter burst into tears. It was too much. His mind raced, anger raging through his veins. Nadia was kicking the front seat, causing him to jolt forward. He wiped his tear-soaked face with the back of his hand, his eyes were blurry, and his head pounded. Stronger now, pushing through his forehead. He felt his heart pulsing at the side of his head; his skin felt tight, like clingfilm pressing against his face.

He saw the shutter to his left, moving upwards, the buzzing sound as it lifted. A person stood in the doorway, peering towards him. They wore black jeans, a jumper, and a black ski mask covering their face. Peter watched as the person beckoned the car over towards where they stood.

He pressed the accelerator and rolled the car forwards. When Peter was close enough, the person held their hand up for him to stop. Peter opened the driver's door and stood for a moment. The sea air hit him, like a sudden lease of life. He watched as seagulls crowed below the clouded sky. He could hear music in the background. Memories flooded back of Peter's childhood. The times he'd come here with his family as a kid, spending hours in the arcades.

'Where is she?'

Peter heard the man's voice. He was English. His accent was possibly from London or Kent. Through the ski mask, Peter saw deep grey coloured eyes, wild, ferocious. 'She's in the backseat.'

The guy walked forward, watching over the car park. He opened the back seat and dragged Nadia out. 'You did well. My brother says she's just as hot as the first girl.'

Peter was speechless for a moment. He watched the guy dragging Nadia across the ground. Her hands and feet were tied with rope. He heard her screaming under the gag. The fear in her eyes. She glanced at Peter for a moment and he turned away in shame.

* * *

Peter stood by the doorway. The guy had been gone a few minutes. He debated whether to wait out here or in the warmth of his car. He hoped this was over. He'd kept up his side of the bargain. He'd brought them Nadia, killed a woman by mistake, and the body of his dead wife was in the passenger seat of his car. He was broken. Peter couldn't take anymore.

He looked across the room; the shutter was wide open. There were shelves of food, neatly stacked. Cartons of orange juice and milk. Breakfast cereals and square green trays with an assortment of vegetables. He saw a small forklift truck further back against the wall.

A neon light glared from the ceiling. Peter heard a door open. His body tensed as the guy walked towards him, still wearing the ski mask.

'Okay. That's it. I'm done,' Peter announced. As he turned towards his car, the guy spoke.

'My brother tells me you were seen. Your image captured in a selfie as you drove along the motorway. Is this correct?'

Peter recalled a conversation he'd had with the guy who called. He was putting pressure on Peter, making sure he understood that there could be no mistakes. He challenged Peter, asking how Nadia had escaped. When Peter explained that Matt and Lucy were the only ones in the car when Peter had approached the Jeep on the motorway, the caller became agitated. Peter could hear him fidgeting, he huffed, blowing a deep wheezy breath into the phone. Peter had to explain himself. He was worried. They'd already killed his wife. He had to tell him how he'd been spotted. The jacket which Peter used to cover his wife had dropped. Anna had been exposed. Peter was unsure for how long. He remembered when Matt had called him, pleading to let Nadia go. Peter had been to Greta's house. Matt had heard everything. He told Peter he saw the dead woman in the passenger seat. Lucy had captured the image. As he approached the Jeep on the motorway, Lucy was sat in the back seat, taking selfies. She'd captured the image of Peter with the body on the passenger seat.

'I admit, it was reckless. I was under pressure. I lost control for a moment. When I pulled into the service station, I realised my wife's body was on display. I covered her again. Nadia is here. I've done as you've asked.'

'You'll do the same,' the guy insisted.

'What? I'll do what?' Peter's voice was irritated.

'My brother has informed me he instructed you to bring the dead body of your wife into the house and hide her. He made it clear. I need you to understand. Actions have consequences. We are firm believers that retribution can be carried out in many ways.' As the guy spoke, he remembered everything they'd taught him and his brother at the commune. The leader was a figure who'd be a part of their life forever. He'd taught Vincent and Marty so much in the time they'd spent together. How revenge, even the smallest act, can cleanse the soul and make everything brighter. The way he and Marty would live their lives from now on. The rules they'd follow. Vincent repeated the words in his mind. Vengeance cleansed the soul and made everything brighter. Every action against someone must face a repercussion. There has to be a fallout of mammoth proportions. They were the words he and his brother were taught. Dionysius. The God of ecstasy and revenge.

'You will take a selfie as you walk along Brighton pier. The first person to look at the screen, you'll bring here. You will be careful and discreet. If you're caught, it's on you. Make sure to be as cautious as possible. My brother and I are very excited about this. We have a trained surgeon waiting.'

As the shutter went down, Peter stood, open mouthed and unable to move.

18

It was early Saturday morning; Matt was driving with Sean in the passenger seat. Mia and Lucy were sat in the back. They were passing the phone between them, taking turns in playing the latest game Lucy had downloaded. She liked Mia and Sean. From a young girl's point of view, Lucy admired Mia. The clothes she wore, the way she conducted herself. Lucy aspired to be like her.

A signpost declared they were twenty miles from Brighton. Matt gripped the steering wheel tight, the veins protruding through his skin. He wanted to talk to Sean. To explain how terrified he was feeling. He pictured Nadia, the woman he adored so much. His mind flashed images of her lying slumped on a cold ground with her throat slit. He couldn't talk about it. Not in front of his daughter. The atmosphere in the car was tense, surreal, something he'd never witnessed before with Sean and Mia. In recent years, they'd been to parties, had many dinners together; they'd holidayed in Greece as a five-some a couple of years ago. Now, as he drove, he felt the weight of the world bearing down on him.

'Next left,' Sean shouted.

'Bloody hell, Sean, don't ever opt to be the voice of a Satnav. You frightened the shit out of me.'

Sean laughed as Matt turned the steering wheel. He watched signs announcing the A23.

'Are you okay, Matt?' Sean asked.

Matt turned towards his friend. 'I've had better mornings.' He kept his voice low. 'It's killing me having to bring Lucy. Who knows what dangers lie ahead or what's waiting for us. Sean, I need to protect her.'

'You're an incredible father. Everyone knows that. Matt, you had no choice. You're always together. The three of you. I know how you protect your family. You can't beat yourself up. I'm not going to let it happen.'

Mia was asking Lucy about school. Matt heard Lucy mentioning the head girl position. He smiled, hoping she got it. She deserved it more than anything. 'What are we going to do when we get there? God knows what will happen.'

'We explain it wasn't us. What can the caller do? It's a hotel. A public place. I don't think he'll try anything. If he does, if anything happens in that hotel, they better not expect a glowing review on Trip Advisor,' Sean said.

Matt laughed. Thank goodness for Sean and his ability to ease the tension, he thought. He kept his voice low, explaining to Sean what he'd read on the internet. The three women who'd gone missing from The Blair Hotel. The owner found hanging in one of the rooms. Matt feared there may be more than one person, and this had a wider scope. His worry was geared towards the people who ran the hotel.

* * *

Matt followed the A23 around to the seafront. It was cold, and, although bright, the sky was a thick blanket of grey. It had rained heavily on the way down, but the worst of it looked behind them. Lucy leant forward. She gasped as she looked at the sea. The waves were tremendous, rolling over each other, like a washing machine on a low spin.

'Look, Dad. When we find mum can we go swimming?'

'Lucy. That water could give you pneumonia this time of year.'

'Go on, Matt. Take her swimming,' Mia suggested.

Matt turned his body slightly. 'Why don't you?' he laughed.

As they drove through town, Matt saw The Blair Hotel on his right. He realised how creepy it looked, wondering if his mind was playing tricks. The building was large, detached; the brickwork painted white. A sign hung above the arched door announcing the name. To the left, he eyed the enormous, double glazed windows. There were four floors, more windows stretching along the road. He turned into the car park and drove to a bay at the far end. It was quiet. He could see a couple of scooters, a small pickup truck and two other vehicles which were stationary. Matt had hoped the car park would be full. Safety in numbers, he had thought.

He turned off the engine and got out of the car. Sean, Mia and Lucy followed.

'Wow. It's chilly down here,' Mia confirmed. She placed her arm around Lucy, huddling her close.

The two men stepped away from Mia and Lucy for a moment.

'Do you think he's here?' Matt whispered to Sean.

Sean deliberated for a second. 'I think he'll be watching us. I doubt he's anything to do with the hotel. I may be wrong. Chances are, he's a psycho loon who wants to play with us. If we keep our eyes open, try and find out who he is and stick together, we'll be safe.'

Matt looked at the side of the hotel. He glanced up to the fourth floor. 'What if she's not here? What if Peter has brought her somewhere else? Maybe he's killed her already. What if he's taken her somewhere else altogether?'

Sean watched the tears stream down Matt's face. He sniffed and turned away. He couldn't have Lucy see him like this.

'I can't cope without her, Sean. I can't do it.'

Sean moved forward and pulled his best friend close. He held him for a moment. 'We'll get her back. I promise.'

* * *

Matt and Sean grabbed the bags from the boot of the car and checked over the car park. Matt watched Lucy's face. She was captivated by the sea. She could hear the waves pushing against the shore, the beach coated with small pebbles. She glanced along the old wooden pier. Lucy had been excited to come here, and earlier, she'd Googled Brighton's history. Sixty-seven thousand lights illuminated the pier each night, and over four hundred people from around the world were employed on the pier. It opened in 1899 and is home to a fairground, bars, restaurants, and deckchairs to enjoy the sea view. The pier stretches seventeen hundred and sixty feet, and Lucy learned that if every plank in the pier's decking were laid end to end, it would stretch eighty-five miles.

'Dad. The pier is amazing.'

Matt moved to his daughter. He crouched beside her, watching the excitement on her face. Her cheeks were bright red, wisps of blonde hair draped over her face, and her eyes watered with the stiff breeze.

'When we find mum, we'll go, Lucy.'

Matt was awash with emotion. He pulled his daughter tight, kissing her forehead. He couldn't think about her life without a mother. Matt had to stay strong.

The four of them walked to the front of the car park and along the road. They stood outside The Blair Hotel. Matt glanced at the building and immediately noticed how tired it looked. The white brickwork was patchy and awash with deep black stains from pollution. The double glazed windows on each side of the doorway, which provided a view into the reception area, were grubby with grease marks absorbing the wooden sills. Above the door, in black stencil, were the words, Welcome to The Blair Hotel. The writing was smudged and appeared to drip at the bottom as if a child had written the words in haste with a thick marker pen. A sign above the main entrance read, Welcome to The Blair Hotel. Est 1970. For vacancies and private functions, please enquire at reception. Please note we do not allow pets. We hope you enjoy your stay.

Matt turned to Sean, Mia and Lucy. 'Okay. Let's do this.'

They walked towards the main doors. Two steps led to a sizeable solid glass door. Matt followed the instructions written above the door handle and pulled. They stood in the large, bright foyer. When he'd arrived here a month ago, he'd raced to the reception area, checked in, dumped his clothes in a room on the ground floor and hit the bar. He was amazed at his lack of observation the first time around. Very little had registered. The reception area was quiet. A woman dressed in a white blouse, black trousers and a brown waistcoat came out of a door to the right marked, "Staff." She was Asian, possibly Filipino. She was attractive and looked trustworthy. She smiled towards the four of them and looked at Lucy.

'Hello, sweetie. Enjoy your stay.'

Matt immediately felt at ease. He watched her move

swiftly towards the stairs, and a moment later, she was gone. They approached a guy who was medium height, stood behind the long, wooden desk, which stretched halfway across the room. He was jotting something in a notebook. His uniform was crisp, smart. The large white collar of his shirt hung over his jacket, and his waistcoat was buttoned all the way down. He appeared to take pride in his appearance. As he turned to the side, Matt noticed his large, Roman nose. His hair was a bright blonde colour and shone as if he'd recently dabbled with a hair dye. He offered a wide smile with perfectly formed teeth.

'How can I help?' His accent was strong, possibly from the north of England.

Matt straightened his back. 'We'd like two rooms. We haven't booked, I'm afraid.'

'Oh, no need to book. As you can see, it's a quiet time of the year. We're hardly swamped with guests at the moment.'

Matt felt his heart rate slacken. He had feared the task of getting a couple of rooms would be daunting.

'How long are you staying?'

'A night, maybe two. We'd like them together if possible?'

The guy tapped on an old computer, jabbing his left index finger and groaning like it was a task he despised. After a moment, he looked up. 'Okay. Rooms seven and eight on the ground floor. There's an extra bed for the young girl. My name is Fred. Please ask if I can assist in any way. Will anyone else be joining?'

Matt couldn't explain his next action. Call it a spur of the moment decision or desperation. He'd wanted to wait, settle in and suss the place out. To be patient. He reached into his pocket, removing his phone and pulled up a picture of Nadia. 'I'm wondering If you can help?'

'By all means.'

Matt opened the phone to a picture of his wife and held it

in front of Fred. 'My wife is missing. Her name is Nadia. Have you seen her here?'

They watched as Fred became flustered. His hands shuffled behind the desk. He stuttered, unsure of how to answer the question. His face turned beetroot red and sweat appeared on the brow of his forehead.

'I'm sorry, Sir. I haven't seen her.' He pointed a shaky hand towards the far end of the reception area. 'Through the door on your right, along the corridor towards the end on the left. Rooms seven and eight. Enjoy your stay.' He disappeared into a room at the back and closed the door.

* * *

Lucy pressed the card against the door of room Eight. They heard the loud clunk, and she pushed hard. 'Yuk. This is horrible, Dad.'

They stepped inside. Matt immediately noticed the worn carpet, which appeared to have small circular holes from recent cigarette burns. Matt tried to think when the smoking ban came into the UK. Surely they can't have the same carpets, he thought. He looked around the small space.

There were two large, triangular burn marks in the middle of the floor, possibly from an iron. The bed was large but looked flimsy and stood on four rickety old wooden legs. The front right leg protruded outwards and looked ready to snap at any moment. The pillows were worn with yellow stains, and the white quilt cover had faded to an almost brown colouring.

Matt was astounded that he hadn't noticed this before. Lucy's bed was small, weak-looking and resembled a cot. The white walls were bare, with damp patches towards the bottom, and the wooden skirting had cracked and splintered through lack of care.

'Dad. It's no use just sitting here. Let's go and see if we can find mum. Maybe someone has seen her.'

Matt suddenly felt guilty. He'd dragged Lucy to the Cotswolds with the promise of a fun weekend. He'd driven halfway across the country in the last twenty-four hours. His daughter had been extremely understanding and tolerable. Even though he hadn't told her the full story. It wasn't fair.

They could go to the pier, and also show the recent picture of Nadia around too. Maybe someone has seen her.

Maybe someone was brave enough to talk.

* * *

Sean sat on the edge of the bed in room seven. Mia was unpacking her bag. She removed a couple of warm jumpers and a pair of jeans. The room was identical to Matt and Lucy's and in the same shit state. Sean was having flashbacks. He recalled the room where Billy stayed across the hall. He heard voices: Peter, Billy, the severe panic. Billy's voice was running through his head like a worn recording. *I'll bring you all down with me. I'll say we were all involved.* His body started trembling, the trauma of that night, playing out in his mind.

'Hey, Sean. Come on. We'll get through this.' Mia's voice brought him out of his trance. She watched her partner. They'd been through so much in the last few hours. She wasn't going to sit back and watch him crumble. As she sat on the bed, watching his hands shake, the clouded, blurry expression which adorned his face, she held her hands in his, clutching them, then pressed them against her chest. His hands were cold, clammy, and he sobbed uncontrollably. She pressed the back of her right hand against his cheek, feeling his dank, cold skin. He shivered as his teeth began to chatter, and she held him close.

'What have we done, Mia?'

She caressed his back, feeling the damp through his jumper. 'We'll sort it out. We'll find the caller responsible for this chaos. Surely it's Billy's word against yours. Against Peter's. We'll find Nadia and get the hell out of here. Then we'll go to the police.'

Sean clasped Mia's face between his hands. He peered into her hazel green eyes, looking at her long lashes, her perfectly shaped eyebrows, her full lips and her long, wavy hair that seemed effortless to manage. Christ, she was so beautiful.

As they held each other, Sean and Mia felt they never wanted to let go.

* * *

Lucy was pulling Matt's arm as they sprinted across the road and stood on the pavement, glancing into the distance. The sea was calmer, a sheet of blue stretching as far as they could see. A small boat rolled gently across the horizon, and Lucy wished at this moment that she was on deck, feeling the cold on her skin, watching the icy water lap the wooden base. She'd never been on a boat. They'd been abroad a few times as a family. Italy, Greece, Spain but Matt disliked the water and often suffered from seasickness as a result. Nadia had offered to take her a few times, but if it meant her father missing out, Lucy would miss out too.

The air was filled with the aroma of sugar and chocolate. They hadn't eaten, and Lucy spotted a kiosk selling fresh doughnuts. She pointed to her father with a wide grin, urging him in the direction of the small cabin. He brought a box of doughnuts with an assortment of jam, raspberry and cinnamon, handing them to Lucy and watched her face light up.

'You're the best dad in the world.'

Matt laughed. 'Yeah. Today I am.'

'Look, Dad. A fortune-teller. Let's do it.'

Matt looked to the left of the pier. A small, white trailer with large wheels was standing alone. The door was closed. A placard detailed the price, the woman's name and recommendations.

'Lucy. I don't know. I'm not really into this sort of thing.'

'Oh, Dad. Come on. It will be fun.'

Matt was worried about time. He'd have to start asking around, showing pictures of Nadia. A chill suddenly flooded his body as he thought about her. He didn't want to scare Lucy. Bringing her here put both their lives in danger. The caller could be anywhere. Out there. Watching. But he had no choice. It wasn't safe leaving Lucy on her own. Greta, Nadia's mum, wasn't able to look after her and there was always the slight possibility that Peter could return. He'd tried his number a few times this morning; every call went to voicemail. He had to find the bastard.

Lucy pulled her father towards the old trailer. 'Are we going to, Dad?'

Matt huffed. He gazed around. The pier was quiet. He could wait until it got busier and then enquire about his wife.

Matt gently knocked the door with the knuckles of his left hand. 'See. No one home. Come on. Let's go.'

'Dad.'

A few seconds later, the door pushed outwards, almost hitting Matt on the head. An elderly lady stood in the doorway. Her body was leaning forward, the tip of her nose pointing towards the ground. She tilted her head upwards, revealing a toothless grin. She was precisely how Matt had envisioned her. She wore a dark green headscarf which covered her forehead, and the tip rested on her eyebrows. Her skin was heavily wrinkled; deep lines cut into her flesh, giving her face a saggy appearance. A red shawl was draped loosely over her shoulders, and she wore an assortment of weird-looking commodities around her neck, dangling on a flimsy dark piece of string.

Matt stood back for a moment. 'I'm...'

'I know who you are. A desolate wickedness has brought you to my door. I sense despair, anguish in your aura. Forty pounds for ten minutes. Cash only.' The woman walked back inside, leaving the door open.

Lucy looked at her father. Her eyes were beaming, filled with confusion and excitement. Matt stood by the door and pushed his head inside. The decor was overbearing. Large tarot cards were enclosed in wooden frames. Small ornaments, which Matt guessed were lucky charms, filled a black cabinet towards the far end of the trailer. A four-leaf clover stood at the front on a stand. He spotted a horseshoe, a rabbit's foot, several pennies in perfect symmetry; the number seven painted in a light green colour and a handful of pocket lighters. There were hundreds of objects; each one had a different meaning. For such a cluttered place, the old lady seemed to take pride in the design. Matt climbed the step and Lucy followed. He could hear the anticipation in his daughter's breath.

As they went inside, Matt saw more pictures. One of a Ouija board freaked him out; others were photos of people who had visited in the past. He noticed the image of a teabag, the palm of a hand with a description of each lines meaning and an astrology chart. Matt was captivated.

A loud voice frightened them as the old woman pushed aside bright beaded curtains and entered the room from her kitchen. 'Young man. I don't pussyfoot around.'

Matt looked at his daughter, perturbed by the woman's choice of language.

Her frame was arched, and her head was hanging to the side. As she spoke, her eyes seemed to roll as if she were possessed. Lucy gripped her father's arm. The woman held her hand out, and after a couple of seconds, Matt removed forty pounds from his jeans pocket. Her grin widened and her eyes focused on the two strangers stood in front of her. She muffled something to herself, then began to hum a tune they struggled to make out. They watched her move hastily towards a

small round table, pushing her hands in the direction of another seat. As Matt and Lucy walked towards her, she raised her voice.

'You cannot join the table.' Her instruction was barked at Lucy. 'Over there. The sofa, young lady.'

Matt took a seat. 'Why can't she join? Is it something to do with hindering the communication of the spirit world?'

The old woman peered up at Matt. 'You've only given me forty pounds.'

'It's okay, Dad. I can watch from here.'

'Be still. If it's conversation you require, I suggest the pub at the end of the pier.'

Lucy began laughing, and Matt scorned her with an embarrassed glance.

'If it's delight, wonder or an enchanted story you're seeking, you've come to the wrong place. I tell it as it is. I won't apprise you with euphoria and prosperity. So, if you choose to go, all well and good. The door is there. No refunds.'

Matt rolled his eyes at her abruptness. She threw her head towards him for a moment as if she'd seen him, then removed a black cloth, revealing a small crystal ball. The object looked heavy, mysterious. Two things went through Matt's head as she started to make a circular motion around the ball with her hand. How did this thing assist in her predictions, and the second thought, what the hell was he doing here? He was too frightened to get up and walk out in case she placed some kind of curse on him. How much worse could my life get? he thought. He watched the old lady appear to enter a trance. Her eyes rolled, giving her a zombified appearance. She muttered words that Matt assumed was her, calling the spirit world, possibly a spell. He gripped the edge of the table and darted his eyes towards Lucy, who was sat forward on the sofa, her legs, swinging with anticipation.

Suddenly, she opened one eye. Matt thought she looked like the witch in Snow White and prepared himself for an apple.

'I see a woman.'

Matt waited for her to proceed. He watched her hands placed on top of the globe.

She continued. 'A pretty thing she is too.'

'Who? Who do you see? What does she look like?' Matt asked.

'Her smile is divine. Such a beautiful face. She's caring. Considerate. I see an old lady. Something has happened to her.'

'Yes. Yes, it's her mother. She was looking after her. Her name is Nadia.' Matt stopped suddenly, not wanting to give too much away.

'It's dark. She's calling out.'

'Who's calling? What is she calling?' Matt urged.

'She's on her own, in a room, I believe, or a container. I see her kneeling on the floor, crying out.' The old lady paused for a second, her breathing became rapid, and she looked at the ball on the table. 'The door is opening; someone is entering the room, making their way towards her. She's so scared. She's trying to get away, but her hands are tied. You must get to her before it's too late.' The old lady raised her voice to a scream. 'No. You need to help her now.' She lifted her head, her eyes wild with fear. 'They're close. They're right beside us.' As her voice became louder, one of her candles blew out. The woman slammed her hands on the table and began to rock in the chair. 'No. No.'

Matt jumped up, pushing the chair back frantically. 'Where the hell is she? Where's Nadia?'

'You need to leave. You've brought this anguish to my door. Get out, both of you. Out.'

* * *

Matt and Lucy stood on the pier, listening to the sound of waves lapping against the base. Above, seagulls hovered. Their cries had a sudden calming effort.

Lucy looked at her father. Tears were rolling down her face. She still had questions, realising her father was distorting the truth. 'Was it mum she spoke about, Dad? She's in trouble, isn't she?'

Matt crouched, staring into his daughter's eyes. 'We'll find her. That's a promise.'

'I'm scared, Dad. What if she's...?'

Matt pulled his daughter close. 'I'm not going to let anything happen to her. Do you hear? We're a team. The three of us. Lucy, I need you to be brave, okay. I love you so much. We'll find her.' As Matt looked around the deserted pier, he began to doubt his words. He also missed the guy, further along, leaning against a stall, watching them.

19

Bella Reynolds loved Brighton. She grew up here. Eager to be a success, she left home at nineteen and moved to London. She took a course in business studies and worked part-time with a local estate agent. At the age of thirty-two, she now ran a project management company specialising in new build homes. Her work was demanding: early starts, late finishes, but, best of all, she was loaded. She owned a two-bed house in North London, the mortgage was almost paid, and she was engaged to the man of her dreams.

For Bella, life couldn't get any better.

She stood on the pier, blowing into her coffee cup, waiting in anticipation for her friend to arrive. It had been a couple of years since she'd seen Nancy. They'd met at high school and were best friends from the early days. Although Bella had moved away, they rang each other weekly, keeping the other informed of how their lives had progressed. They were going to spend the day shopping, a bite to eat and a couple of drinks. Bella had promised herself she'd get back to her parent's house early. They'd be upset if she made the journey and didn't spend time with them. She watched the girl making her way towards her. Nancy hadn't aged. Her hair was much longer; she'd lost weight, but, if anything, she still looked like the girl from school.

They embraced, the excitement evident, then Nancy stood back, giving Bella the once over.

'Wow. It's so good to see you. You look amazing. How's the high life suiting you?' Nancy asked.

'Oh, you know, long hours, not enough time in the day. The usual complaints. But I wouldn't have it any other way.'

'How are you? Nancy, you haven't aged. Like, not a frigging day.'

'Oh, I feel it. Thank you. So, shall we do a little retail therapy? I need to spend lots of money,' Nancy stated.

'Sounds good to me.'

The ladies began walking away from the pier towards The Lanes. Bella pulled her jacket tighter around her waist. The chill in the air stabbed against her body, and she turned slightly as the wind moaned around her, a piercing grate that rang in her ears.

'It's so good to see you, Bella. I've been counting the days.'

'Me too. Visiting makes me realise how much I miss this place. It's bloody freezing. I don't know how you cope.'

'You've been gone too long,' Nancy laughed. 'It's made you a wimp.'

Bella saw a man, just ahead of them, dressed in a suit. He was tall with thick grey hair. She noticed he had a mobile phone held in front of him. He was frantically turning, spinning in circles, pressing the screen as if taking selfies. His behaviour was eccentric, giving him an erratic presence. She watched as people moved around him. The guy kept jabbing at the screen, like he was willing people to notice him. As the women walked past him, Bella watched. She saw a picture on his phone, her face, staring, her image captured. Suddenly, he turned. His excitement was evident. The guy watched Bella as she walked away, grinning to himself.

'What the hell is his problem?' Bella asked.

'Who?'

'That guy back there. Taking pictures.'

'There are weirdos everywhere. Ignore him. You should feel honoured.'

'It's just creepy,' Bella said.

As the women walked towards The Lanes, Peter Simpson watched them, then began moving in the same direction.

20

Matt and Lucy spent another half hour on the pier. They approached families, couples, dog walkers and anyone who had drifted in from the street. Matt watched the weary faces as he held a recent picture of Nadia in front of them. No one had seen her.

'Dad. I'm cold.'

'Come on. Let's go back to the hotel. You must be starving?' Matt asked.

'When have you ever known me to turn down food?'

Matt and Lucy exited the pier and raced across the street towards the hotel. They entered the lobby and made their way along the corridor to Sean and Mia's room. Matt tapped on the door of room seven, and a few seconds later, Sean answered.

'Matt. Lucy. We were worried. Any news?' Sean asked.

They walked into the room and sat together on the edge of the bed. Mia was having a bath. Matt noticed the room: it was just as worn out as theirs.

'Nothing. We asked a few people; no one's seen her, Sean.'

Sean hesitated for a moment. He glanced around the

room, thinking, feeling completely hopeless. They had to do something, but where did they start? Sean jumped as his mobile phone rang from his back pocket. He lifted the screen to his face, seeing "No Caller ID," displayed across the glass. 'Hello?' He glanced at Lucy.

'How is your room?'

Sean darted his eyes at Matt, signing with his hands the urgency of the call. 'Who is this?'

'You know who it is. I'm glad so many of you are in one place. It will make my work much easier. I saw you this morning when you arrived. I watched from the street. You parked the Jeep around the back. You and your male friend were looking around, thinking no one could see. How wrong you were.'

'What the fuck do you want with us?' Sean asked.

'Oh, patience. Tolerance is a must when we speak. I dislike bad manners. I trust the four of you are comfortable and settling in for a cosy stopover?'

'This needs to stop. We weren't involved.' Sean raised his voice. 'We had no part in it.'

'Oh, but you did.'

The phone went dead.

* * *

A few minutes later, Mia came out of the bathroom wearing a dressing gown and complimentary slippers, courtesy of the hotel. She was towelling her hair and noticed a sudden change in the atmosphere. 'What's happened?' she asked.

Matt explained the phone call, how the guy had watched them when they entered the hotel and his remark about four of them being here.

'Christ, he's watching us.' Mia felt unsteady.

'I think we need to stay in the rooms. He may be out there, waiting to pounce,' Matt suggested.

'Is he part of the hotel? Bloody hell, he could be a waiter, a chef, one of the porters. A guest. He could be anywhere,' Mia stated.

'He saw us arrive, which means he was waiting outside,' Matt said. 'He could be watching our every move.'

'There's four of us. I doubt he'll try anything while we're here. I think it's best to lock the doors, keep as silent as possible and hope he gets bored,' Mia announced.

The four of them glanced towards the door as the handle flipped downwards.

'Dad. I'm scared.'

They sat, muted, waiting.

'Keep quiet. No one make a sound,' Matt ordered. He glanced at the back window, hoping it would open far enough for them to escape. A loud, banging noise echoed through the room. Someone was kicking the door.

'What do we do?' Sean asked.

Matt raced to the window at the back. There was a large doubled glazed panel with rotten frames and two small hooks towards the base. He lifted, glad to see there was ample space for them to jump. He peered into the garden, watching the shadows cast their threatening shapes in the distance. Matt turned to Sean. 'Okay, I say we answer the door. If it's him, we'll grab him, hold him down and call the main desk.'

Sean deliberated. 'What if he has a gun?'

Matt hadn't thought of that. 'Well, you crack the door open, and I'll peek out. Slam the door on my command, shield the ladies and dive for cover. I doubt he'd shoot a gun in here, but you never know.' Matt walked towards the door, hearing another pound against the wood.

Sean stood silently. He reached his arm forward, touching

the handle. His eyes were blurry, and he tried to blink them clear. He could feel his heart race, his hands shaking.

'On three,' Matt said. 'One, two...'

'No, wait. Go backwards. Then say go.'

'Why backwards?' Matt asked.

'One, two, three, go is four instructions. I never know whether to go on three or go.'

Matt smirked. 'Right. So, three, two, one, go is the same.'

'No. You say, two, one, go. Simple.'

'Just open the bloody door. What the hell?' Mia was lying on the floor, holding Lucy's hand.

Matt turned towards his daughter, then started to count. 'Two. One.'

Sean opened the door before the instruction. He reached out, pulling the guy towards him. Matt leapt on him and the two men wrestled him to the floor. The silver tray he was holding flipped upwards, and the food went everywhere.

'What the hell is wrong with you?' The young man stood, clearing up the mess.

'I'm sorry,' Matt offered. He recognised the man from the main desk. The person they'd spoken with while checking into the hotel. 'We heard the heavy banging. We thought you were someone else.'

'I was holding the tray; I had to knock the door with my foot. Someone ordered room service. I spoke with a lady.'

Matt and Sean peered back to Mia. 'Oh shit. I forgot. It was while I was in the bath. That was quick. Sorry.'

Once the apologies were out of the way, the guys returned to the room with shameful expressions. The four of them tucked into the food Mia had ordered. An array of hot toasted sandwiches of melted cheese, bacon and smothered with Mayonnaise.

'Wow, I needed this,' Mia confirmed. 'What are you two like? I doubt he'll call again.'

'Thanks, Mia. Next time alert us if someone's coming,' Matt stated. He laughed, breaking the tension between the four of them.

Once they'd finished their food, they sat, pondering their options.

'I say we go look for him. He's here somewhere,' Sean suggested.

'No, Sean. We're safer here. The door's pretty robust. If we stay together, nothing can happen,' Mia said.

'I can't do it, Mia. We can't stay here, locked up like caged animals. We have to find this prick. He has one over on us. He knows we're here. While we stay put, we're sitting ducks.' Sean looked towards Matt.

'I think you're right. Staying put is too risky. I say we search for him. He won't expect it.'

The four of them waited, weighing up the options. Mia broke the silence.

'Okay. But we stay in this group. If anything happens, we're in this together. Whatever has to be done.'

They stood, huddling each other, then made their way out to the corridor and walked towards the main reception.

Matt walked in front, holding Lucy's hand. Sean followed with Mia close behind.

'I want to take a look on the other floors. Maybe there's a porter, someone cleaning the rooms. There must be someone we can talk to.' Matt was stood by the lift doors and pressed the call button. The light glowed a bright, white colour. Ten seconds later, the doors edged open, revealing a large, brown coloured box room. They all got in, watching the guy behind the reception desk. It seemed he hadn't noticed them. As the doors closed, Matt confirmed his plan.

'Let's start at the top and work down. Someone must know something.'

He pressed number four, and the lift began its slow ascent. The lift jolted, feeling more like a chairlift rising over the side of a mountain. It was rickety and shook like a washing machine on its last legs. They all held on to the side of the large box, hoping they'd make it out alive. The lift stopped on floor three, and the doors opened.

'That's weird. Hold on, don't get out. I pressed four.' Matt jabbed the button; the number four began flashing on the sidewall. The doors closed, and Matt breathed a sigh of relief.

They stood still for a few seconds; the lift didn't budge.

'Come on you piece of shit. Move,' Matt demanded. Again, he jabbed his finger on number four. The doors opened, and the lift remained stationary.

'This is ridiculous.' Matt looked at Sean.

'Let's take the stairs,' Sean announced.

Again, the lift doors closed. Ten seconds later, they opened again. They stepped out into the corridor. The lights were off, and they struggled to see anything. Matt removed his phone torch and held it in front of them. Sean did the same.

They strolled along the hall, clustered close together, listening to one another breathing, the anticipation rife. They reached the end of the hall, seeing a large red door with "Emergency Fire Escape," written above. Matt pushed the bar, and they stood on the freezing steps. The icy chill was something they hadn't expected, and the wind pelted towards a cracked window opposite where they stood. They glanced at the concrete steps, strong, robust, which lead to the floors below. A black handrail that had long fallen off its clips and looked as much use as a dissolving condom curved along the wall. They turned, seeing a solid metal door leading to the fourth floor. Matt reached forward, yanking the handle. He crouched, seeing the lock fastened.

'This is madness. Why is there no access to the fourth floor?' Matt banged the door and pulled on the handle.

'Come on. It's no use,' Mia stated.

They moved back into the darkness, Matt and Sean, shining their torches in front, moving slowly forward.

'Dad, why can't we get to the floor above?' Lucy asked.

'I'm not sure, Lucy Lou. But we'll find a way. Are you okay?' Matt shone the torch towards his daughter's face, watching the fear begin to manifest, the tension evident.

'I want Mum. Is she going to be alright? Where is she, Dad?' Lucy began to panic. She felt claustrophobic. Thoughts began to fester inside her head, imagining never seeing her mother again.

Matt knelt beside his daughter, embracing her tightly. 'We'll find her. I don't want you to worry.'

'How am I supposed to do that?' Lucy asked.

'You need to trust me. I won't let anything happen to her. I love you both so much.' Matt kissed his daughter's cheek, then stood up.

They slowly walked along the corridor, keeping silent, listening for anything unusual. Lucy pressed her ears against the door of each room they approached, either side, confirming to her father that nothing seemed untoward. Matt was unsure what they were listening for:

- A Scream.
- A cry for help.
- Anything that would indicate his wife was being held at the hotel.

So far, nothing had remotely clarified this. Once the four of them had reached the end of the hall, they turned.

'How are we going to find her? She could be anywhere. Poor Nadia. I'm so scared for her,' Mia said.

Matt shone the torch towards Mia. 'Look, we can't give up. I know she's here somewhere. Someone knows the answer. We just have to find them and make them talk.'

They approached the lift, creeping along the worn carpet, their feet sticking with the grime. Matt pressed the call button. The neon light glowed, and a second later, the doors opened.

Once all of them were inside, Matt pressed the fourth floor. The doors closed and the lift remained stationary.

'Come on, you bastard. What are you hiding up there?' Matt jabbed the button with his finger, then pounded it with his fist. The lift shook, and for a moment, they expected it to drop to the basement.

'It's no use, mate,' Sean announced. 'We may as well check the other floors. Maybe we'll try again tonight.'

Matt continued to pound the button with his fist as his hand began to turn a bright red colour. 'Something is going on up there. Why are there four frigging floors and only access to three? What the hell are they hiding? Are you telling me they closed off a quarter of the hotel for no reason?' After a few seconds, Matt pressed the button indicating the second floor. The lift jolted, the cables began churning, and the lift suddenly stopped. The four of them gasped as the lights went out. Matt and Sean had turned off the torches on their phones to save their batteries. The bleakness hit hard.

'Dad. What's happening?'

Matt reached forward, pawing in the dark for his daughter's hand. He squeezed it, rubbing his thumb along the knuckles. 'I'm here, Lucy. Nothing's going to happen.'

'Err. That's my hand,' Sean stated.

'Oh. Sorry, mate.'

'It's fine. I thought it was rather comforting.'

Lucy moved away from the wall, swiping the darkness

until she found her father. She had visions of being stuck in the lift and never getting out. She struggled to control her breathing, not wanting her father to know how she felt. Matt placed his arm around her, and they huddled close.

'Sean. Your phone. We need light. Matt, you too,' Mia ordered. 'Lucy, don't panic; we'll get out of here in a minute.' Mia pawed her hands along the row of numbers, then, aided by the phone lights, she saw the emergency button at the bottom. Mia pressed it. Nothing happened. She expected an alarm to ring or a bell to sound a piercing echo through the third floor. She looked back, watching the lights shining into her eyes. She hesitated a second and pressed the button again. 'For Christ sake. What the hell is wrong with this dump? I wouldn't board my dog here. What a shit hole.' Mia was struggling to catch her breath as panic formed, rising through her body. She closed her eyes, counting to ten, then pressed the button again.

Matt felt Lucy's hand clasp his, squeezing tight.

Sean was breathing heavy, the phone torch shaking in his hand.

'Hello. Can anyone hear us? We're stuck. Hello.' Matt banged his fist against the side wall. Again, the lift jolted. 'Anyone fancy a game of I spy?' Matt asked sarcastically.

Mia continued to press the emergency button, jabbing the middle and forefinger of her right hand against the panel, then moved upwards, frantically trying to force the lift to move. In desperation, she pushed her fingers between the gap of the doors and pulled. 'Hello. Help us, someone. We're stuck.' She turned to Sean. 'We could die in this box. No one knows we're here.' Mia watched Lucy, realising what she'd just said.

'Dad. Are we going to get out? Are we going to die?'

Matt shot an irritated look towards Mia, who mouthed an apology.

'Lucy, I don't want you to worry. We're going to get out. We'll find Mum and the three of us will be home this evening. Do you hear me?' Matt needed his daughter to believe him although he had doubts they'd get out alive. He watched his daughter's face as she gazed towards him. Her eyes were glazed with tears and her lips quivered as she spoke.

'Dad, we're not getting out, are we?'

Matt pulled his daughter and held her tight as she broke down.

Mia crouched, pushing a hand through Lucy's hair and kissing her flushed cheeks. 'Do you know how brave you are? I've never met a young lady like you, Lucy. We're going to find your mum and then get the hell out of this dump.'

Matt pushed back the lump which had developed in his throat, causing a burning sensation which he tried to swallow away. He turned to the side, fighting to compose himself. He listened as Mia reassured his daughter.

'You are so very brave,' Mia continued. 'You know, when I was your age, what are you, fifteen?'

Lucy nodded, wiping the tears from her face with the back of her hand.

'Fifteen. Christ, the world at your feet. Anyway, all I cared about were boys and alcohol.' Mia lowered her voice. 'Don't tell Sean.' She watched the smile on Lucy's face, her lips widening, and her eyes becoming more focused. 'I didn't care much for my parents at that age. Yes, I was close to my mum, but I know I gave her a hard time. I'm probably responsible for the odd grey hair or two. What I'm trying to say is you, Lucy, are the bravest lady I've ever met. I'll let you into a secret. I often wish I'd been like you as a teenager. I caused my parents no end of grief. I rebelled, I stayed out way too late, I smoked. The girls and I used to meet on a bench in London on a Friday night, and all we cared about was getting wasted.'

'Don't go getting any ideas, young lady,' Matt dictated.

'The boys in my class are gross, and I hate alcohol.'

Mia laughed. 'Keep it that way. If anyone deserves the honour of being head girl, It's you, Lucy.'

The lift jolted, and the four of them slammed their hands against the side wall of the cabin. The lights returned and the doors began to vibrate.

'What's happening?' Sean asked.

Matt, Lucy and Mia remained silent, consumed with apprehension. The heavy, metal doors rattled and began to part.

Mia saw her first. The lights in the hall were off, drenched in darkness. As Matt shone his phone torch towards the open doors of the lift, a woman stood still, staring at them. Mia screamed, stepping back towards the other three.

'Who the hell are you?' Matt shouted.

The woman covered her face, shielding the light from the phone, showing her discomfort. She wore a white blouse, black trousers and a brown waistcoat. Matt noticed the badge declaring "Staff," pinned to her waistcoat and suddenly recognised her as the lady who'd greeted them earlier in the lobby.

'I'm so sorry if I startled you. I'm the housekeeper.'

Matt pushed out a sigh of relief. 'We were stuck in the lift. Why can't we go up to the fourth floor?'

The woman looked awkward, her smile replaced by anguish. 'It's locked. No one can go up there. It's for refurbishment purposes. It's not due to open for a while.'

Matt watched the way her expression altered. Her cheeks became a bright red colour, her eyebrows knotted, the creases now visible on her brow. She darted her eyes towards the floor as if covering the lie she'd told. As they stepped out of the lift, Matt and Sean shone the torches, the light dancing over the walls opposite, tackling the bleakness surrounding them.

'I'm sorry if I startled you. How is your stay at The Blair Hotel?'

Matt wanted to return the question with, "Have you got all day?" He decided to suppress the contempt. 'Fine. What's not to love?'

The woman looked towards Lucy. She offered a comforting smile, then peered towards the lights, watching Matt and Sean. 'If you need anything, ask for me at reception. I'm only too happy to help. I'm Angela by the way.' She wheeled a large trolley with dusters, clothes and detergent spray into the empty lift. 'Have a good afternoon.'

As they walked along the hall of the third floor towards the stairs, the lights came on. Lucy turned back, watching the woman enter the lift, the trolley bouncing over the rough frame. Lucy stopped for a moment, watching the lady forcing the trolley, standing at one end, shoving hard.

As the wheels bounced, Lucy watched an arm drop from the right-hand side of the trolley which had been shielded with a bed cover. The woman entered the lift and turned towards Lucy, who was stood, open-mouthed. Lucy noticed the heart-shaped tattoo. The tattoo her mother had on her forearm. The woman grabbed the arm, lifting it and tucking it back under the sheet.

Lucy raced towards the lift as the doors closed. She was screaming hysterically. 'Dad. Quick. It's mum.' She pounded on the doors, hammering her fists in desperation. 'Let her go.' She turned to her father. 'Mum's in the trolley. I saw her tattoo. She's got mum.'

Matt turned. 'What are you talking about, Lucy?'

Matt joined his daughter. Sean and Mia followed, trying to force the doors open, listening to the loud squeal of the machinery in the lift shaft.

'That lady, she has mum on her trolley.'

'Lucy, are you sure?'

'I swear, Dad. It was mum.'

They watched the outside of the lift as the neon light shone brightly and the cabin began its ascent to the fourth floor.

21

'I think it's a little short. I don't have the legs anymore.' Bella held a bright red summer dress below her neck, pressing the fabric against her skinny frame. She was standing at the back of a shop on The Lanes, outside one of the dressing rooms. A full-length mirror rested on the floor supported by a wooden stand.

'I think it's divine. The colour brings out your eyes.' Nancy was batting off the shop assistant, hovering around the two ladies, eager to push the sale. *Yes, we're fine. No, we don't need your help, we have our own taste in clothes. Yes, we'll call if we need assistance. Fine, we know you'll be around if we need you.*

Bella moved back inside the changing room and pulled the curtain. She squeezed into the dress and reappeared a few seconds later in the corridor.

'It's perfect, Bella. And so cheap.'

Bella wanted to correct her friend, to brag that money was no concern. She stopped herself before the boastful remark threatened to spoil their outing. She'd worked hard, earned the right to spend her money, but she wasn't going to rub her friend's nose in her lavish lifestyle. 'Okay. I'll get it. I think I'll take the black one too. I think the green one would look good on you. My treat. Go and get them.'

Nancy smiled and moved back out to the shop. The assistant was waiting behind the till, eager to pounce with as many clothes that she could pile into Nancy's hands. Her phone rang. Nancy removed it from her handbag and moved to a corner of the shop. The assistant watched as pound signs literally bulged from her eyes. She lived for days like this. It reminded her of the film, "Pretty Woman," when Julia Roberts spent an excessive amount of money in a shop in Beverly Hills. She knew the labels were a little less lavish, but it didn't stem the eagerness.

Bella stood in the changing room, balancing on one leg, her hands pressed against the wall as she stepped out of the dress. She lifted it off the ground, folded it and placed it on the plastic bench. 'Nancy. Have you picked a dress yet? Don't forget to bring the black one for me too.'

'Be there in a second. I'm on the phone,' Nancy shouted.

Bella stepped into her jeans and placed her jumper over her head, pushing her hair off her shoulders. The curtain opened slightly and a dress was presented to her, pushed through the gap. 'Thanks, hun. Are you going to get the green one or what? My treat.'

'It won't fit.'

Nancy was still standing out in the shop. She heard Bella, screaming. At the same time, the shop assistant charged over to the changing rooms. Nancy hung up the phone and dashed after the assistant. The fire escape door was open, banging against the back wall; the light pushing through caused a sudden haziness making it difficult to see. The curtain to Bella's changing room was closed and the weeping cries echoed along the corridor. Nancy pulled the curtain back and saw Bella, kneeling on the floor, the shock evident on her face.

'He was here,' Bella confirmed.
'Who, Bella? Who was here?' Nancy asked.
'The guy who took the selfie. He's after me.'

* * *

'Are you sure it was him? I was on the phone. Maybe it was my voice you heard?'

Bella and Nancy were sat at the back of a modern bistro pub towards the far end of The Lanes. A large bottle of red wine rested in the centre of the table. They'd left the clothes shop without buying anything, much to the dismay of the shop assistant.

'It was him. I heard a man's voice. He pushed a dress through the gap and grabbed my arm. I freaked out. I thought it was you. He was standing on the other side of the curtain. He was pulling my arm, Nancy.'

'What a freak. I'm sorry you've had to deal with this shit. He's gone now. You scared him off. Don't let it put you off enjoying your day.' Nancy sipped her drink from a tall glass, watching her friend, the closed, fearful expression, her legs pulled up onto the wooden frame of the chair, huddled into herself like a hedgehog forming the shape of a ball.

'Christ, I thought London was bad.' Bella smiled, an attempt to break the tension. She glanced around the room. Although it was mid-afternoon, the lights were off, contributing to the dull atmosphere. A tall guy with a black apron wrapped around his waist stood behind the bar and greeted a young couple walking towards him. Bella noticed the array of wines behind the counter, placed in rows, four of five shelves high. The menu which stood on the table in a dark, plastic stand offered swanky bar food: Sushi, Grilled Ratatouille Salad, Croque Madame, Potato Gratin and extravagant nuts. She craved a roast dinner or pie and chips. It wasn't her type of place, but Nancy was her best friend, and she didn't want to insult her taste.

'Nice here, isn't it?' Nancy asked as she downed the remainder of her wine and filled the glass back up to the brim.

'Yeah. It's certainly different,' Bella added.

The waiter had finished serving the young couple and then made his way to Nancy. 'Hey. Good to see you. Can I get you another bottle?'

Nancy placed her hand on the brim of her glass. 'Are you trying to get me drunk?'

The waiter blushed. Bella watched the flirtation between the two of them. He was handsome, his dark features and chiselled face made him appealing, and he smelled great. Bella glanced at his chest; the top button of his white shirt was open, and his chest muscles bulged through the material. As he walked away, Bella caught Nancy giving him a quick once over.

'What?' Nancy laughed.

'So this is why we're here?'

'You have to admit he's bloody hot.'

'Yeah. Absolutely. How do you know him?' Bella asked.

As Nancy spoke, Bella glanced a figure, standing in the corner of the large window towards the front. A man, facing towards her. Bella stood, making her way across the floor.

'Is the story that boring?' Nancy asked.

Bella moved to the window, looking across the lanes at the shops opposite. People were standing, chatting, the sound of laughter. She turned to her friend. 'Sorry, I thought I saw him.' Bella turned and made her way back to the table.

'Saw who?'

'The guy. The one who took my picture. The same guy in the changing room. I think he was standing at the window.'

'Oh, Bella. There's no one there. You're safe. Have your drink and stop worrying about him. He's long gone.'

'Do you think?' Bella asked, almost childlike.

Nancy stood, placing her arms around her friend. 'Let's enjoy our time together. Don't let anyone spoil it. Do you hear me?'

Bella nodded and sat back down.

They stayed for another couple of hours. The waiter joined them and gave the ladies a free bottle on the house. Bella was feeling quite drunk. She stared at her friend, watching her finish the final glass of her Pinot Noir, her face flushed, the sparkle in her glazed eyes. Her brown hair was dishevelled, resembling a scarecrow on a bad day, her lips were stained red, and she struggled to focus. She missed Nancy. Yes, they spoke every week, but it wasn't the same.

Nancy reached for her handbag under the table. 'Right. Shall we call it a day?' She fell forward, placing her hand on the table for support.

As they passed the waiter, Bella lifted her hand, thanking him for a great afternoon.

Outside, the chill awakened them from their drowsy slumber. The alcohol hit them hard, and they linked arms, relishing the contentment of their friendship. They walked slowly, drenched in the buzz of the wine they'd consumed, giggling like naughty schoolgirls.

'I wish you'd come here more often. I miss days like this. Not giving a shit, getting pissed and the worries of being an adult pushed to the back of my mind.' Nancy looked towards her friend.

'I know. I miss Brighton. But I'll visit more often. Being away has made me realise how much I crave this place.'

They approached a taxi rank. A row of cars pulled forward.

Nancy turned to her friend. 'I'll drop you off on the way to your parents.'

'Don't be daft. It's the opposite way. 'I'll call you during the week. Nancy, it's been great. Love ya, chick.'

The girls embraced, and Nancy stepped into the first car, waving enthusiastically.

Bella watched as the car pulled out onto the road. She waited for a second, glancing behind her, watching for the guy who had ruined her day.

'Where to, love?'

Bella swung around and looked at the driver of the next car in line. She suddenly felt alone, her body soaked with fear. She imagined the guy who had taken the selfie, leaping out from the back seat, grabbing her, pulling her into an alleyway.

Bella gave her parents address and cautiously opened the door of the car, stepping into the passenger seat. As they pulled out of the taxi rank, the driver made small talk, but Bella was too occupied watching around her to hear what he was saying.

* * *

Ten minutes later, Bella produced a credit card from her handbag, tapped the small machine and thanked the driver. Now, she stood alone on the pavement, glaring at her parent's house. A three-bedroom semi-detached, situated towards the end of the street. Bella suddenly felt emotional as she stared at the house. The memories of her childhood flooded through her mind. She felt guilty for moving away, an only child leaving home to make a better life, to be a success, more money, respect. She struggled to comprehend why she'd fled. The time she'd spent earlier with Nancy made her think only of her own greed. Did she look down on these people now? Had she been away too long? Did she have anything in common with her parents? Bella's mind raced with questions, and, at this point, she wanted to open the front door, clutch her parents and never leave them again.

The memories of her childhood were magnificent. As Bella moved towards the brown wooden gate which separated the pavement from the front garden, she recalled the times her father had spent helping her balance on her new bike. The hours he'd invested, patiently running alongside her, holding her when she fell to the side. Her mother, trimming the hedge as her father washed the car. The neighbours popping over for drinks at the weekends. Bella felt choked. Although she'd made a decent life for herself in London and had a partner she loved dearly, she missed home.

Bella removed the front door key from her handbag. The taxi had long gone, and although it was early evening, darkness had set in almost instantly. The sky was smothered in a grey, hazy bleakness and the streetlamps provided little support for the loneliness she felt.

Bella opened the front door, hearing her mother's voice calling from the kitchen.

'Bella. Is that you?'

Bella broke down. She stood with the front door open, sobbing like a child.

'For heaven's sake. What's happened?' Her mother came racing along the hall wearing an apron over her green jumper. She wore black trousers and was barefooted. Her grey hair bounced on her shoulders, and her arms were held out in front of her.

Bella closed the front door. 'I'm sorry. I've had a drink with Nancy, and I'm feeling emotional. I love you so much, Mum.'

'Oh, you daft mare. I thought something had happened. We love you too.'

Sheila reached forward, pulling her daughter into her arms

and gripped her tight. She could feel her daughter trembling. 'Now sit down, and I'll make us a cup of tea. Christ, you frightened me for a second. How was Nancy? I haven't seen her for so long.'

Bella followed her mother along the hallway and walked into the living room. 'She's great. God, she still looks the same. She hasn't aged. Where's Dad?'

Sheila watched her daughter sit in the centre of the sofa, then looked towards the ceiling. 'He's gone for a nap. Poor bugger can't handle it anymore. Lazyitis is the word I'd use.'

Bella laughed as she kicked off her high heels and allowed the large cushions to consume her body. She watched her mother leave the living room, wallowing in the familiar comfort she'd craved for so long. She listened as her mother poured water into the kettle, then the loud hissing noise as it began to boil. Bella looked over the room, her body sinking further into the cushions, the adrenalin from the copious glasses of wine now stimulating her mind, making her anxious. She breathed deeply, inhaling the aroma of her mother's perfume which hung in the air: citrus, grapefruit. The scent of coriander and chilli powder worked its way from the kitchen. Her mother's latest cooking recipe. Now she smelled the essence of strong mint from a couple of plants that stood either side of the telly.

Bella closed her eyes for a moment, smiling to herself as she thought about Nancy. How great it had been seeing her today. As she opened her eyes, a figure moved into her vision. A man, standing at the front window. Bella jumped up, the room suddenly spinning. He waited for a moment, staring at Bella, a crazy grin adorning his face, then he moved to the side of the house. Bella screamed as the kettle came to a halt. Her mother called out.

'Bella. Are you okay?'

She ran to the hallway. 'Lock the back door. Quickly,

Mum. The back door.' Bella watched her mother turn, reaching for the door handle on her right.

'It is locked. What on earth is wrong, Bella?'

Bella shouted, alarming her mother. 'Move away from the door.'

She watched the awkward figure of her mother as she went to the centre of the kitchen, now flustered.

'Bella. What is it? What's happened, my love?'

Bella was standing in the hallway, too frightened to move. She kept her voice low, controlled, aware of causing any more dismay. 'I think there's someone outside.'

Her mother smiled. She wanted to say the alcohol had caused Bella's fear, made her uncomfortable. She chose her words carefully. 'Bella. There's no one outside. Go into the living room and relax. I'm making us a curry. Although I doubt your father will have any. He's awkward like that.'

'Mum. You're not hearing me. A minute ago, someone was standing at the window. Someone is outside.' Bella moved closer to her mother, now standing at the kitchen door. She looked out of the window above the kitchen sink, staring into the darkness. Bella eyed the door. The key in situ and the lock secure.

'Bella, why on earth would someone want to break in at this time? It's early evening.'

They both jumped as the security light came on, shining towards the neighbour's wall. Bella glanced at her mother, seeing the sudden confusion on her face.

'It's probably a cat.' Her mother was now agitated.

'Move to the hallway, Mum. Now.'

Sheila did as she was told. The two women stood together, watching the bright light outside, looking for a shadow, anything to confirm Bella's fear.

Bella switched off the kitchen light, then the hallway.

They stood in silence, waiting. Both were exhaling short, sharp breaths, controlled, listening tentatively.

Bella moved into the kitchen, taking light steps towards the back door.

'Bella. What are you doing?'

Her daughter turned slowly towards her mother. 'I'm going to see if he's still outside.'

'I'm sure it's just an animal. Should I call the police? Where's your phone?'

'It's in the living room. I'll check first. If there's someone outside, we'll call them.' Bella pressed her body to the kitchen door, feeling the cold from the tiles against her feet and placing her left ear against the wood. She listened hard, hearing her mother, the wheezing sounds from her chest as she stood in the hallway.

Bella remained in a crouched position, waiting. A minute went by, then another. She heard nothing to confirm that someone was outside. She turned, facing her mum. 'I think they're gone. I'm going to check.'

'Bella. No. Keep the door locked.'

'I need to check, Mum.' Bella gently straightened her legs, placed her hand on the key and turned. The lock made a loud, snapping sound. Too loud. She placed her hand on the door handle, bringing it downwards, a slow, exaggerated movement, then pulled the door towards her. Outside, the lights were still on, the glow filling the area where she stood. She looked at the wall opposite, then along the concrete path towards the front of the house. To her right, the garden opened out in a web of darkness. Bella moved out onto the step, pushing her body further, her frame almost horizontal. She felt dizzy, a rush of adrenalin as she thought about the guy earlier. He'd taken a picture of her. He knew what she looked like. The same guy she'd seen while trying on clothes in the shop. The same guy who was watching her while they'd had a drink. Was it possible that he'd followed her home? Could he be here? Surely Bella couldn't be imagining this. He was real. He'd ruined her day. Now, had he come for her?' The lights going off caused Bella to retract from her thoughts. She stood in the darkness, backing away, then stepped into the kitchen and locked the door.

As Bella made her way across the tiled floor, she listened to the voice of her mother in the darkness.

'See. No one there.'

'I had to check,' Bella replied. She stood at the door between the kitchen and the hallway, pawing for the light.

A mobile phone sounded, coming from behind them, towards the front of the house.

Bella turned on the kitchen light.

Peter Simpson was standing in the hallway.

22

Matt, Lucy, Sean and Mia were stood on the third floor of The Blair Hotel, watching the light above the lift as it changed to number four. Matt was pushing his fingers into the gap of the doors, trying to open them from the hallway. A few minutes ago, his daughter had said she'd seen her mother, her hand dropping from the trolley.

'There has to be a way to get up there. I think it's where they're holding her,' Matt stated. He pounded the lift door with his fists, the rumbling sound filling the hallway where they stood.

Mia crouched, then held Lucy's hand. 'If it's your mother, if you saw her, we're going to get her back. Do you hear me?'

Lucy nodded her head, her eyes fearful with the image she'd seen a few minutes ago. Lucy had never felt more frightened. She saw the arm drop, her mother's tattoo, her body being loaded into the lift. She wondered if her mother was still alive; the frightening scene of her body on the trolley was too much to think about. Lucy tried to push the image from her mind.

The lift began to descend, and the display which showed the number four above the doors was now blank. They watched, listening as the cart moved towards them. Matt hit the call button, and a few seconds later, the lift stopped. They waited as it aligned itself and the doors slowly opened. They stared at the empty box.

'Where the hell is she?' Sean shouted. 'She went to the fourth floor. If it's closed off, what is she doing up there?'

Matt stepped inside and pressed button number four. As the doors closed, he eyed the three of them as they watched in anticipation. Matt stood, waiting for the lift to move. A few seconds later, he pressed number four again. The lift remained stationary. He jabbed the button in frustration, then pressed for the doors to open. 'She must have a security pass or something. An area where only members of staff can go.'

'But why have they blocked it off? What are they hiding?' Mia asked.

Matt stepped out of the lift. 'We need to get a pass.'

* * *

Matt led the way, followed by Lucy, Mia and Sean. They walked out through the doors marked "Fire Escape," which lead to the communal stairs. Again, Matt tried the door to the fourth floor.

'How are we going to get a pass?' Mia asked.

'We'll steal one. We have to find the woman who's gone up there and take it,' Matt declared.

'Dad. That's too dangerous.'

Matt smiled at his daughter. 'It's what we have to do, Lucy. I think Mum's being held up there.' Matt turned towards the stairs. 'I say we go back to the rooms, keep a low profile for a while. I haven't seen any security cameras, but whoever is involved in this may be watching us.'

Mia looked around the communal stairs, fighting the dread which began seeping through her body.

They made their way down the stairs, struggling with the smell. It was like blocked drains. The nearer they got to the ground floor, the stronger the stench. The building was hugely neglected. Matt struggled to see how they made money. The rooms were repulsive with damp and rot, the staff seemed like they were in a trance, and the place was depressing. How had he not noticed any of this when he came with the guys?

Matt opened the fire escape door, and they walked out to the reception area. The first thing that hit them was the silence. The desk was unoccupied, the restaurant doors were closed, and the lights were out. He checked his watch. It was almost 6pm. Where was everyone?

Matt turned. 'What now?' He watched as Mia walked along the floor to the main entrance. She pushed the handle.

'It's locked. What the hell?' She pushed both doors, then leaned her body against them, trying to force them outwards.

Sean raced over. As he crouched, he saw the doors were locked. 'I think we should go to the rooms. The more time I spend here, the crazier it gets.'

'Are we locked in, Dad?' Lucy asked.

'I don't think so. Maybe it's protocol. The person behind the desk may have gone for a break. Let's go to the room. We can look around again later.'

'There's nobody here,' Mia said more to herself. 'How are we going to get out of this place?'

Sean gently clasped her hands, grabbing her wrists. 'We're going to get out. Don't panic. I need you to stay strong.'

Tears began to fill her eyes, and she turned away to prevent Lucy from seeing her. Once she'd composed herself,

Sean linked her arm, and they walked along the foyer towards their room. Matt and Lucy followed.

Sean opened the door to room seven, and once he'd made sure it was safe, the others joined.

Mia turned on the telly, a distraction from what was happening around her. Lucy sat on the end of the bed, waiting as Mia searched for something to watch.

Matt signed to Sean that they needed to chat. He stepped outside, and Sean followed.

'I'm thinking that whatever is going on here, the staff may be involved,' Matt suggested.

'I was thinking the same thing.'

'I say we should call the police. The sick games are getting out of hand,' Matt confirmed.

Sean cupped his hands over his nose and pulled his fingers along his face. 'What happens then?'

Matt hesitated. 'Well, they can help. We're sitting fucking ducks here.'

Sean's frustration was visible. 'Okay. They have footage of that night.' Sean couldn't bring himself to say what had happened on their weekend away. 'They've also got Nadia. As soon as they hear the sirens, it goes one of two ways. They kill your wife as they make a run for it.'

'And the other scenario?' Matt asked.

'They show the footage. The recording of what we have done. Maybe they'll do both.'

Matt itched so badly to say he wasn't involved. He'd gone to bed before the others. Before the horrible incident that started all of this. He'd been dragged into it. The only reason that stopped him from calling the police was the others possibly framing him. He trusted Sean. But Billy. Peter. He wouldn't put it past them. Sean had a point. If Matt did call for help, it wouldn't end with a handshake and a pat on the back. 'So, we just stay here? Wait? Is that it?'

'We have no choice. While we're together, we're safe. We need to ride it out. Find a pass to the fourth floor, get to Nadia and get the hell out of here,' Sean said.

* * *

Matt and Sean joined Mia and Lucy in the room. The atmosphere was tense between the four of them. Matt needed to protect his daughter. The later it became, the more he worried for Nadia. For her safety and his daughter's. He sat beside her on the bed, watching her. He struggled to say the words of encouragement that she needed to hear. The hotel was locked, the staff had done a disappearing act, there was no way up to the fourth floor, and it was too dangerous to leave the room. How the hell could he find the words to put Lucy's mind at ease?

'How are you bearing up, kid?' he asked.

'Oh, I've had better days. It wasn't how I'd imagined my first trip to Brighton, that's for sure.'

Matt ruffled her hair. 'We're going to find mum. You hear me?'

Lucy glanced at her father with tear-soaked eyes. 'Do you mean it?'

Matt fought the burning pain in his throat. He reached forward, placing his hands on her shoulders. 'I mean it. I'm so very proud of you. Other teenagers would have crumbled with the pressure. But not you. You are a remarkable young lady. I love you so much.'

The phone rang in room seven. Matt glanced towards the table. Sean, Mia and Lucy watched in anticipation. The noise was deafening, like a grating church bell ringing out early on a Sunday morning. The clanging sound bellowed through their ears. Matt stepped towards the table, lifting the receiver. 'Hello?' He waited, listening to the silence. 'Who is it?' Matt glanced towards the other three, watching their eyes on him. 'Hello?'

He hung up. A few seconds later, the phone rang again.

Matt grabbed the receiver, holding it to his ears without the greeting this time. There was a muffling sound that made the hairs stand on his arms. It resembled someone desperately trying to talk, moaning in discomfort. Now there were more, other sounds, muted and crying for help. 'Who is this?' Matt asked. As he placed the phone down, they heard footsteps moving along the communal hall. Matt grabbed Lucy, moving backwards away from the front door. Sean and Mia followed.

'Someone's coming. What are we going to do?' Mia asked. She'd heard the voices coming from the phone.

'Keep quiet. Don't make a sound.' Matt watched the fear on Sean's face as he held Mia. 'They're taunting us. I think they have people held here. Against their will. They're sick bastards,' Matt said.

The footsteps paused outside the room. Suddenly the handle moved slowly downwards. They could hear someone gently pushing against the door. Matt waited, praying they hadn't left the door unlocked. He listened for a click, anything to suggest the person had a key. The four of them stood, holding their breaths, staring towards the front of the room. The muffled sounds a few minutes ago played over in Matt's head. He wondered if he'd ever see his wife again. Matt feared if the person got into the room, they'd all die here.

'Sean. Do we run for it?' Matt asked.

'I don't know. Christ, Matt, we're fucked if they get in here.'

A knock rattled on the wood, sounding like someone tapping with their knuckles. Matt stepped forward, edging to the door.

'Stay there. Don't open it, Matt,' Mia ordered.

Suddenly the footsteps began to fade. They stood motionless until the noise had disappeared into the distance.

They heard Mia gasp as an image appeared on the screen. Matt shot a look in her direction. She stood by the telly, the remote control resting in her right hand.

You okay, Mia?' Matt watched her as she watched the screen.

'It's Billy.'

'What are you talking about?' Matt asked. He looked towards the screen.

'Look. It's Billy and Lydia.' Mia held the remote control at the telly and turned the sound up.

Sean moved towards the bed. The picture showed two people, a live feed, their movements being recorded.

'What the hell is this? Matt asked. He stood, then moved slowly towards the screen. He watched as Billy and Lydia stood in a room, similar to the one they were in, holding each other. They looked frightened. Suddenly, there was sound.

'What is going on, Billy? I thought you'd whisk me away to Paris, a weekend in Barcelona. This is a shithole.' Lydia smiled, a way of retracting her words.

'No, it's great here. I came with the lads recently; you'll love it,' Billy replied. 'It's just a night away. A break from the pressure, if you like.'

Matt looked at Sean. 'What the hell is going on?'

They watched as Billy and Lydia unpacked a small bag. Lydia moved to the bathroom and shut the door. Then there was silence.

They continued watching, mouths open, unable to speak. They had so many questions. The fact that Billy and Lydia could be here, their movements monitored, drove terror through the four of them.

Matt stood and began turning everything over. He lifted

the bed, crawled on his hands and knees through the room and ran his arms along the wall. He was sure there was no camera here. But it was possible. Now, they were the size of a small coin, often hidden in pictures, walls, smoke alarms. Matt glanced to the ceiling. The room didn't have one. He was sure it went against safety regulations, but then nothing would surprise him with this place. Matt moved to the bathroom. Water dripped from the shower hose; the toilet was slanted on one side, balancing on a piece of old timber. The white mastic around the sink and bath had long been discoloured. Again, the walls were bare. If there was a camera, Matt struggled to work out where it could be hidden. He moved back to the room, watching the screen. Lydia had returned from the bathroom; she was looking for a towel to dry her hands. Billy was sat on the edge of the bed in silence. Again, they could hear the conversation.

'Why have you brought me here?' Lydia sat on the bed, holding her stomach. Matt remembered she was pregnant. He hadn't noticed at first. The image was slightly grainy. He recalled when Billy had told him. The phone call, Billy's jubilation. He sounded thrilled. Then the stupid bastard went home with a woman from the casino. Matt wanted to find him, tear him limb from limb for what he'd put them through. He listened as Billy replied.

'Lydia, can't you just enjoy the break? We came here a few weeks back, the lads and me. It's a great place. I'm only thinking of you. Let's just enjoy ourselves.'

Mia turned to Matt and Sean. 'She doesn't know, does she?'

'Know what?' Lucy asked.

Matt interrupted. 'He hasn't told her about the weekend. It's obvious. She doesn't know the dangers of this place.'

'Know what, Dad?'

'Lucy. It's nothing for you to be concerned about, okay? I'm not having you worry unnecessarily.'

'I can handle it, Dad.'

Billy was tapping on his new phone. He'd had to explain to Lydia how he'd lost the other one, making an excuse that he'd left it at a pub while drinking with the lads.

They could hear Billy and Lydia talking. Billy was asking Lydia if she was hungry. He placed his arms around her, then tried to remove her dress. Lydia pushed him away, and he sulked like a small child. For a moment, Matt held his breath, aware that his daughter was watching and thankful the embarrassing moment had passed.

After a few minutes, Billy stood. Matt, Sean, Mia and Lucy were watching the screen.

'Let's go and eat. I'm starving,' Billy confirmed.

Lydia stood, again moving to the bathroom at the back of the room, the only difference between their rooms. A minute later, Lydia came out, rubbing the remainder of a face cream into her cheeks. Billy opened the door, let his wife through to the communal hall and then closed it behind him.

They watched the screen, unable to look away. The empty room. Vacant. Haunting. Suddenly, the door opened. Mia leaned forward. Lucy gripped her father's hand. Sean was standing silently. A man walked inside, cautiously checking the storeroom at the front of the room, which housed the water heater. Matt looked towards their front door, seeing the same cupboard.

The guy moved slowly, looking behind him, making his way to the back of the room. He opened the door to the bathroom and stepped inside. A second later, he closed the door.

23

Peter Simpson stood in the hallway, holding a hammer in his right hand. His eyes were both vicious and fearful at the same time. He moved forward, hearing the screams from the women stood in front of him. A few minutes earlier, he'd managed to find an open window at the front of the house after checking around the back. He'd hoisted his body up, pushing himself forward over the ledge and landed on his hands. He'd kept as silent as possible. Now he was inside. He gazed at his phone, which he held in his left hand. "No Caller ID." Peter knew who it was. The puppet master, pulling the strings. Playing with him. The evil deeds were just starting. Peter glared at the young woman stood in front of him, the same woman he'd taken a selfie with earlier. He'd followed her, walking inside the shop. He'd heard Bella asking her friend to bring the dresses. At the last second, he panicked, racing out through the fire escape. Peter had watched her while she drank in the posh Bistro pub. As the girls came out, he saw her taking a taxi. This was his chance. He couldn't blow it. He'd parked close by and had jumped in his car, following the taxi.

Now, Peter stared at the phone and pressed the answer button, summoning the speaker. The familiar voice, his demands.

'You have thirty minutes to bring her here. Otherwise, you know how it works out for you. I know where your daughter lives.'

Peter wiped the saliva that dripped from his chin. He held the phone in the air, watching the fear on the faces of the women standing in front of him.

'I'm with her now. Please. I have her. Do you know how difficult this is for me?' Peter heard a noise upstairs, someone walking along the floorboards. 'Wait. There's a third person in the house.'

'Great. I'm going to make the game a little more challenging. Now you are going to bring two people here. You decide which ones.' The phone went dead. Peter grabbed the younger woman by her wrists, pulling hard. She fell to the floor, kicking out.

'Don't make this more difficult for me. They're going to kill me. Do you understand?' Peter shouted.

Bella's mother reached forward, and Peter turned her around, gripping her waist from behind.

'Leave her alone. Mum, run.'

The older lady pushed her arms outwards, but Peter's grip was vice-like.

He thought about hitting her with the hammer. He couldn't and wouldn't. He wasn't a violent man, but the person on the phone was driving him to the edge of his sanity. As he held the older lady, Bella kicked from the floor, hitting Peter on the knee. He let go for a second, winching in pain.

'Why is nothing easy?' he shouted. Peter lifted the hammer in the air, holding it above his head. 'I swear, if you make this difficult, I'll kill her.'

Bella moved backwards on the floor towards the front door. 'Mum, run. Please.'

There was a voice from the top of the stairs. A man, shouting, asking if everything was okay.

'Oh, for Christ's sake. Get down here. Move,' Peter ordered.

'What the hell are you doing? Get away from my wife this instant.'

Peter looked up the stairs. The guy was around sixty, frail-looking. He had tossed, unkempt hair. He slowly made his way down the steps, bare-chested, but wearing dark blue pyjama bottoms and slippers.

'Don't come any closer.' Peter grabbed the older lady and pushed her into a store cupboard. He closed the door and leaned against it. 'I need to bring you with me.'

'You're out of your bloody mind. Go on, piss off. Leave us alone.' The guy was now standing on the bottom step.

Bella was almost at the front door.

Sheila was banging the storeroom cupboard from inside.

'Can you just listen to simple fucking instructions? Get in the car. Now.' Peter's voice was raised, and he watched the startled look on the guy moving towards him.

As the front door opened, Bella screamed. 'Help us. Someone help. There's a madman in our house.'

Peter felt fear rise through his body. His stomach turned over, and for a moment, he thought he was going to be sick. He listened to the woman at the door. Any second now, a neighbour would appear, and Peter's life was over. He considered running around the side of the house. The phone call from a few minutes earlier played in his mind. He had about twenty-five minutes to get the girl and her father, he assumed, to the hotel. Otherwise, his daughter would be in danger and everything that happened would come out, including the contents of his stomach at this moment.

Again, Bella screamed, frozen at the front door. 'Someone help us!'

The older man raised his fist, pounding it on Peter's head. He fiddled with the lock, now struggling to shield the blows to his face from the woman in the cupboard. Peter pushed his head down, trying to defend himself, listening to the screams from the front door. He managed to force Sheila back in, then he pushed the door, feeling the weight against it and locked the storeroom door. Peter turned, placing the hammer down the back of his trousers and grabbed the bare-chested man in front of him. He spun him around with ease, gripping his wrists together behind his back, holding him tightly, and walked him to the front door. Peter stood for a moment. His head ached, his nose was bleeding, dripping onto the floor. He removed a handkerchief from his trouser pocket, then wiped the stain. Bella turned, straining to move with fright. She attempted to push her body off the floor, collapsing in a heap. She looked behind, seeing Peter now standing over her.

'I need to bring you with me. You and your father. I'm truly sorry for all this.' Peter gripped the man's wrists with his right hand. 'If you call the police, or try to escape, I promise I'll kill him. Don't try me. Not today.'

Peter moved along the front garden, listening to Bella, weeping at the door. He watched both sides of the house. The street was empty. He prayed silently, hoping no one could see him. He'd been instructed to place his wife in the boot. He opened the hatch of his car, placing Bella's father beside his wife's dead body, then he went back into the house, grabbed Bella's phone from the living room, and closed the front door. He placed Bella in the back seat, again warning of the repercussions if she tried to escape.

As he sat in the driver's seat of his car, he eyed the watch on his wrist. He had twenty-two minutes to get to The Blair Hotel.

* * *

Peter waited at the black gates. When they opened, he drove close to the metal shutters. He waited, knowing a security camera had picked up the image of his car. He'd managed to get to the hotel with only minutes to spare. He listened to the muffled cries of the woman in the backseat as the door to the warehouse began rising. Peter was petrified, vigorously wiping the sweat from his cheeks, his glasses steamed up, and his body felt on fire.

The man wearing a ski mask stood at the entrance of the warehouse. He signed for Peter to come over. He stepped out of the car, his legs aching, then moved to the boot. Peter opened it, grabbing Bella's father, one arm under his back, the other over his mouth. He lifted him as ski mask man watched him struggling, then Peter pulled him out of the boot. He glanced around, then dragged him along the hard floor. Peter slumped the body in front of him. He waited for a response.

'No gag? Rope? Extremely careless.' His voice was muffled under the ski mask.

Peter felt like a naughty schoolboy being scorned. 'It wasn't easy. I'm done. This is where we draw the line. I can't cope anymore.'

Ski mask man stood calmly. 'Now bring her.' He pointed to the back seat. Bella's head was leaning against the window.

Peter walked to his BMW and dragged Bella out of the car. She fell onto the floor and Peter placed his hands under her shoulders, dragging her in the same way.

Ski mask man had placed Bella's father towards the back of the warehouse, tying his hands to a radiator pipe. He walked towards the entrance, watching Peter, then placed his foot on the woman's chest as she lay on the floor, pressing her body against the ground. 'You fail to understand the consequences of your actions. You and your friends. You know what happened, what you have done. My brother will be extremely peeved if I just let you go. Where's the retribution in that?'

'Why are you doing this? I can't cope anymore. You've ruined my life, don't you see?'

'It's only the beginning.' The man pulled out a gun from the inside pocket of the jacket he wore. He held it to Peter's head. Bella screamed out. Now the gun was pointing at her. 'Do you know what they've done?'

Bella shook her head, her body quivering on the cold ground. She felt his large boot pushing against her throat.

Peter watched the gun aimed at Bella's head, her eyes wild, her face flushed. The guy took his foot off Bella's throat, and as he turned, Bella stood. Suddenly, she charged forward, her arms extended, and she grappled with the guy.

The man in the ski mask was too quick. He hammered the butt of the gun hard on the side of Bella's face, watching her drop to the ground in agony.

'That was a very foolish thing to do. You know you'll pay for that. Actions have consequences.' He leaned forward, dragging Bella by her shoulders, her body sliding along the ground, into the warehouse. Then he returned, instructing Peter to join them. Once they were both inside, the shutters slowly moved downwards.

'Give me your phone.' They were standing in the dark warehouse; a small light hanging from the centre of the room provided enough glow for them to see.

'I don't have it.' Bella struggled to talk.

The man turned to Peter. 'Please tell me you brought her phone?'

Peter dipped into the pocket of his trousers, handing Bella's phone over.

The man pressed the screen, seeing the command for 'Face ID.' He held it in front of Bella, and a second later, the phone opened. 'Because of your stupidity, you are going to play selfie. A game, it would seem, which has derived from our antagonists.

'What? What are you talking about?' Bella asked.

'You see, your friend here, he made a grave mistake. A weekend away. Lads together. Fuelled by alcohol and lust. But they fucked with the wrong people.' The guy turned to Peter. 'Do you know how long we had planned the operation? Trafficking the right woman. We're practically on our knees here. The only saving grace, my brother has plans to get The Blair Hotel prospering again, to keep us in employment. It was handed down in a lacklustre state. It is a hindrance, a deterrent, a derelict hovel of a place, but my brother is a fighter. There are plans, huge ideas. My father neglected the hotel towards the end. He had started to brighten the place up. But he ran out of money. Now, all I have left is my brother. He is everything to me; we're a community here, but you've put a large spanner in the cogs, and your actions have fucked everything up for us. Now, you will pay, and so will anyone who obstructs the operation of The Blair Hotel. We have to send out a message.'

'Please, we didn't mean it. I didn't kill her. It wasn't me.' Peter watched as Bella's eyes glanced towards him.

'You hid the body. If a car went over the edge of a cliff and dropped to the bottom, you're in the passenger seat, and it's crushed beyond recognition, would your life be spared? I think not.' The guy started to swipe the phone, flicking his finger from left to right. He stopped at the first selfie. It was a picture of the woman standing in front of him. Bella. She was with an older lady. He held the screen up. 'Who is this?'

Bella made a gurgling sound from deep within her throat. 'It's my mother.'

She eyed the man wearing the creepy ski mask.

'Well, we have a winner. You have precisely one hour to

bring her here, or I'll kill the old man. Then Peter.' He pointed the gun at Peter, then back to Bella, watching the fear in her eyes. He reached for the remote control to open the shutters, then reminded Bella of the tracker under Peter's car. 'One hour, starting from now. If you fail, they both die, then I'll come for you.'

24

'What the hell is he doing in the room?' Mia was staring at the screen. They'd just watched a man enter Billy and Lydia's room, and hide in the bathroom. 'Does anyone recognise him?'

'I doubt it's room service,' Matt said. He turned to Sean. 'If they're here, we need to find them. They don't realise the danger they're in.'

'I think Billy knows only too well. He wouldn't come back here off the cuff. He's been ordered here. Like we have.' Sean moved towards the front door. 'I think it's safer if you and Lucy stay here. Keep the door locked.' Sean directed the suggestion towards Mia.

'You think it's safe going out there?' Mia asked. 'I suggest we stay here. It's safer if we're together.'

'Look. The doors are solid. It would seem the only benefit with this cruddy dump. Keep it locked, Mia. Matt and I will be as quick as we can. We'll find Billy and Lydia. We have to warn them what's going on.'

'Dad, I want to come.'

'Lucy, it's not safe. People are out there, trying to hurt us.

You're safer in here with the door locked.' Matt hugged his daughter, then smiled at Mia.

A few seconds later, Matt and Sean moved out to the communal hallway, and Mia locked the front door.

* * *

As they moved along the hall, Matt tried to digest everything that had happened. His wife going missing. Peter calling over to Nadia's mother. Finding the bracelet. The medium on the pier. Lucy seeing her mother's hand dropping from the trolley. Billy and Lydia. The guy hiding in their room. The fourth floor. His head ached with the confusion of everything. Now, as he followed Sean towards the door leading to the foyer, he struggled to breathe. His body ached with tiredness. His mind, trying to unknot the past twenty-four hours and make sense of it all. He needed to protect Lucy. She was too young to deal with this. He wanted to bring her, but what if they were jumped? Whatever was going on at The Blair Hotel, Matt and Sean would protect Lucy and Mia. He was going to make sure they were safe.

Sean reached the door at the end of the corridor and pushed. He turned to Matt. 'It's locked.'

'What?' Matt moved in front, shoving his body against the door. 'This is ludicrous.' He stepped back and hurled his body against the wood. It was too robust. They stood in stillness, anticipating each other's words.

Sean finally broke the silence. He slammed the palms of his hands against the door. 'Can someone help us? Hello. Anyone? Is anyone there?' He stopped, listening intently to the quiet. 'Billy. Lydia. Can you hear us?'

'It's no use, mate. Let's go back.'

Again, Sean called out. 'Billy. Lydia. It's Sean and Matt. Open the door. You're in danger.'

Matt reached into the pocket of his jeans. He dialled Billy's mobile and waited. Billy had lost his phone but had managed to keep the same number. Matt had called him a few times since that fateful weekend, but he hadn't answered. As the phone began ringing, he glanced at Sean, seeing the apprehension in his eyes. A few seconds later, he hung up.

'Wait. I have an idea.' Matt Googled, The Blair Hotel, Brighton. Then pressed the call button. The front desk had been empty a few minutes earlier, but he needed to try. The phone call connected, and Matt heard a voice. He summoned the loudspeaker so Sean could hear. He waited, then someone spoke.

'Hello. The Blair Hotel. How can I help?'

Matt heard the English accent. The same man who they'd met earlier when Matt had asked about Nadia. The guy with the food who Matt and Sean had jumped outside their room. 'I need you to put me through to Billy and Lydia's room. It's a matter of urgency,' Matt ordered.

There was a short pause before the man spoke. Matt could hear tapping, like he was searching for the number.

'Putting you through now.'

The phone rang. Matt and Sean listened. The loud dialling tone was blaring in their ears. Matt was about to hang up, then someone answered.

'Who is this?'

Again, the accent was English, the voice deep. Sean whispered to Matt that the voice was familiar. The same person who had called him this morning with instructions to bring Mia here.

Matt had to be clever. He couldn't say they were watching the room on the screen, that they knew what was happening, or ask straight out for him to leave the room and give them Nadia back. 'I'm at the front desk. I'm one of the maintenance team for your lift. We had a report earlier that it was stuck. Someone pressed the alarm button.'

'I don't know anything about the lift. Who called you?'

'Like I said, someone pressed the emergency alarm. I need to take a look.'

'Show your ID to Fred. Once he's cleared it, go to the basement. That's where the plant room is and access to the machinery.'

Matt held his breath for a moment, then glanced at Sean. 'I need access to all four floors. Can you give me the lift pass?'

The phone went silent. Matt thought the guy had hung up. A minute went past. Matt began pacing the floor with anticipation. Again, he took a deep breath. 'Where are you?' Matt asked.

'I'm in Billy and Lydia's room. Then I'm coming to room seven.'

The phone went dead.

* * *

Matt and Sean walked back down the corridor, panic evident in their breathing.

'Keep this quiet. I don't want to scare Lucy and Mia,' Matt insisted.

'That goes without saying.' Sean reached an arm forward and stopped Matt. 'We need to get out of here. Now.'

'I'm not leaving until I find Nadia. I have to get up to the fourth floor.'

'Matt, It's not safe. You heard the guy on the phone. Billy and Lydia are in trouble. They've locked us in here, for Christ's sake. We can go out of the window. Race across the grounds and around to the front of the hotel. We can get help once we're out of here.'

'Listen to yourself, will you. You're not seeing the bigger

picture here. They know what you've done. You, Billy, Peter.' Matt wondered for a split second if Sean would bring his name into it. He didn't. 'Billy murdered a woman in his room; the three of you hid the body. For fucks sake. What the hell were you all thinking?'

Sean dropped his head in shame. 'Don't you think I've suffered? Don't you think I picture her every waking moment of my life?' Sean turned away for a second as he composed himself. 'Billy said he'd blame all of us. He was losing it, Matt. He didn't want to go down for what he'd done, but he made it clear if we didn't help, he'd say we were involved. What the hell was I supposed to do? He went on and on about Lydia, the baby on the way and not being able to handle prison. Christ, we wanted to get help. Report what had happened, but he had us. We were there, in the room. Our DNA, our fingerprints were everywhere. I have no doubt Billy would have brought us all down with him. He framed us. Getting rid of the body. That's the long and short of it, Matt.'

There was silence for a few moments as both men contemplated the situation.

'What are we going to do?' Matt asked. 'I guarantee someone is watching the grounds. We know the staff are involved. The second we make a run for it, they'll be on us.'

'Then we stay in our rooms, wait it out. It's the only option we have,' Sean stated.

* * *

Matt tapped the door to room seven. 'Lucy. Mia, it's us.'

Mia opened the door, and Matt walked into the room, followed by Sean.

Mia went to her partner, and Lucy to her father. They all

hugged, then Matt turned to the screen. He watched the empty room.

'What happened? Did you find Billy and Lydia? Mia asked.

'The door to the foyer is locked,' Sean pointed out.

Mia explained that the man hiding in Billy and Lydia's room came out of the bathroom to answer the phone. She'd seen it on the flat screen telly. Then he returned to the bathroom and closed the door. She glanced from Matt to Sean. 'So, we're trapped?'

'Mia, we'll get out. We need to keep it together, okay?' Sean placed his hands on her shoulders. 'I love you so much. We're going to get out of here. All of us. Then move on with our lives.'

They all turned to the screen as the front door opened. Billy and Lydia walked back into the room. They could hear the conversation clearly.

Billy moved across the room and sat on the edge of the bed. Lydia walked to a shelf to the right side and dipped her hand into a small holiday bag. She removed a sandwich and joined her husband.

'I'm sorry. I don't understand why the restaurant is closed.' Billy proclaimed.

'It's fine. Do you want one of these? Cheese and pickle.' Lydia held the sandwich in front of her husband.

'No. I had the burger and chips on the way. I'm okay for the moment.'

Lydia opened the packet and took a bite from the sandwich. 'Billy. What's going on? Why were the front doors locked? The restaurant?'

'You heard the guy behind the desk. He said there were staffing problems. Let's just chill here in the room. You and me.'

'So they lock the front door? Keep us here? Is that it?'

'Lydia. Relax. We're together. Just enjoy the evening.'

Matt moved closer to the screen. He eyed Sean, who was listening intently.

'I think they're struggling to keep the place afloat. It's nothing to worry about.' Billy removed his shoes, then lay horizontal on the bed.

They watched Lydia pacing the floor, moving towards the bathroom door. Matt, Sean, Lucy and Mia gasped. Lydia grabbed the handle of the door and at the last second, Billy called her to show her something on his phone.

'I can't just stand here and watch this. We need to get help,' Matt stated.

'Then we all go together.' Mia stood, then reached her arms to Lucy, holding her tight.

'Let's try the foyer again. We need to move fast.' Matt walked to the door and stepped out into the corridor. Sean, Mia and Lucy followed. At the end of the hall, Matt pushed against the door, surprised to find it unlocked. He walked out, seeing the blonde guy from earlier now behind the desk. He was sat on a swivel chair, tapping on a keypad. Matt walked over.

'Hi. There was a couple here a few minutes ago. I think they tried to get into the restaurant.'

The guy looked up and spoke in a calm, relaxed voice. 'The restaurant is closed, sir.'

Matt looked towards the doors. 'I understand it's shut. I'm asking about a couple who were here moments ago. Where are they now?'

'Sir, I can assure you, I haven't seen anyone come in or out of the hotel for a while. Maybe an hour or so. It's quiet this time of year.'

Matt rubbed his face in frustration. 'We came out here earlier. The front doors were locked. The desk was vacant, and the lights were out.'

The guy behind the desk peered at the other three, then back to Matt.

'Yes. We had a power cut. It was too dangerous to leave the doors open in case someone hurt themselves. Health and safety. All that palaver. You know how it is, don't you?'

'So, you didn't see a couple? A few minutes ago? A man and woman, staying here, trying to get into the restaurant?'

'I can assure you, Sir, as I've said, there was no couple here. You must be mistaken.'

'Look, Fred, is that your name?' Matt glanced at the name tag on the guy's shirt.

'Yes, it is.'

'Fred. I've had a long day. My wife is missing, I think my friends are in danger, and I'm not feeling very welcome here if I'm honest. I'm asking you to be straight with me. What the hell is going on?'

'I can assure you, Sir, nothing is going on. As I said, we had a power cut and...'

Matt interrupted. 'Yeah. You said. Are the doors open now?' Matt looked to the front. He moved over to the main entrance, then opened the doors. He glanced back to the guy behind the desk. 'Could you come with me for a second? I want to show you something?'

'Sir, I'm busy at the moment. If there's something...'

Matt walked back to the front desk, leaned over and grabbed Fred by the shirt. 'You're coming with me now. Do you understand?'

'Yes, Sir. I do.'

Matt led the guy along the corridor and into room seven.

'What seems to be the problem?'

Matt looked up at the blank screen. He grabbed the remote control, searching for the footage of the room where Billy and Lydia were staying.

He skipped through the channels, Sky News, CNN, BBC

World News, old recordings of Oprah Winfrey, Jerry Springer, The Cartoon Network, Sky One.

'Is there a problem, Sir?'

Matt threw the remote control down on the bed. 'What's happened to the footage? The recording? Our friends are in one of the rooms here. We were watching them. A man walked in and hid in the bathroom. They're in danger.'

'Sir, I can assure you it goes against the hotel's policy to allow anyone to be filmed. Maybe you were watching a re-run. Columbo perhaps?'

'Are you taking the piss?' Matt asked.

'Will there be anything else, Sir?'

Matt turned to Fred. 'Get out of the room.'

'Very well, Sir.'

Matt watched him close the door.

They were all involved.

* * *

Matt sat alone in the room. He felt frightened. Not only for Nadia, but for Lucy. This place was dangerous, of that, he had no doubt. He glanced at the screen, debating whether to hurl the remote control at the glass. He placed his face in the palm of his hands, fighting the fear which began to engulf his body. He started to shake; his skin became blotchy. His neck itched. He sat in silence, thinking of Nadia. Beautiful Nadia. Matt jumped as the front door opened. He saw Sean, Mia and his daughter. Suddenly, his world lit up, seeing Lucy. Although she didn't know it, Matt gained the strength to keep going from her. She was so influential, they were always together, and Lucy gave him the courage to continue. He always seemed stronger in her company. Maybe it was a father thing, needing to be courageous in front of his little girl.

'Dad, are you okay?' Lucy walked towards Matt.

He held her close, smelling the familiar scent of apple shampoo from her hair. Although they'd been on the road all night, Matt could still detect the fragrance. Lucy only ever used apple shampoo. 'I'm hanging in there, kid. And you?'

Lucy pulled back, staring into her father's eyes. 'I don't like this place much.' She smiled, which filled Matt with hope.

'You and me both.'

Suddenly, the live recording returned. A news station had been on in the background. Now, they could see Billy and Lydia again. Matt, Lucy, Sean and Mia watched. The atmosphere was one of dread, confusion. Billy was still clothed, lying on the bed. Lydia stood, again, pacing the floor, moving around the room, placing a couple of dresses from the holdall into a cupboard and hanging them up.

'How long do you intend on staying here?' she asked.

Billy sat up, leaning his head against a pillow. 'I don't know. A night, two at the most. Can't you just enjoy yourself? We're away. Let's have a good time.'

As Matt watched, he found himself feeling sorry for Lydia. Billy most likely had a call with instructions to come to the hotel. Matt doubted he had told Lydia the reason, that he'd played away when they came here for the lad's weekend, that he'd taken part in a kinky sex game and murdered a woman, hid her body and then ran. 'I'll be back in a second.'

'Dad, where are you going?'

'Wait here, Lucy.'

Matt walked out of the room, along the darkened corridor then pushed the door at the end and stood in the foyer. He glanced over to the desk. Fred was gone. Matt turned, eyeing the doors to the restaurant which were also closed. He walked over, cupping his hands against the glass. The place was in complete darkness. *How can they make money?* he thought to himself. Matt looked across at the main entrance, then back to a door opposite which he assumed were more rooms. He couldn't remember the layout of the hotel from his recent visit. He had to find Billy and Lydia's room. Although they hadn't spoken since that fateful weekend, and Matt was still pissed off with his friend, he needed to let them know the danger.

Matt walked across the foyer, trying the door, which he was certain led to more rooms. He saw a placard announcing eleven to twenty. The door was locked. Matt banged on the wood. 'Hello. Is anyone there?' He waited. 'If you can hear me, open the door. Hello.' Matt stepped back. He glanced around, looking for security cameras. He spotted one above the desk, pointing towards the front door. It seemed to be the only one, unless there were others, hidden. Matt waited, standing between the restaurant and the door leading to their rooms. He needed to find Fred. Show him the screen. Ask again about Billy and Lydia. The more time he spent here, the more he hated it. Regrets began to play out in his mind. Why the hell had they come here a few weeks ago? Why did Matt go to bed before the others? He would have got help, even though Billy would have tried to stop him. He suddenly felt guilty. Guilty that Nadia had been taken. A stupid, crazed, revenge act devised by the lunatics who ran this place. Dragging them here like pawns on a chessboard for their sick depravity. Peter wasn't like this. He loved Matt and Nadia. They'd killed his wife, driven him to murder an innocent woman by mistake. To kidnap Nadia. Where would it stop? He knew what they were capable of, the twisted retribution they had planned. Matt had to find Nadia. He had to get his family out of here.

As Matt walked along the corridor towards Sean and Mia's room, he heard gasps. For an instant, he visualised Lucy, missing, being taken by the people who were running this hideous dump. He raced to the door and knocked. A few seconds later, Sean answered. Matt saw Lucy and blew out a sigh of relief.

'What's going on?' Matt asked. He looked towards the screen. Billy was still lying on the bed. Lydia had moved beside him, sat up and combing her hair.

'Where did you go?' Sean asked.

Matt was transfixed with the screen. Although he knew they shouldn't watch, they needed to make sure their friends were safe. 'I went looking for that prick, Fred. He's gone. I couldn't find him. I also tried a door on the other side of the foyer. I think it's where Billy and Lydia are staying. 'It's locked, Sean.' Matt watched his friend, the disoriented look on his face.

Sean's voice was low. 'How the hell are we going to get out of this? Are all the staff involved?'

Matt hesitated for a moment. 'It looks that way.'

The two men glimpsed at the screen, knowing a man was hiding in the bathroom.

Suddenly, Lydia stood. 'I need to take a pee.'

Billy didn't answer.

'No. We have to stop her,' Matt said, louder than he intended.

Mia and Lucy were staring; the anticipation was rife.

Lydia moved around the bed, then slowly stepped towards the back of the room.

'Don't open the door. Lydia. Get out of the room.' Matt started pacing, pushing a hand through his hair.

Lydia placed her hand on the bathroom door and opened it. She walked inside and the door closed behind her.

Matt, Lucy, Sean and Mia held their breath in silence. They waited, their eyes fixed on the screen, Billy on the bed, Lydia out of view. The seconds slowly ticked past as they watched. Suddenly, the bathroom door opened. The four of them seemed to lean forward with apprehension.

Lydia walked back out. As she made her way to Billy, the intruder came bursting out behind her. They watched as the man grabbed Lydia from behind and held her tight around the waist. Billy looked over in shock. He clambered out of the bed and raced towards his wife. The sound was slightly muffled. Billy was shouting as he tackled the imposter. All of a sudden, the man produced a weapon from his back pocket. Lydia kicked him as Billy grabbed for the claw hammer which the guy held in his hand. He lifted it high in the air and caught Billy on the side of the head with the handle. Lydia was screaming, trying to tackle the guy. He pushed her out of the way, and she landed on the bed.

'Look away, Lucy. Now. Turn away,' Matt shouted. 'We need to help them.'

Billy was lying on the floor, wincing in pain as the guy brought out a small plastic bottle from his jacket pocket. He began pouring the liquid over Billy. Then he dragged him by his feet and pulled him into the bathroom. A few seconds later, flames engulfed the room. Lydia was screaming as she banged on the bathroom door, pulling the handle down in desperation as smoke seeped from underneath.

Matt, Lucy, Sean and Mia listened to the blood-curdling cries coming from the room as Billy lay in the bath, his body engulfed in flames.

A few minutes later, there was silence coming from the bathroom, only Lydia's screams as she continued to pound on the door. When Billy went quiet, the man grabbed a fire extinguisher from the front of the room. Lydia lay on the floor, wailing like a mad woman. The guy moved to the bathroom, sprayed the foam over Billy's corpse, then calmly walked out of the room.

'Turn it off. I can't stand it anymore. Turn the telly off,' Mia shouted.

Five minutes later, the phone rang in room seven.

Matt picked it up, listening to the man he'd spoken with a few minutes ago.

'I hope you enjoyed the show.'

'You're sick. You hear me? You'll never get away with this,' Matt insisted.

'I'm coming to room seven next.'

25

Bella sat in the driver's seat of Peter's BMW. She struggled to put the car into drive, having never driven an automatic before. Moments ago, the guy in the ski mask had pointed a gun at her and the creep who'd brought her here. Her father had been dragged to the back of the warehouse. She'd been instructed to go to her mother and take her here. How the hell was she going to do that? The last sentence played in her mind, over and over like a recording, as she watched the closed shutters to the warehouse.

You have precisely one hour to bring her here, or I'll kill the old man. Then, Peter. One hour, starting from now. If you fail, they both die, then I'll come for you.

Bella glanced at her watch. It was just gone 6pm. She drove out of the car park, the BMW jolting forward like a fairground ride. Almost five minutes had passed, and Bella hadn't reached the main road. She calculated the route, visualising the roads leading to her parent's house. If the traffic was light, she guessed she'd get there in twenty minutes. That left her ten minutes to persuade her mother to get in the car and go with her. What the hell did she say as she opened the storeroom cupboard? *Hey, sorry about that. An old flame. We split up years ago but wow, how he loves his games. Anyway, he's sincerely sorry for his behaviour earlier and feels a tad embarrassed with the whole episode. So, he's cooking a meal in the way of an apology. Come on, Mum. Get ready. You'll like him. Honestly.*

Bella followed the road away from Brighton seafront with visions of meeting Nancy this morning powering through her mind. What the heck had happened in those few short hours? How could her life turn upside down so quickly? She watched the road ahead, the lights from the streetlamps glowing, lighting the path. She felt weak; her body was exhausted from everything that had happened. If only she'd blown Nancy out, stayed with her parents and avoided the shops. Bella hated hindsight; she firmly believed our paths are our destiny. That everything happens for a reason. So why did she bump into that freak, the lunatic who took her photo, who broke into her parent's house and kidnapped her? Now she was part of their sick game.

As Bella drove, she recalled the guy in the ski mask, mentioning something about a lad's weekend. An accident. This was their way of revenge. How the hell did she get tied up in all this chaos? Bella glanced at her watch: 6.17pm. The last few minutes had been a haze. Like she'd been transported via a parallel universe. She struggled to remember the roads she'd taken, the people she'd seen or the cars she'd passed. Bella watched the windscreen wipers, her eyes following them, hypnotised, left, right, her mind in a trance. She slammed the brakes as a young lad stepped out onto the road. Bella unwound the window.

'I'm so sorry. Are you okay?' Bella called out.

'Piss off. Get a bike, you stupid bitch.'

Bella sat for a moment, tainted by the guy's remarks. She watched him stroll down the road, pulling a vape from his front pocket and then disappear around a street corner. Someone honked loudly behind, and Bella closed the window, lifting a hand up to apologise. She burst into tears, sobbing hysterically, the pressure building inside her, needing to be released. She glanced in the mirror, wiping the stained mascara from under her eyes, then she took a deep breath, composing herself as she turned into her parent's road.

Bella parked outside and looked from the car, over to the house. The lights were on in the living room. The living room where only a short while ago, she sat, mesmerised by the aroma of her mother's cooking. Bella whacked her fist on the steering wheel, pounding it hard, then stepped out of the car. As she walked along the path, her stomach doing somersaults, fighting the anxiety and taking deep breaths, she fished the front door key from her pocket and rehearsed the conversation she was going to have with her mother. She placed the key in the door, pushed it back and stared along the hallway.

The storeroom door was open.

Her mother had escaped.

* * *

Bella raced desperately along the hall, first checking the storeroom. She already knew it was empty. 'Mum. Where are you?' She checked her watch: 6.30pm. 'Shit.' Bella screamed, more intensely than she'd meant. She was running out of time. She moved to the kitchen, then the living room, preparing for the worst. She turned, then charged up the stairs, checking each of the rooms. 'No. No. No. Where are you?' Another flick of her eyes to her watch: 6.33pm. Bella raced to the top of the landing, moving downstairs, taking two steps at a time. She stood for a moment in the hallway, breathing deeply, her head pounding with stress, her body more fatigued than she could ever remember. 'Mum.' Bella turned sharply and moved along the hallway towards the front door, listening intently. Outside, the road was peaceful. It was dark; heavy clouds had veiled the sky and threatened more rain. Bella stood on the doorstep, the chill causing her body to feel numb, considering her next move. She paused, then raced to the car. As Bella got into the driver's seat, turning on the engine and battling to move the gearstick to drive, she remembered the man in the ski mask telling her a tracker had been placed underneath. 'Shit. Shit. Shit.' Again, she whacked the steering wheel, thumping hard with both fists.

They knew where she lived.

* * *

Bella tried a three-point turn, managing more of a five-point procedure, battling with the car as it jerked forward. She drove slowly along the road, watching the neighbour's houses on each side. Bella glanced at her watch: 6.37pm. Suddenly, she saw her mother. She hit the brake and wound the window down. 'Mum. Are you okay?'

Sheila turned. 'Oh, Bella. Thank goodness. Where is that bastard?' I can't find your father either.'

'I don't have time to explain. Quick, get in,' Bella ordered.

She watched her mother stepping away from a neighbour's front garden.

Sheila moved into the front seat. 'Where did you get the car?' she asked.

'It's a long story. Mum, we have to do something. It's going to be alright. Have you called the police?'

Sheila put her seatbelt on, then looked at her daughter. 'I didn't have time. I found an ornament. Remember the small elephant we bought from Devon?' Well, I managed to bash the lock. It took me a while. I ran along the road, thinking it was safer to leave the house, you know, after that man came and locked me in the storeroom. Anyway, I tried a couple of other houses. Where is your father?'

Bella stepped on the accelerator, throwing them back into the seats. 'Mum. Take a breath.' Bella looked at her watch. She had just over twenty minutes. 'He's being held at a hotel.'

'Oh, for goodness sake. Who was that man? Why is your father being held? What's going on, Bella?'

'These men are dangerous.'

'I can see that for myself.'

'The guy who was here. He drove us to The Blair Hotel. That's where they're holding dad.'

'I never liked that place.'

Bella took a deep breath. 'Anyway, they know our address. If I'm not back by 7pm, they'll kill him. I have to get there. The car is tracked. We'll think of something. I won't let them harm us.'

'Heaven's forbid. What a carry-on. .'

Bella eyed her mother, seeing the terrified expression on her face.

She pulled out onto the main road and prayed they had a clear run.

* * *

As Bella drove, her mother's voice became a haze, a vague buzz of drivel in the background. She pressed the accelerator, pushing it to the floor, the haunting image of her father being dragged to the back of the warehouse playing out in her mind. The creep taking her picture, his voice coming from the other side of the curtain as she changed. His frame, standing outside the living room window, watching her. Had all this happened in one day? Her mother continued yapping, but Bella seemed immune to her sentences, unable to hear her words. She eyed the road where earlier, the young lad had shouted insults, the streetlamps, the oncoming cars, drivers oblivious to her situation. Another glance at her watch showed 6.53pm. The minutes ticked, her heartbeat quickened, now pulsing through a vein in her neck. As she drove, the shapes in front came and went like thoughts in her imagination. She peered towards her mother, her mouth moving, her hands exaggerated, white noise, like a muffled cry in the distance. Bella felt like she was going mad, falling into a pit. The world around her appearing artificial.

'Bella.'

She turned, a perplexed expression on her face. 'What, Mum?'

'We're here.'

Bella looked to the right, seeing a sign for The Blair Hotel. She steered the car around the back, waited for the black gates to open and parked the car, staring at the shutters in front. Her watch showed 6.58pm. Bella pushed a hand through her damp hair, then got out of the car.

Sheila followed. They listened to the buzz of the shutters, the mechanical cogs in motion. They waited, Bella conjuring an array of scenarios waiting for them inside the hotel. She darted a look at her mother and waited.

* * *

Bella moved forward after a moment, the watch on her wrist displaying 6.59pm. She'd made it. She stepped inside, peering towards the back of the warehouse, whispering her father's name. Sheila moved behind her. The room was dimly lit, only the sound of the stutters as they began to fall behind them.

As Bella walked further inside the room, she saw a figure towards the back wall. A man, hanging upside down by his feet. She screamed, feeling her mother's hand clinging onto her. As Bella moved closer, she saw the creep from earlier. His throat had been slit and drops of blood were still dripping onto the floor.

Her father was gone.

26

Matt replaced the phone in room seven back in its holder. The voice repeated in his mind. I'm coming to room seven next. The hairs stood on Matt's arms. Moments ago, he'd listened to Mia, crying out not to answer it. The sound of Billy's blood-curdling cries rang in his ears. 'We need to get out of here. It's not safe.' Matt turned to Lucy. 'Are you ready?' He saw the petrified look on his daughter's face.

Lucy stood. Mia joined her.

Sean was still glaring at the phone, struggling to control his trembling body.

Mia looked at Matt. 'Where are we going to go?'

'We need to find the woman with the trolley. We have to try and get up to the fourth floor. I'm sure it's where they're holding Nadia. I think it's where they'll bring Lydia too.'

Mia turned to the screen on the telly. The dark glass, displaying only their images like a mirror, the dust visible across the top. 'Oh my goodness. Lydia.' Mia pondered turning the telly back on, making sure she was okay. The last image they'd seen was her, lying, screaming on the floor. As she reached for the remote, Sean grabbed her arm.

'Mia. No. We'll find her. We have to go.'

'Dad, I need the loo.'

'Okay. Be quick.' Matt watched his daughter, the embarrassed look on her face.

'Really, Lucy Lou?' Matt realised it wouldn't be a quick visit to the toilet.

'Sorry. I have to go.'

Matt opened the door to room seven. He pushed his head out, peering along the corridor. 'Okay. Quick. Let's go.' He turned to Sean and Mia. 'This could take a while. We'll see you back here shortly.' Matt removed the key from his jeans and placed it against the lock to room eight. He listened as Lucy followed along the corridor. 'Wait here a second. I need to take a look.'

Lucy was stamping her feet, crouching where she stood. 'Hurry up, Dad. I can't hold it much longer.'

Matt listened to the clunk as the door unlocked. He pushed it open, gazing at the room. The bathroom door to his right was open, the buzz of the extractor fan intense. He stepped inside, scanning the area, moving his eyes towards the beds, the curtains towards the back. Were they moving? Matt walked slowly, his steps intense, exaggerated. He stood inside the bathroom, eyeing the toilet, the shower screen, a plastic sheet, pulled back. He stepped away, moving across the room, listening to his daughter by the front door.

'Come on, Dad. I'm desperate.'

Matt reached his left arm in front, his trembling hand gripping the curtains, shielding the room of its natural light. He prodded the material, walking along the length of the window and finally dropping to his knees, inspecting under the beds. 'It's clear.'

'Finally,' Lucy said, the irritation evident.

Matt listened to the bathroom door close, and the lock engage. This was his moment. The brief time he needed to himself. Matt knew he couldn't show his emotions in front of his daughter. Inside, he was dying. Suddenly, his body craved to spill the anguish, the agony which had built up inside, like a volcano, spewing its hot lava, overflowing with its release.

He lifted a fist to his lips, biting on the knuckle of his forefinger, and he sobbed. Matt's body shook, his shoulder's bounced, his head dropped, and images of his beautiful wife played out in his mind. A recent picnic on Hampstead Heath, the smell of pine, damp moss, tree trunks, the collection of bright flowers clung in the air, the wildlife at his feet, Lucy delighting in the wilderness. Matt and Nadia held hands as Lucy ran in front, hopping with excitement. A trip to London, a swanky eatery in the West End, Matt wore a black suit, Nadia shimmered in a red summer dress. Christ, she looked breathtaking. As Matt wiped the tears from his face, he craved Nadia's touch, sceptical as to whether he'd see her again.

He couldn't think this way. Matt fought with the hostile intrusion his brain conjured. He thought about Peter, played like an instrument. Billy, the womaniser, another string to his bow, only this time, it was rope, and he'd got entangled in it.

'Lucy. Come on. We've got to go.'

'One second.'

Matt composed himself. The time alone had eased the pain of their situation. He wet his fingers, wiping under his eyes. Matt faced towards the curtains at the back of room and jolted as a door slammed. The walls were flimsy, and he could hear footsteps. Matt initially thought it was Lucy, but the bathroom door was closed. He called out, 'Are you okay in there?'

'Yes. I'll be a minute.'

He heard the toilet flush, the gush of water emptying into

the bowl, the extractor fan whirling, the water filling the cistern, Lucy washing her hands, the bathroom door opening. Lucy stood, watching her father. A cry resounded through the room, a woman, wailing, roaring for help.

Matt looked at his daughter. 'It's Mia. Lucy, go back in the bathroom, lock the door. Now.'

Matt raced to the front door and pulled the handle. 'Come on. Open. What the hell?' He grabbed it again, forcing it down, the screams from Mia louder in his ears. Matt rushed to the wall, the thin plasterboard adjoining rooms seven and eight. 'Mia. Can you hear me?' Matt listened. He stood back, again moving to the door, pulling hard. He peered between the gap. The door had been locked from the outside.

'Let us out. Do you hear me? Let us out of here.' Matt hammered his fists on the door as Mia's voice became mute.

'Dad. What's happened?'

Matt turned, facing the bathroom door. His fists ached from banging on the wood, and red blotches had appeared. He needed Lucy in his sights. 'Come out. It's okay. I'm here.' Matt heard the door gently unlock.

Lucy stood, glaring at her father, trying to read his expression.

'Someone has locked us in here. But we're safe. I don't want you worrying,' Matt said.

'Oh. Okay. I won't then. Thanks for clarifying that, Dad.'

'Lucy. Please don't be difficult. Not now.'

She edged closer to her father, watching along the room, expecting someone to jump out at any moment. 'Dad. I'm so scared.'

Matt reached his arms out, holding his daughter. 'I know. But you have to be brave. For your mother. I know you can keep going.'

Lucy's eyes began filling with tears. She blinked, trying to focus. 'I don't think I can.'

Almost in sync, they turned towards the front door. Someone was outside. They listened as a door slammed. Now, the sound of heavy footsteps moving along the hall. Matt estimated the person was outside room seven. Sean and Mia's room. He walked to the front door, signalling for Lucy to keep silent by placing his forefinger on his lips. Matt pushed his ear against the door, listening. He jumped back as a floorboard creaked, right outside their door. Matt waited, holding his breath. Was this it? Fight or flight? The time when Matt had to kick into action, tackle the people who'd put them in danger? Billy's voice, screaming for mercy as he lay in the bathroom, his body ablaze, resonated in his mind. Mia, shouting for help, her voice chilling, eerily soaring in the air. Matt's mind raced; noises brewed like a ride through a ghost train. His brain, so busy, a concoction of turbulence, like an explosion set off in his head. The sound of a lock being opened, the heavy clunk was legitimate. Matt didn't imagine it. Someone was trying to get into the room. He desperately grabbed the handle, holding it upwards with everything he had. A moment later, the footsteps became distant. Matt waited a minute, then turned, watching his daughter. The footsteps were further along the hall. Then the sound disappeared.

Matt braced himself. He reached forward, placed his hand on the door handle, the brass, warm against his skin and he gently pulled down. He tensed his body, stiff, rugged, anticipating the worst, then moved the door towards him, shielding his daughter in case there was someone on the other side. Matt observed his surroundings, his senses on high alert, then poked his head out like a jack in the box, looking one way, then the other.

'It's clear. Come on, Lucy. Let's move.' He listened to his

daughter's fearful breaths as she barged against him, like they were bound with rope.

Matt and Lucy walked along the communal hall and stood outside Sean and Mia's room. There were no signs of a break-in. If someone was there, they had a key. Matt tapped on the door, the warm air from Lucy's mouth heating his skin, causing him to itch.

'Mia. Sean. It's Matt. Are you in there?'

'Dad. I have the key. I opened the door earlier. Remember?'

Matt took the card from Lucy, then pressed it against the door. The loud clunk resonated, a green light appearing on the lock.

'Wait here a second. Let me go in first.' Matt steadied himself. He pushed the door, whispering the names of both his friends. A muffled sound came from the back of the room. Matt moved forward, continuously checking the room. Then he saw something. Mia, tied with thick rope to the bedpost. He could see the top of her head. As he moved closer, he noticed the gag tied around her mouth. Mia's obscured voice became louder. She was fearful, her eyes wild. Matt crouched on the ground, untied the rope and removed the gag.

Mia gasped, forcing air from her lips. She looked at Matt. 'They've taken Sean. Someone's in the bathroom.'

Matt froze. Suddenly, his life flashed in front of him. He stood, then staggered backwards, like he'd been poisoned. His body swayed, and he thought he was going to vomit. The bathroom door opened. He glanced at Mia; her eyes closed as she mouthed a prayer. Matt turned on his heels, facing the intruder. The woman from the lift was pointing a gun at him.

Matt felt a bead of sweat roll onto the tip of his nose as he stared into her eyes. He braced, watching the end of the gun as she cocked it. She'd done this before. Her body language was confident, assured.

'I'm sorry I have to do this. I'm only following instructions.'

As Matt squeezed his eyes shut, he heard a heavy thud. He opened them, focusing on the floor. Lucy had crept into the room, held a small bin above her head and brought it down on the woman's arm. The gun lay on the floor, the woman, kneeling, writhing in agony.

Matt sprung forward and landed on the floor like a diver bellyflopping onto water. He grabbed the gun, then stood, pointing it at the woman in front of him. The skin on her arm had turned red, and it looked like it might be fractured. Matt looked at his daughter. 'Lucy. That was quite something.' He held the gun, his arm stretched, guiding it across the woman's body like a torchlight in a cave. 'I'm going to count to three. If you don't answer, I'll put a bullet in your kneecap, so help me, God. Where is the key to the fourth floor?'

The woman covered her face, squealing like a pig.

'One. Two.'

'Okay. Please. Okay.' She dipped into her blazer pocket, pulling out a card slightly bigger than the door pass.

'Throw it to me,' Matt instructed.

The woman swung her good arm, and the card landed by Matt's feet. He bent down, lifting it as if it were The Holy Grail. He turned to Mia who was now stood behind him, then back to Lucy. 'We're in.'

27

'We can't just march up there, bold as you like,' Mia pointed out.

Matt, Lucy and Mia were stood towards the back of the room. The woman from the lift was sat on the floor, rubbing her arm and weeping like a terrified child.

'What do you suggest we do?' Matt asked.

Mia could hear the desperation in his voice. She wanted to hold him, tell him everything would be alright. She'd gone through so much with Sean after that weekend. She could see the torment in Matt's eyes, but Mia needed to be strong, for all of them. Mia nodded her head towards the woman. 'Let's grill her. She knows where they've taken Sean and the mechanics of this place. How it all works.'

Matt stepped away from Mia and his daughter. He held the gun in his right hand. 'I need answers.' He watched the woman nodding. He could see she was scared. 'How many are there?'

She stared at him. At first, he thought she wouldn't answer. As Matt went to ask the question again, she opened her mouth.

'Three. In total. Two of them are brothers. They own the hotel. Marty and Vincent. The other man is a friend of theirs. A Spanish guy who works here. He's part of it too. He's with them.'

'How are you involved?'

She hesitated. 'If I told you I answered an ad in the paper, would you believe me?'

Matt huffed, a sign he was losing his patience. 'Cut the bullshit, or I swear to God...'

'No. Really. A couple of months ago, I saw an advert. A small, two-sentence announcement that they were looking for help. The picture looked surreal. A family-run hotel just a stone's throw from the beach. Anyway, I had an interview, and they called the next morning offering me the job.'

'What does it entail exactly?'

'I was busy at first. Cleaning the rooms in the morning, making the beds, the usual. I'd manage the bar from around 1pm until late. The problem was it was always vacant. I'd clean the rooms, but they'd be untouched from the night before. Often, I was alone in the bar. They don't even open the restaurant much. They can't pay the staff.'

'So how do they make ends meet?' Matt inquired. He recalled the weekend here a month ago. Matt thought he recognised her now.

The woman looked to the floor, awash with embarrassment. 'I needed money. I'm supporting my mother. She's poorly. We have a room outside of town. It's not much, but it's a roof over our heads. Before this job, I hadn't worked for months. I couldn't afford to lose it. I noticed the guys were more quiet, secretive. I thought, at first, they were busy. They often mentioned the plans they had for this place. Then, nothing. I'd wave at them when I'd start my shift, and they'd gaze past me. I'd greet them, passing along the hall and it fell on deaf ears. Then, one of them called me into the office. I thought they were getting rid of me. The younger brother sat, leaving me stand. He told me what they had planned. He said if I didn't follow their instructions, they'd kill my mother.'

Matt eyed Lucy and Mia; then he turned back to the woman. 'What's on the fourth floor?'

She hesitated. 'Your worst nightmare.'

***

Matt stood in front of the woman. 'You need to help us.'

She glared up, like a lone child who'd lost their parents, her eyes, pitiful.

'I can't. They'll kill my mother. You don't know what these men are capable of doing.'

'Oh, I do.' Matt removed his phone from his pocket and produced a picture of his wife. He held the screen in front of her face. 'This woman. Have you seen her? She's my wife.'

'You don't get it, do you?'

'Get what?' Matt asked.

She raised her voice; her eyebrows elevated, saliva now dropping from her mouth. 'They tell me nothing.' She screamed out, 'Nothing. You hear? I'm asked to cart a trolley around the corridors with Christ knows what under the blankets. I'm too scared to look. Do you think I want to see? I couldn't look even if I wanted to. I don't want to know what they're doing. It's better that way.'

She completely broke down. Mia and Lucy moved forward, crouching beside her. She was in meltdown, unable to function. Her eyes were busy, rolling like a runaway tyre. She rocked, banging her head against the plasterboard behind.

'I don't want to know what I'm carting around.'

Mia leant forward and cradled her as the woman sobbed into her shoulder.

Matt could see she didn't want to play a part in what was happening here.

The woman had now composed herself. Matt held her hand, and Lucy was telling her it would all be okay.

'Do you know how many cameras are on this floor?' he asked.

'One. At the end of the hall. In some of the bedrooms too.'

Matt pictured Billy and Lydia. He struggled to push the image from his mind. 'What about this room?' Matt braced himself.

'No. Not here. I have to clean them, so I know where they are. Only a couple of rooms. The other side of the foyer.'

'Where else?'

'On every floor. At least one at each end of the corridors.'

'Where is the generator?' Matt asked.

'The what?'

'Where do you shut the power down?'

The woman looked fearful. 'You can close the cameras off in the basement. It's locked, but the keys are in the main office out the front.'

Matt was thinking. A couple of hours ago, they'd met the woman on the third floor. Lucy had seen Nadia on the trolley. Just before that, the three of them had got stuck in the lift. He realised they were being monitored. A sick game for their amusement. 'Is someone watching the cameras?'

'Not always. I see the Spanish guy, and sometimes Vincent, the taller one of the brothers, going down there occasionally'

Matt directed the statement to Mia. 'We need to shut off the cameras.'

'You'll never get down there. If someone is watching, they'll realise instantly. They'll see you,' Trolley lady clarified.

'Do you ever go down there?' Matt asked.

'Yes. It's where I keep my cleaning equipment.'

Mia watched the lady as she placed her hands over her face and bawled. She'd snapped, unable to cope. Her body slumped further down the wall.

Mia pulled her close. 'I need you to listen for a second. Can you do that?'

Again, she nodded.

Mia continued. 'Your mother is going to be okay. Do you hear me? I'm not going to let anything happen to her. They are bad men. We can't call the police. As soon as the sirens ring out, they'll kill my partner.' She pointed to Lucy. 'And her mother. We need to get to the fourth floor. I'm only going to ask one thing of you. Just one. I need your clothes.'

'This is ludicrous.' Matt watched as Mia helped the woman to her feet. They were the same height, more or less. Both were slim with similar builds. 'Mia. Are you hearing me? I won't let this happen.'

'Please go to the bathroom and remove your clothes. You need to hurry.'

Mia moved to her holdall by the bed. She grabbed a pair of white tracksuit bottoms and a brown jumper, then handed them to the woman.

The bathroom door closed, and Matt sunk his head in his hands. 'Mia, I'm begging you. Don't do this.'

'We have no choice. If we go waltzing out of here, brave as you like, skipping along the yellow brick road, we may as well sign our death warrant. You heard her. There are cameras everywhere. It's the only way, Matt.'

'I'm with dad. Please, Mia. Don't do it.'

Mia turned, facing Lucy. 'I'm so proud of you, Lucy. If I ever have a daughter, I want her to be exactly like you.' Mia turned as the bathroom door opened. The woman handed her the uniform. Mia walked into the bathroom, removed her clothes and placed them in a neat pile under the sink. Then, she stepped into the black trousers, the slip-on shoes and pushed her arms into the blazer. She glanced at herself in the mirror.

Her hair was slightly longer than the woman's and a tad lighter. She took a deep breath, her skin numb, her stomach churning, then she stepped out into the room.

'You'll need the trolley. You won't look suspicious if they see you. I'm rarely without it.' The woman slumped back on the floor. You'll find a key to the basement behind the front desk. Go into the room, a little to the left; you'll find a rack. It's the key with the red tag. A long, brass one. Then go to the basement. When you come out of the lift, it's the door immediately to your left. The power switches are at the back of the room. Everything is labelled. I've often had to push the trip switch when the power goes out on different floors.'

'What about Fred? Is he involved?' Matt asked.

'Yes. But he's like me. He does as he's told without asking questions. His shift finishes at 7pm.'

'Who else is in the hotel?' Matt asked.

'There are no other guests. Just the three men. I think we're all alone.'

Mia hugged Matt, then Lucy. 'I'll be back before you know it.'

Matt saw the fear in Mia's eyes. Her lip quivered, her face, wild with anticipation. 'Mia, I'm asking you, please don't risk this.'

Mia reached out her hands, clasping Matt's. 'We have no choice.' She grabbed the gun which Matt had placed behind the curtain at the back of the room, then walked out of the door.

***

Mia stood outside room seven, straightening her jacket. Her trousers were tight, her shoes uncomfortable with the gap at the back. She glanced at the trolley she'd wheeled out of room seven. A white blanket was spread over the top. A pink duster clipped to the left side and a compartment holding an array of clothes and detergents. Mia gripped the handle. It was deep and long, resembling more a surgeon's trolley, easily able to hide a body. Mia had visions of a hand, reaching through the blanket. She closed her eyes, bracing herself, then began to walk.

The trolley bounced along the floor, the wheels unstable, noisier than she'd expected. It sounded like a train, climbing a steep track in a theme park.

Mia reached the end of the corridor, keeping her head down, remembering the mention of a security camera. She pushed the door open, moving into the foyer. The front desk was unoccupied. Mia turned to her right; the doors to the restaurant were closed. She watched the main doors across the hall, expecting them to open at any second. The trolley was hard to wheel over the carpet. Mia forced the handle, like pushing a piano up a steep hill. This is all she needed now. She dug her feet into the floor, forcing the cart. The wheels turned sideways as she heaved from behind. Once at the desk, Mia eyed the camera. She waited, wondering if it would turn towards her. A few seconds later, she moved to a door marked 'Staff.' Mia let go of the trolley handle and opened the door.

The room was large, messy. Papers were strewn across the table, takeaway food cartons in silver aluminium trays decorated the sides. Mia saw two laptops, powered down and a monitor, which displayed parts of the hotel. She froze, listening, wondering if they were watching her now. Mia waited, frightened to take a step. She turned, seeing the key rack, the long brass one with the red tag. Mia stepped to the side, her face still, her arms by her sides. She thought about the gun which she'd placed on the trolley. Mia should have held on to it, kept it with her. Was this her first mistake? She'd gone hunting with her father, and, although not used to firearms, she'd shot his rifle a couple of times. If it came to it, she'd have no hesitation firing the handgun. *Point and pull. Surely that's it?*

Mia reached her arm forward, clasping the key, lifting it off the hook. Her heart raced, her legs unstable. She felt like a baby horse, lifting itself off the ground, legs everywhere, spreading to hold its weight.

She backed out of the room, reaching behind her, feeling for the door, then pulled it back, stepping out towards the main desk. The foyer was still empty. Mia clasped the handle of the trolley and steered it over to the lift. She eyed the buttons and pressed to call it. She listened to the mechanics, the whirring sound as the lift crept to the ground floor. As the doors opened, Mia looked behind, then pushed the trolley into the lift. As the doors closed, Mia had flashbacks to earlier. Her, Sean, Matt and Lucy, shouting to get out. She gripped the handle of the trolley, holding her breath, praying it didn't happen again. The lift jerked, Mia fell to the side, and the doors began to open.

The basement was a simple layout. Plain, rugged grey brickwork gave a bleak, cold appearance. The floor was uneven, rough, with potholes. The ceiling had damp patches caused by watermarks due to neglect.

Mia pushed the trolley, forcing the wheels over the uneven frame. The lift struggled to align itself, like it had a mind of its own, purposely making it difficult. Mia glimpsed a short corridor with a room facing her. The door was closed. Immediately to the left of the lift was another room with double doors. Mia moved closer, seeing the words "Machinery" marked with a small, gold-coloured badge. Next to this door was another with the word, "Deliveries." She dipped into her trouser pocket, removing the brass key and placed it in the lock with the door marked, "Machinery." She turned it gently anti-clockwise, slowly tugged the handle downwards and opened the door, leaving the trolley outside. A continuous tapping noise sounded across the room, like a printer spilling out pages of A4 paper. Mia looked to her left, seeing a large black rope, a tall mesh cage, displaying the machine which operated the lift. The wheels were turning slowly, clunking as the rope moved. Mia spun around, wondering if someone had called the lift. She walked across the floor, her shoes hanging off her feet, the button of her trousers pushing hard against her belly. At the back of the room, Mia saw the large consumer unit. She lifted the flap, seeing every switch labelled. A power source to the entire hotel. Along the top, she spotted one marked "Security Cameras." Mia steadied herself, feeling like a dictator about to launch a nuclear missile. She placed her hand on the black switch and forced it downwards. She listened, expecting to hear something. Anything that indicated it was safe to wander around. Nothing happened. Mia backed away, then turned to face the door. The clunking noise still resounded, the rope still moving. Mia had to get back to Matt and Lucy. She tripped up as she walked, then reached down and removed her shoes, carrying them in her hands. She opened the door, reaching her right arm to the trolley handle and placed her shoes back on her feet. As she lifted herself back up, the lift bumped, the display flashed, illuminating the letter "B" on the side of the door. Someone was here. They'd seen her. Mia pawed under the blanket, gripping the handle of the gun. As the lift doors opened, Mia stood, pointing the weapon. The elderly couple froze, gaping in shock, the trauma evident on their baffled faces.

'Who are you?' Mia asked.

The bare-chested man spoke. 'We're trying to get out of here. Don't attempt to stop us.'

'No. It's okay. Don't worry. I'm...'

Mia spun around as the door opened from the communal stairs. A younger woman raced towards her. Mia fired off a round, watching as the woman fell to the floor.

The bare-chested man screamed. 'Bella. No.' He dropped to his knees beside his daughter as the blood sprayed over the basement floor.

28

Earlier, Bella and her mother had walked around the body, which hung upside down in the warehouse. The body of Peter Simpson. They'd opened a door which had led to the basement. There, they'd taken the stairs to the ground floor. As they walked around the foyer, arms linked tightly together, Bella heard a groaning noise coming from a door to the left side of the restaurant. They shuffled slowly across the room; their legs felt bulky, their bodies weary. The eerie emptiness of the hotel was apparent. On the wall to the right of the door, a placard announced rooms eleven to twenty. Bella opened the door, her father, falling back onto the floor. His leg was sprained, he writhed in pain, but he was alive. Bella knelt, kissing him on his head, then they placed a hand under each arm and lifted him to his feet. The process took twenty minutes between getting him up and moving him to the lift.

Bella took the stairs; claustrophobia meant she couldn't bear confined spaces.

Now, her lifeless body lay on the basement floor, slumped in front of her parents.

'What have you done? My beautiful daughter. What the fuck have you done?' Bella's mother shouted.

Mia watched as the older woman came charging towards her; her fists were gripped tight, her eyes wide and ferocious.

'I'm so sorry. I thought she was someone else,' Mia cried out.

The older woman stepped over her daughter, clawing for the gun. Mia knew she was out of control. She had to do something. There were endless possibilities if she grappled the weapon from Mia's hands.

She stepped away, backing herself up against the door opposite. Mia reached the handle, her arms behind her back. She lifted the gun, pushing the tip against the woman's forehead. 'Get in the room. I won't tell you a second time.'

The woman stood, flicking a glance at her husband.

Mia watched, his face distorted, his puny, white body shaking.

'Get in the room, Sheila. Do as she says.'

As the woman moved, Mia kept the gun pointed at her back. Bare-chested man joined his wife a few seconds later.

Mia watched the terror on their faces.

A minute later, Mia left the room, closed the door and locked them deep in the basement.

* * *

Mia stepped towards the room, marked "Machinery," and pushed the door. Inside, she leaned over and vomited on the floor. She screamed, louder than she could ever imagine. She knelt on the ground, pulling at her hair. Then she bent forward, placing her head on the cold ground and sobbed. At this moment, she didn't care what happened to her. Sean had been taken. Mia was unsure if he was still alive. She'd murdered someone in cold blood, although a mistake, Mia wondered if she could live with herself? She worried about the couple in the basement room. What would happen? Would someone find them?

Mia grabbed a mop and bucket, filled it with water and cleaned up the vomit. Her body was weak, her mind disorientated. She retched again, spitting out saliva. Her stomach was empty, her mouth so dry and sore.

Once the floor was clean, she moved out to the lift. Mia stared at the young woman, the red stain on her jumper. *It's only jam. Jam is good. It's tasty. Only jam,* she kept telling herself. Mia dipped the mop into the bucket, then drenched the area with water, dabbing at the blood, sorry, jam, squeezing the end into the water and bringing the mop back out. She heard banging on the basement door opposite, now unsure if her mind was playing tricks. The older couple, the girl's parents, faces pushed against the door, begging to be released. *No, no, no. Leave me alone. I need to do this. You're pressuring me. I can't cope. Let me do this. When I find my partner, I'll come back. Please, just let me do this.*

Mia crouched, pushing out hard, fast breaths from her mouth, her cheeks bloated with air, her head, light. She clutched the woman's legs and dragged her into the room marked "Machinery."

She wiped the gun of fingerprints and threw it towards the lift cables, hearing it clunk below. Then she dumped the mop and bucket, locked the door and moved out to the communal stairs.

* * *

Mia pushed the door leading out to the foyer. She saw the security camera hanging on the wall behind the desk; the light had gone out. Job done. Mia watched the lift as she made her way towards the back of the foyer. A door opened opposite. The badge to the right of the door announcing rooms eleven to twenty.

Mia stopped; she was standing halfway between the desk and the entrance leading to her room. She glanced over. Was someone watching her? For a moment, she wondered if someone was peering through the crack. The door opened, she was certain. Mia held her breath, backing away. She could turn around, walk back to the communal stairs, call the lift, or lock herself in the basement. Mia had to do something. She watched, her mouth open, her body static. We're the only ones here. Trolley lady's words played in her mind. She visualised three men racing towards her, grabbing her, bringing her to the fourth floor. A terrifying portal to another world, never to be seen again.

'Hello. Can you help me?'

Mia heard a voice, a woman, whispering across the hall. 'Who are you?' Mia asked. She stepped forward, closer to the door. She watched it open further. Now she saw her. A sympathetic figure, hiding, like a child in the woods, so vulnerable. 'Lydia. Is that you?'

The door was now fully open. Mia eyed the bump, the lost soul, clutching her stomach. Lydia had crawled out of the room, along the hallway on her hands and knees, collapsing at the door. Then, lay helpless in a slump, crying, fearful for her life after witnessing what these people had done to her husband.

Mia broke into laughter, her way of showing how pleased she was to see a familiar face.

'Mia. What the hell is going on?'

The two women moved closer, now holding each other. They broke down, crying into each other's shoulders. Mia, relieved to see her friend and compassion for what she had to witness. Her husband, murdered in their room. Lydia, seeming so alone, lost and delicate.

Mia stood, holding Lydia's hand and filled her in with what had happened. Lydia listened without interruption. They'd both been through a hellish nightmare. Now, they'd gain strength from one another.

Mia felt for the key in her blazer.

The key to the fourth floor.

It was possible the nightmare was only beginning.

* * *

Matt glanced at his watch: 8.02pm. Mia had been gone for over half an hour. He'd wait another ten minutes, then he'd go and look for her.

Lucy was sat beside him. Trolley lady was slumped on the floor. Although Matt took pity on her, he didn't know her. Earlier, she was hiding in the bathroom, then pointing a gun at his head. She was capable of murder.

A knock on the door distracted him from his thoughts. He stood, moving across the floor.

'Matt. Lucy. It's Mia.'

Matt slowly opened the door. He stared at the pregnant lady standing behind Mia.

'Christ, Lydia. Am I happy to see you!' He hugged her tight, unable to stem the flow of tears. 'I'm... Jesus, Lydia, what the heck do I say? There are no words.'

'Matt, let's make the focus on Nadia and Sean. I'm so sorry for what has happened. I don't know why they're doing this, but we need to take these bastards down. I'll grieve when we get out of here.'

'That's the spirit. Right, I have to go. It's getting late,' Matt stated.

'I'm coming, Dad.'

Matt sat for a moment beside his daughter. 'It's not safe.' He turned to Mia. 'The three of you need to leave here. Find a pub, sit tight and wait. If you don't hear from me after an hour, call the police. Understood? I am not taking you all to the fourth floor. It's too dangerous.'

'Matt, my partner is missing. I'm coming with you. Please don't try to stop me. Lucy can leave. She's a child. Lydia can go with her.' Mia pointed to the baby bump. 'Lydia's in no condition to go through any more stress. They can leave. I'm staying with you.' Mia was dying inside. She had to be brave for Matt. A few minutes ago, she'd wiped the gun clean of her fingerprints and hid it in the basement. She was in shock. Terrified of the consequences. Now wasn't the time to break down. She'd deal with it afterwards. 'I'm coming with you, Matt.'

Matt hesitated. He tried to find the words, but Mia was adamant.

'Fine. Okay, as I've said, calling the police is signing a death warrant. The security cameras are switched off. We have a key to the fourth floor. They won't expect us. We need to find Nadia, Sean and then get the hell out.'

Matt lifted trolley lady to her feet. He directed the instruction to Lucy. 'Bring her with you.' He turned to trolley lady. 'No funny business, do you hear? We're helping you. As soon as we rescue Nadia and Sean, then and only then, we call the police. Let's go.'

29

Matt held the door open at the main entrance. He watched Lydia and trolley lady wander out into the street. The wind pushed hard in their faces, and they tasted salt in the air. Lucy stopped at the door. Matt crouched, looking into her eyes.

'Dad.'

'Lucy Lou. You are my angel. The most special young lady in the world. I'm so very proud of the woman you're turning into. I'm going to make our family complete again. Mum needs to come home. Now go, sit tight and don't worry about your old man, you hear?'

Lucy's eyes filled with tears. She nodded, gripped her father's hands and walked out.

* * *

Matt stepped back inside and closed the door. He was tempted to go with them. Dial 999 and let the police do their job. He pictured the blue lights, the sirens, the shouting as they stormed the place. The men would undoubtedly see from one of the windows. The phone call played out in his mind. *Call the police, and we'll kill them.* He had no choice. The security cameras were powered down, but it wouldn't be long until someone noticed. Matt and Mia walked side by side, keeping watch, their eyes busy, scanning the foyer and then stood by the lift. He stretched his right arm, pressing the button, and the lift began moving from the basement. It bounced, shaking harshly as the doors opened. Matt stepped in first, Mia followed. Together, they eyed the strip of numbers as Mia lifted the card from her blazer and touched the small pad. A light switched from red to green. She pressed button number four. For a moment, the lift remained stationary. Seconds ticked by while they stood in silence. Suddenly the lift doors closed, and it began to climb.

They stood, facing each other on opposite ends of the lift wall. They remained silent, muted by their apprehension. Matt's mind went into overdrive. The last twenty-four hours flashed by like an explosion, a mass assault, plaguing his head. Lucy, showing him her phone at the petrol station. The selfie which she'd captured. The car, chasing them to the hotel. Peter, a lifelong friend, kidnapping Matt's wife, playing their twisted game. He struggled to recall the last time he'd spoken to Nadia. It seemed like so long ago. Matt tried to remember her voice, the high pitched, husky tone, which felt so reassuring. Now he remembered. As he'd left the hotel with Lucy, he'd called her at her mum's house. Peter was there. Matt had turned up, finding her bracelet by the front door.

The feelings came flooding back, how he'd tried to explain to his daughter what had happened. His beautiful Lucy. How would they cope without Nadia? How could they go on? The thoughts caused anxiety. Matt felt the feeling of dread wash over him, blanketing his thoughts and the ability to function. The lift walls seemed to move, closing in on him, squeezing ever closer like a vice.

He heard a pinging noise, removing him from his subconscious. Button number four illuminated and the lift doors began to open.

30

Matt stepped out of the lift first, and Mia followed. They faced a bare wall that resembled something you'd find in a cave, ravaged by water, lapping against its sides, deadened by shadows that permanently concealed its existence. A putrid smell of rust, bones and death clung to the air like a baby with its toy. The floor was concrete, stained from years of neglect. Crater-like holes were etched into the ground along its path, deep, piercing gaps which they stepped over. A double door exposed a gloomy corridor, stretching like an abandoned drawbridge leading to an uninhabited island. The ceilings were low, once a glossy white but now stained with a dark yellow tone like the sky, decorated with thick clouds that smothered its richness. The walls were etched with symbols, so many, like the owners were part of a cult, a medieval practice they had become a part of and worshipped.

A security camera faced them, planted on the wall where they stood. Matt stared into it, hoping it had been turned off. He leant against the double doors, composing himself, watching Mia. Christ, she was so brave. He wondered how she felt inside, up here, with him, searching for her partner. Now wasn't the opportunity to have a conversation; there would be plenty of time afterwards. He envisaged them gathered in the local pub, recalling this day. Somehow, he didn't imagine them smiling.

A whirring sound started behind them. Mia began to speak, and Matt placed his finger over his lips. He turned around, peering through the glass of the double doors. The space was vacant. He pushed the doors, stepping closer to the lift. It was making its way down.

Someone had called it.

* * *

'Quick, Mia. Move.' Matt pushed the double doors. Mia turned to face him.

'What's going on?'

'The lift. Someone may be coming. They're going to find out about the cameras. We need to hurry.'

They stopped outside the first room to his left. Matt pushed the thoughts from his mind, the men, realising the cameras had been turned off, calling the lift and on their way here. 'Where's the master key?'

Mia pulled it from the breast pocket of her blazer and handed it to Matt. He pressed the flimsy card against the lock, hearing the clunk and then slowly opened the door. The room was furnished. The usual basic mod cons: a bed, a flat-screen telly on the wall and a drinks bar. Apart from that, it seemed empty. Matt stepped inside, first checking the bathroom to his right, the storeroom, under the bed and behind the thick curtains. He heard the door to the room open.

'Anything?' Mia asked.

'Nothing. Christ Mia, what if we're in the wrong place?'

'We need to keep searching.'

They moved to the next room along, finding much the same. Again, the basic furnishings, but the room was unoccupied.

'I have to check something.' Matt moved back along the corridor, out of the double doors and stood beside the lift. He watched the display. The lift had stopped on the second floor. Moments ago, he'd heard it moving.

Now it was stationary. He waited, wondering if it had all been for nothing. He'd presumed this is where they'd taken Nadia and Sean. But what if he was wrong? They could be anywhere. No, it had to be this place. Why lock the entrance with a steel door? Why had they needed a staff pass to get to the fourth floor? Trolley lady had stepped into the lift on the third floor. Lucy was convinced she'd seen her mother, a hand, dropping from the side of the cart.

The lift began to move. Matt stood back, watching the display. Was it moving upwards? Were they coming? He waited, watching the digital display. One of two ways. Where was it going? *Come on. Show me something?* Suddenly the number changed. One. Then, the basement. Matt could hear the cogs in motion through the lift shaft.

Mia was stood by the double doors. 'What's happening? Are they coming?'

Matt kept his voice low, controlled. 'They're at the basement.'

'Do you think they know about the cameras?'

'I think so. It was only a matter of time.'

Mia screamed as the lights went out. They were drenched in darkness.

* * *

Matt removed his mobile phone from the pocket of his jeans. He listened to Mia's voice, close to him, her heavy breaths, her steps, her wrists cracking as she pawed the bleakness.

'Matt, are you there?'

'I'm here. The bastards have turned the lights out. It won't be long until they're here.' Matt turned on the torch. He leapt back, seeing Mia's face so close. 'Shit, you frightened the life out of me.'

'How? You knew I was here. What are you like?' Mia pawed the pocket of her trousers, taking out her phone. She pressed the screen and watched as it remained motionless. 'Oh no. The battery is dead.'

Matt looked at his screen. He hadn't charged his phone. He had twelve percent. The torch would eat into the battery. He grabbed Mia's hand, steering the light to the walls on either side, eyeing the symbols, drawings, words he didn't recognise. He pointed the phone torch ahead, watching as the light carved into the blackness in front. They reached the third room on the left. Matt pressed the key against the door, again, hearing the loud, clunking sound. He opened the door, listening intently, guiding the torch ahead. Immediately, he could smell something resembling a blocked drain. Fleshy, like a slaughterhouse, its meat decaying, abandoned and situated in the middle of the woods. Matt pointed the light to the bathroom; a noise came from further along the room. The rustle of a chain, a bed moving. Matt glanced into the bathroom, then steered the phone in front. He walked, stepping gently, gripping Mia's hand tighter as she pushed close to his body. Their fear, palpable, more obvious now. Mia gripped Matt's jumper, blowing warm air on his neck. He moved, slow, paced, flicking the torch across the room. A shadow seemed to move in front of them, swaying one way and the other, a lone figure in the darkness. Matt wondered if his mind was playing tricks. The stench filled their lungs, a rancid, vomit odour or excrement. He was uncertain. He retched, his mouth full, cheeks aching, spitting out saliva. Again, they moved awkwardly together, like their bodies were joined. Matt stepped, Mia mirrored his movements. As Matt lost his balance, a hand grabbed Mia's foot. She screamed, a piercing wail. Now jumping, dancing like a ballerina on hot coals. Matt spun around, pointing the torch towards Mia's legs. A woman in a blood-soaked nightdress, one arm chained to a pole on the wall; her other arm was free. She knelt, clawing the air, desperation in her eyes.

'Please help.'

Her voice was foreign, but Matt struggled to recognise which country.

He shone the torch in her face, watching her eyes dilute. 'What have they done to you?'

She lifted her nightdress, showing the scar which ran along her stomach.

Matt held her face. He remembered the story he'd read. The three missing women who had stayed in The Blair Hotel. 'I'm going to get help. Don't be scared.'

'Please. Don't leave me here. Please.' She yanked the chain; her arm bounced, the pain evident on her face.

'I need you to stay calm. You're safe now. Are there others?'

'Help me,' She whispered. Suddenly she raised her voice. Now screeching. 'You have to help me.' The woman ripped her arm downwards, forcing her body away from the wall.

'Keep quiet. They'll come. Please,' Mia stated.

They heard a rustle coming from the centre of the room. 'Wait here with her. I'll check the rest of the room out. If anyone grabs me, run.'

'Where? The only way down is the lift,' Mia stated.

Matt watched Mia as she knelt by the woman, pushing a hand through her hair, trying her best to calm her down. She smelt like she hadn't showered in weeks. Mia saw the tray set out on the floor. The empty glass. They'd held her here, God knows for how long.

Mia wanted to ask questions but now wasn't the time. She watched the light against the back wall as Matt walked across the room.

'Mia. Talk to me,' Matt whispered.

'I'm here.'

Another clanging sound came from near where Matt stood. He shone the torch towards a woman lying on the bed, her body held in a straitjacket. A drip attached to her arm with a purpose-made hole in the material. She looked drugged, sluggish. Matt touched her face. She was wriggling, resembling a mummified figure trying to free herself. The bed jolted, her eyes rolling as if she were in a trance. Matt tried to talk to her, but she just smiled, now focused, staring at the ceiling. Matt feared her kidney had been removed, judging by the scar on the woman they'd just met.

He reached down, brushing a strand of hair from her face. 'I'll get you out of here.'

Again, the woman grinned.

Matt pointed the torch towards the back of the room. The display showed eight percent. Panic rose from the pit of his stomach as he realised they didn't have much light left. Again, he saw something, stood towards the far end of the room, hiding in the shadows on the edge of the light. He steered the phone to his left, holding his breath momentarily. The shape was large, still, and then dropped to the floor. Matt walked, listening to the sobs from the woman Mia was comforting. The smell was getting worse, causing his nostrils to sting, filling the room with a pungent odour.

As Matt directed the light to the floor, a man was crouching, one knee on the floor, the other rose, like a sprinter on the blocks. He charged towards Matt.

Mia screamed, 'What's happening? Matt.'

The guy was about a foot from Matt, racing, ready to jump. At the last second, Matt covered the light with his hand, drenching the area in darkness. He moved to the left, sticking his foot out. The guy tripped, falling heavily into the bed and banging his head on the frame. Matt turned the light towards him. His head was bleeding, he lay on the ground, and Matt punched him twice in the face. He grabbed his shirt, pulling the upper part of his body off the ground.

'Who the fuck are you? Where's my wife?' Matt asked.

'I don't know, man. I just work here.'

The guy was smaller than Matt had imagined. He was puny and weak looking.

'I carry out their operations. I remove kidneys. They make money. I haven't seen your wife. I swear.'

Matt pulled the guy off the floor. He checked to see if he had a phone and then locked him in the store cupboard. He wanted to grill him, make him talk, question everything about this place. Matt didn't have time. Six percent glowed in the corner of the phone screen. Matt pointed the light towards Mia. 'We need to leave the room. We'll get help as soon as we're out of here.' Matt reached to the floor and lifted Mia.

'That was quite impressive,' she said. 'I heard the punches.'

Matt smiled. 'If anyone asks, he was six foot three and built like a brick shithouse.'

'Oh yeah, he had a baseball bat too, I suppose?'

'Don't push it.' Matt opened the front door and stood in the corridor.

They tried more rooms along the hall, each of them empty, a reflection of the first two. They walked together, side by side to the last room on the left. Again, Matt pressed the key to the door.

Clunk.

Handle down.

Four percent.

Matt pushed the door and stepped into the darkness.

He stood for a moment, his body tense, exasperated. The only noise was Mia, shuffling behind him. Matt shone the torch deep into the room, watching the light cut through the dimness. Again, he scanned the bathroom. Empty. He slid the handle down to the store cupboard. Empty. Matt backed away, pointing the torch to the walls, the light from his phone washing over them. Something moved.

'Mia. Are you okay?' Matt whispered through the room.

'Yes. Have you found them?'

'Not yet. Let me know if you hear anyone coming.' Matt faced towards the end of the room. Again, he heard a shuffle. He moved one leg in front of the other, creeping, holding the torch at arm's length. 'Is someone there?' Matt kept his voice low, faint, tiptoeing across the concrete floor. 'Hello?'

Matt moved the torch to the ceiling, the floor, the curtains draped over the window at the back, moving, edging deeper into the room. Suddenly he heard a muffled cry. He saw a bed to his right-hand side. The shape of a body covered in a white sheet. Matt crept towards it, then gripped the edge of the material and began to draw it backwards. More muffled cries, a hand clutched his jeans. Matt shone the torch towards the face. 'Sean. Oh my goodness.' Matt turned. 'Mia, I've found Sean.' Matt removed the gag from his mouth. Thick rope secured him to the bed, wrapped around his biceps and legs.

Sean clenched his fists, sobbing. Tears fell to the sides of his face.

'I'm getting you out of here, mate. Hold on,' Matt insisted. 'Have you seen Nadia?' Matt fought with the rope. The knots were tight, but he worked at them, feeling them slacken.

'No. I don't know where they've taken her. I'm so scared, Matt. They held a gun to my head, brought me up in the lift and tied me in here. What the fuck is wrong with these people? They told me they'd be back. You know what they had planned? A surgeon was going to remove my limbs. That's what they told me. What the hell?'

Matt was speechless. He didn't doubt it. These men were capable of anything. Once the rope had been removed, Sean sat up. The two men hugged, their bodies trembling.

'Guys. Guys. I think there's someone coming.' Mia heard the double doors swing open towards the front of the hall. Heavy boots pounded along the corridor.

Matt pointed the phone torch to the bed. 'Hurry, Mia. Underneath. Sean, hide. You too, Mia. I'll get in the bed. Place the blanket over me. Quickly.'

'No, Matt. It's too dangerous. Are you insane?' Sean asked.

'Just do it,' Matt ordered. He turned off the torch, placing the phone into his jeans pocket, then swapped places with Sean. He felt the warm sheet being placed over his body and lay still, listening to Mia and Sean, holding each other, crying.

'Er, hello. Sorry to break up the party, but you need to hide.' Matt listened as they clambered under the bed. He closed his eyes, waiting for the sound of the door being opened.

Clunk. Then a low, creaking noise. Matt opened his eyes, struggling to breathe, pushing air from his mouth. He could see a bright light through the sheet, like a car in the distance on a lonely highway. Matt kept still, forcing his thoughts away from here, to times spent with Nadia and Lucy.

The footsteps were louder, the noise increasing as the

person approached. Matt pictured Mia and Sean, lying under the bed, praying they didn't make a sound. He felt a hand on his face, pawing his features, a laugh, deep and raspy. As the blanket slowly came away, Matt braced himself. This is it. Time to do this. The first thing Matt heard was the voice. A light shone on his face.

'What the hell?' The guy looked wild, his eyes full of disdain.

Matt heard the Spanish accent. Trolley lady had said he was part of the operation here. Matt jumped up and grabbed the guy by the ears. He pulled as hard as he could, hearing the man squeal.

As Matt got out of the bed, the guy hit him across the face with the torch.

Matt fell backwards, holding the side of his face. As the guy charged towards Matt, Sean grabbed his ankle, and he dropped hard to the floor. Matt knelt on him, wiping the blood from his face. At the same time, Sean crawled out from under the bed.

'Where's my wife?' Matt asked.

The guy was trying to push his body off the floor. Matt needed to rough him up. He wasn't going to answer questions any other way. Matt was enraged. The whole time, he'd thought Nadia was here. He had to face the possibility that they could have murdered her. Her beautiful face flashed in his mind, then Lucy. How would she deal with this? The things these people have done, the torment they've caused for their own gratification.

The adrenaline soared through his body, the hatred for what these people had done. Matt reached his hands around the guy's throat. He squeezed, cutting off the airflow. His eyes were blank, his lips wet as he crushed the guy under him. Matt watched his hands, pounding the floor, grasping at

Matt's jeans. He coughed, gasping for breath as his legs kicked out. His face began to turn purple.

Sean was watching, his face awkward.

Matt gripped the guy's throat tighter; it looked like he was about to take his last gasp. Then he let go.

'This is your last chance or so help me, God.' Matt warned.

The guy was terrified. His expression was one of delirium. He choked, wheezing heavily for air. Matt steadied himself, ready to grab him by the throat.

'Cumberland Road. Milton Lodge. Number three on the ground floor. She's been taken there.'

'Who's with her?' Matt asked. Again, he placed his hands around the guy's throat, pressing hard.

The man gargled. His breath was rancid, his mouth open, revealing large gaps where his teeth once were. 'The two brothers. I watched them leave earlier. They left Angela and me in charge. They're going to kill us.'

'Who else is here?' Sean asked, now standing over the bed. He began tying his legs and arms with the rope.

'Just me, the surgeon and Angela. I'm so sorry, man. I didn't want to be a part of this. They made me do it. I didn't want to be a part of it. You have to believe me.'

Once the guy was held securely, Matt lent into his face. 'If anything happens to Nadia, I swear I'll return and kill you.'

Matt, Sean and Mia moved to the front door, listening to the guy calling out.

'I didn't want to be a part of it.'

* * *

Matt removed the phone from his jeans pocket, summoning the torch. One percent flickered in the corner of the screen, enough to see Sean and Mia embracing.

Mia pressed her lips all over his face while Matt watched. 'Guy's. Enough already.'

Seeing the love between them made him all the more determined to get Nadia home.

He was going to the address the guy had just given him.

Matt, Sean and Mia pawed their way through the darkness as they walked towards the lift. Matt eventually found the call button, fearing they'd be stuck up here with no way out. They rode the lift in darkness, Sean and Mia clinging to each other, Matt only able to cling to hope.

On the ground floor, they made their way to the main entrance.

A well-dressed man stood outside the front door. 'At last. What the hell is wrong with this establishment?' He eyed Mia's uniform. 'My wife and I have been waiting to check-in for ages. Why is no one at the desk? Where are all the staff? This is ridiculous.'

'Sorry, we're closed,' Mia answered.

'Well, be assured we'll leave a rotten review of this dump.'

Mia turned to Sean and Matt, then back to the man stood in front of them. 'You and me both.'

31

Matt and Sean walked Mia to the pub, making sure she'd found Lucy and Lydia. Matt gazed through the window from the street as Mia joined them, watching the three of them hold each other, weeping tears of distress and joy simultaneously. Trolley woman was there too, sat silently, watching the tension unfold.

Matt could see Lucy, a confused expression on her face. Mia would explain, but Matt didn't have time now. Although he ached to be with his daughter, Matt had to finish this.

'Right. Let's get the Jeep.'

'Sean. Go and wait with Mia. I can do this.'

'After what you've done for me. I'm with you, Matt. Let's go. Do you have the address?'

Matt recited it out loud, continuing to repeat it in his mind as they walked to the Jeep. Matt got into the driver's seat, Sean beside him. He tapped the address into the Satnav, then pulled out of the car park. He watched the lights of Brighton pier, the pavement full with Saturday night partygoers, the din of the sea through his open window as it gently tumbled over itself. Rolls of water caressing the surface. He plugged his phone in, hearing it ping to life a few minutes later. Then he dialled 999.

'Emergency services. What is your emergency?'

Matt explained what had just happened at The Blair Hotel, from them watching the man in Billy's room, Sean being taken and the people held captive on the fourth floor. He'd left the master key and the lift pass on the front desk, instructing the call handler where to find it. He couldn't risk giving the address they were heading to and jeopardising Nadia's rescue. According to the Satnav, they were minutes away. He knew every moment was crucial. After more questions from the call handler and the woman assuring them the police were on their way, Matt hung up.

Sean digested the phone call. He knew he could still be in the frame for what had happened. The men had killed Billy, and the possible threat of being framed was now minimal.

Oprah Winfrey's voice instructed them to take the next left, a right at the end of the road, drive another mile, a left, then their destination. Matt parked the Jeep in a visitor's spot outside the plush apartment block.

He undid his seatbelt, then got out of the Jeep, peering across the elegant lawn.

Sean joined him. 'How do we play this?' he asked.

As they walked towards the main entrance, Matt glanced at the numbers. Apartment three was on the ground floor. Matt looked through the glass door, seeing a short corridor and stairs to the right-hand side. 'We go around the back. We can't chance pressing the buzzer. Who knows what could be waiting inside?'

Matt moved left along the path made up of white paving slabs, leading to the side of the building. The apartment block was a new build. The brickwork was clean, graceful looking. A spotlight glared over small rockeries behind them, an array of bushes shaped and clearly maintained regularly. The plants gave off a pleasing aroma, and the soil was a deep black colour.

Matt moved around the side of the building, pressing his body against the brick. Sean followed. The first window on the right was huge, double glazed and gave a view into a kitchen. Matt stopped, about to push his face to the glass when an elderly lady appeared. She pulled a cord, and wooden shutters dropped, obscuring their view.

'Can you make it a little more obvious?' Sean asked sarcastically. 'Quick, keep going. We're looking suspicious.'

Matt kept walking. A security light jumped to life, shining over the grass behind them. Matt turned, seeing a wooden bench, a small play area with a slide and two swings. They waited, listening for movement coming from the front. After a few minutes, they came to another window. Matt crouched, signing for Sean to get down. He stabilised himself, placing one leg behind the other, then rose slowly, looking in the window.

'I see someone,' Matt announced. 'There's a guy wearing jeans and a shirt.'

'What's he doing?' asked Sean.

'He's just standing there. He has a glass of whisky, I think. He's talking to someone. I can't see the other person. Wait, let me move a little. He's definitely having a conversation.'

'Maybe it's his wife?'

'Maybe?' Matt said. 'He's moving forward. He still has the drink in his hand. I can see his eyes. There's a lust to them, like he's eyeing a prize. Something's wrong, Sean.'

'What do you mean?'

'He's stood beside the living room door, practically facing me. There's someone in the room with him. I know him, Sean. I've seen posters when Lucy and I went to the pier. I think it's Mayor Tomlinson.'

'Well, shit. We're in the wrong place,' Sean answered.

Suddenly, Matt's jaw dropped. The guy standing in the living room placed the glass on the side counter, reached forward and pulled a woman close to him. His expression was one of delight, his lips widened, and his body trembled. Matt could see the figure standing in front of the Mayor. She was taller than him, slim, her hair a golden brown colour. Her hands were tied behind her back, and a gag placed over her mouth. She was facing away from Matt, standing like a possession, paraded in front of the Mayor. He began unbuttoning the front of her dress. He lifted it off her shoulders, dropping it to the floor. The woman stood in a bra and knickers. Mayor Tomlinson reached out, clasping one hand on her shoulder, the other on her hip, then gently turned her around, his eyes burning into her body. He watched her as she turned, his lust evident. This semi-naked woman on parade for his sexual gratification. She winced, pulling her head back, tears streaming down her face.

As Mayor Tomlinson dropped his trousers and pulled his pants down around his ankles, he heard an enormous crashing sound coming from the kitchen.

Matt dropped the brick, then handed Sean his phone and asked him to take pictures as he climbed onto the ledge, pushing his body over and landing on the kitchen floor. Matt watched as the Mayor fled, racing towards the front door. The woman turned, facing Matt.

'Nadia. Oh my God. I'm here. I'm here, baby.' As Matt removed the gag from her mouth and untied the rope holding her hands together, she fell into his arms, sobbing until she had no tears left.

Sean watched from the outside window. He had the photos that would destroy Mayor Tomlinson. He watched Matt and Nadia. He couldn't help but shed a tear himself. He recalled the words Matt had said to him when he and Mia

had been reunited on the fourth floor of The Blair Hotel.
'Guys. Enough Already.'

Matt stuck his middle finger up at Sean, then pulled his beautiful wife closer, promising to never again let her out of his sight.

* * *

Lucy kept her eye on the pub's front door as she sat with Mia, Lydia and trolley lady. She was sipping her third diet coke, chewing on the straw and listening to Lydia, asking how she was for the umpteenth time.

'They'll find your mum. Don't worry. Your dad is so brave. How are you feeling? Are you tired? Do you want another drink?'

Lucy knew she meant well, but her anxious state made the questions more annoying. Suddenly, the door of the pub opened. Lucy rose off the stool, like she'd seen an apparition. Matt and Sean stood behind Nadia, and Lucy walked, almost in slow motion, savouring the sight of her mother across the room of the pub. Lucy held her tight, her body quivering with excitement. Then, the young girl burst into tears. 'I thought you were dead. Don't do that to us again.'

Nadia smiled, reaching her hands towards her daughter, crouching and pulling her close to her body. Nadia shook, tears spilling down her face.

Lucy couldn't let go as they placed her heads together and cried tears of elation.

Nadia turned to Matt. 'Get me a drink. A large whiskey.'
'Nadia, are you sure...?'
'Matt. A large whiskey. Christ, I need it.'
'Coming up.' Matt stood for what felt like hours, staring at his wife. He watched her hug Lydia, feeling her baby bump. Lucy smothered her, gawking at her mother's every move.

Police sirens sounded out on the street, and Matt saw at least three ambulances making their way to The Blair Hotel.

People stood, their bodies pressed to the window, whispers rang through the pub as punters tried to see what the commotion was all about. Matt watched Nadia through all the distraction. He had her back. Nadia was back.

'Matt. A large whiskey.'

'Oh yeah. Sorry, Nadia. Coming right up.'

* * *

Matt sat down, unable to draw his eyes away from Nadia. He watched her sipping her drink, elegant, graceful. He held her hand, his fingers trembling in hers. Lucy was perched beside her. She'd left her phone on the table for once.

'I can't believe you're back. Christ, Nadia, I didn't think I'd see you again.' Matt watched the tears emerge in her eyes.

'It was horrible. A nightmare I'll never forget. One minute I was with mum, the next thing I heard a knock on the door. As you know, it was Peter. Suddenly he grabbed me by the wrists, tying me up and dumping me in the back of his car. I could make out your voice, screaming down the phone. All I could hear while Peter drove was him, apologising. He took me here, The Blair Hotel. I remember seeing two men, coming to the car. A hood was placed over my head, and I recall riding in a lift. They shackled me to a post in a dingy room. I screamed until I was hoarse.' Nadia gazed into her husband's eyes. 'All I kept thinking was I'd never see you again, or Lucy.' Nadia broke down. Matt reached forward, wiping the tears from under her eyes. Her face was marked, dirt smudges on her cheeks. She had scratches running along her arms. Her fingers were grubby and oil-stained. 'I remember a man coming to the room. He told me they had rich clients, and I was going to make them shit loads of money. He said it was a way to compensate for what had happened. I didn't know what the hell he was talking about. He said if I didn't cooperate, they'd kill my family.' Nadia took a swig of her whiskey. 'How the hell was Peter involved?'

Matt took a deep breath, then went on to explain what happened the weekend they went away. He told her about Billy, the woman he killed and how his friends helped bury the body while Matt slept. The selfie Lucy had taken. Peter chasing them to the hotel. The receptionist joining them in the restaurant, telling them of the strange man trying to get into their room. Sean, Mia, Lucy and him watching the screen at The Blair Hotel, seeing the guy entering the room and Billy burning to death in the bathroom.

'Billy's dead? Oh my God, Matt.' Nadia stood, placing her hand on the table to steady herself. She walked over to Lydia, placing her arms around her. 'I'm so sorry. Matt has just told me what's happened. Lydia, if there's anything I can do, we're all here. We have to support each other.'

Lydia wiped the tears from her face. 'We need to make sure these bastards pay for what they've done.'

Nadia glimpsed at her friend's stomach. She was heartbroken for Lydia. Now the baby would never meet her father. 'We will. You can be assured of that.'

The women spoke for another ten minutes. They'd been through so much; they'd become friends through their partners. Now, they'd be a rock for each other.

* * *

Matt moved across to the table. Customers were still standing at the window. A few more were standing outside, cigarettes in one hand, phones in the other, taking pictures.

'We need to give a statement. The police are at the hotel now. Are you up for it?' Matt asked.

'No time like the present.' Nadia looked towards Lydia. 'Are you ready?'

Lydia stood with Matt's help. Lucy grabbed her mother's hand, Sean and trolley lady followed.

They walked along the street, the blue lights flashing around them as more police cars pulled up outside The Blair Hotel. As they approached the front, they saw two men handcuffed and led to the back of one of the vehicles.

Matt approached a policeman. 'We need to talk.'

'Sorry, sir. You'll have to step back. This is a crime scene.'

'Yeah. I gathered. I can tell you everything you need to know.' Matt went on to explain what had happened; the people held captive on the fourth floor, where he'd left the lift pass, the master key, right up to when he rescued his wife from the clutches of Mayor Tomlinson.

The policeman stared at the small entourage in front of him. Matt, Nadia, Lucy, Sean, Mia, Lydia and trolley lady glared back.

'This all happened today?' he asked.

Everyone nodded.

'Let me take a statement. I never liked that bastard Tomlinson. I knew he was a bad one. Have you people got somewhere to stay?'

Matt looked up at The Blair Hotel. 'We're going to drive home. We've had enough of hotels for the moment.'

* * *

The following morning, Matt, Nadia and Lucy watched the news from the comfort of their living room in North London.

Last night, The Blair Hotel had been stormed by police.

Several bodies had been found. One had been doused in petrol and burned so badly the person was unrecognisable. The report stated that at least two women, thought to be illegal immigrants and trafficked by the owners, had been rescued from the fourth floor. Three women who were reported missing a few months ago and had stayed at The Blair Hotel were also found, bound and gagged in a room. It was reported they were kept as prisoners and scars indicated their kidneys may have been removed. The women had been taken to hospital, and their families had been notified.

Marty and Vincent Blair, two brothers who recently took over the hotel after their father committed suicide, had been charged and remanded in custody to appear at the local magistrate's court where they'll be committed to the crown court to stand trial. Two other members of staff had been arrested while police continued their enquiries. In a turn of events, pictures of Mayor Tomlinson had surfaced on the internet where it's thought he may have paid the brothers a large sum of money as part of a prostitution ring. Mayor Tomlinson was arrested in the early hours of the morning and released on bail, pending further investigation.

A few minutes previously, he appeared before reporters at his home in Brighton and said the allegations were completely false, insisting he'd be consulting his solicitor. He has asked for privacy at this difficult time and has said he loves his wife and children more than anything.

'Yeah. Right, mate, sure you do,' Matt shouted at the telly.

The press dubbed the place, "Hotel Hell." All British newspapers ran with the story on the front page.

Once the report had finished, Matt turned off the telly. 'I want you to see a psychologist, Nadia. You've been through so much. Maybe a bereavement counsellor. Will you do that for me?'

'Please don't worry about me. I just need rest. I can cope. A cup of tea would be nice.'

Matt stood. 'Don't think you can use this free pass forever. I know your game,' he laughed.

'Just make me tea,' Nadia joked.

Lucy held her mother's hand as the phone rang.

'I'll get it.' Matt picked it up. 'Hello.'

'Matt. Can you talk?' Sean asked.

'Yes. We've been watching the news. Crazy, isn't it?'

'The police are here. They've found a security tape from The Blair Hotel. I heard Mia explaining to them that she turned off the cameras in the basement.'

'Yes. She did, Sean. She dressed as Angela, trolley lady and went to the basement. I begged her not to, but she was adamant she could make it. Why. What's happened?'

'Apparently, they had a couple of other cameras. They work through Bluetooth. Mia didn't turn all the cameras off, Matt. The police have found footage. They say it shows Mia, shooting a woman in the basement.'

Matt paused. 'Mia. What do you mean?'

'They're arresting her. She swears it was an accident. I don't know what to do, Matt.'

'Don't say anything. Call a solicitor. Tell Mia not to admit anything.'

'That's not the worst of it,' Sean continued. 'It also shows Mia hiding the gun and the body, then marching two elderly people into a room and tying them up.'

ONE MONTH LATER.

* * *

Matt and Nadia sat in the assembly hall. Lucy stood on the stage.

The headteacher approached her, holding a mic. 'Saint Bernadette's High School has great privilege in awarding the title of head girl to Lucy Benson.'

Matt held Nadia's hand. They proudly watched on, seeing the delight on their daughter's face. The hall was packed with students, standing and clapping wildly.

'I'm so bloody proud of her. This is all she wanted. If anyone deserves this, it's Lucy.' Matt stood, and Nadia joined him.

Once the students had drifted back to class, the headteacher walked over. 'She was always the lead runner,' he said, grinning profusely. 'Especially after, well, you know.'

Matt and Nadia didn't need him to finish. They knew what he was talking about.

'How is she coping?' the headteacher asked.

'She has her good and bad days,' Nadia explained. 'Sometimes she wakes in the night, screaming. She still can't talk about that place. The horror she went through. We've been having counselling, you know, to deal with the trauma. It's helping, but it's a long road to recovery.'

The headteacher nodded. 'I can only imagine.'

Lucy came up behind them. 'Mum. Dad. Can we have a selfie?'

Matt froze, taking Lucy's phone and passing it to a student. 'Can you take our picture?' He turned to Lucy. 'I think we've had enough of selfies to last a lifetime.'

* * *

That evening, Matt put on his jacket and made his way out to the front door. 'I'm popping over to see Sean. I'll grab a curry on the way back.'

Nadia was in the living room with Greta. Her mother was on the road to recovery, and they wanted her to stay with them for a while. Greta still asked why she'd ran off with Peter. Nadia just smiled.

The telly was on low. Lucy was revising for a mock exam upstairs.

'What are you going to say to him?'

Mia had been arrested without bail. She'd been charged with manslaughter. The security camera had captured everything. The woman she'd killed was an accident, but Mia was caught on camera, hiding the body and dumping the gun. It also showed her marching the dead woman's parents into a room in the basement and tying them up. She was pleading guilty. Everything was caught on camera. Sean had been told that Mia would most probably spend a long time behind bars.

'I don't know yet, but I have to be there for him. I've been trying to call him for days. He's not answering the phone. I'm worried. I'll see you later.'

Matt closed the front door. On the drive over there, he rehearsed what he'd say. How do you comfort someone, knowing their partner could end up in prison for years? It's like a death. Matt hoped he could find the right words.

* * *

He parked outside and walked to the house. Matt tapped the knocker and waited. The key was in the front door. He worried when Sean didn't answer, knowing the stress he was going through. He tapped again. Nothing. Matt moved his hand to the key and twisted. Inside, the house was drenched in darkness. Matt braced himself. Visions flashed in his mind. Sean was suffering. He had backed away, not answering Matt's calls. He'd been through so much. Matt whispered softly. 'Sean. Are you okay?' No answer. As he moved onto the stairs, edging up, he heard sounds. Moans, coming from the bedroom. A woman was crying out.

'Yes. Oh yes. That's it.'

Matt stood, astounded. When they'd finished, he heard them speaking.

It was Sean. He was with Lydia. Billy's wife.

No. No. No. This isn't happening. What the hell is going on? Matt thought to himself. He could hear them speaking.

'What if someone finds out?' Lydia asked.

'It's not your fault. Stop blaming yourself. How were you supposed to know?'

Know what? Matt thought. He was standing halfway up the stairs, his body numb with shock. Sean and Lydia. Making love upstairs. Her, pregnant with Billy's child.

Sean continued. 'Okay. Let's see it for what it is. You called your friend, Marty. You went to school together, right?'

'Right,' Lydia answered.

Sean continued. 'He and his brother had recently taken over The Blair Hotel. That's how you recommended the place to Billy. I know he mentioned it to us. That's how we ended up there. You wanted to catch Billy out, set a honeytrap. Someone he couldn't resist. Lydia, you were sick of his womanising. Your friend, Marty, said he could help. He'd asked how you and Billy were getting on, and you poured your heart out to him. He had a woman and a camera. You weren't to know how it would end up, Billy killing her. He brought it on himself.'

'But I feel responsible. If I hadn't made that call. The crazy thing is they were doing me a favour. Once I'd transferred the money that Saturday evening, they set the wheels in motion instantly. The woman was with someone else at the casino. An old guy. She was wearing a wire. Marty knew I was desperate. At the last minute, they contacted her, telling her to go after Billy. Marty called me and said everything was set up.'

Sean sighed. 'I'll admit, I was shocked at first when you told me a few days ago. But I've come to terms with it. We wanted so much to be together. Now, here we are. Look, Billy brought her back to the room. He had a choice. It was perfect. Your trap worked, you wanted to get it on film so you could divorce him, and we could be together. Now, you don't need to worry. He's gone. So is Mia. It's worked out perfectly. Don't blame yourself.'

'But the trail of destruction it caused. The deaths. Peter, found beaten to death and hanging upside down in the warehouse. Anna, his wife, in the boot of Peter's car. Your neighbour, Kate. Mia, probably serving the rest of her life behind bars. The young girl and her parents in the basement. Mayor Tomlinson, jumping off the bridge. Unable to cope with the pictures which flooded the internet. Billy, burnt to death in the bath. What if it comes back to me?' Lydia asked.

'Mayor Tomlinson's suicide was partly my doing. Although Matt asked me not to, I couldn't help myself. I had to post the pictures.' Sean pushed the blanket back. He glanced at Lydia's bump. There wasn't long to go. 'You weren't to know how they'd take revenge. How evil Marty and Vincent were. That's on them. The woman Billy brought back to the room seemed to be on her own revenge trip. She knew Marty had a camera. She knew her and Billy were being recorded. They'd killed her husband, and maybe the kinky sex game she'd played out with Billy was her way of sticking two fingers up to them. It was her way of putting on a show; maybe she was making the brothers jealous as they watched. I think she had nothing to lose; it's just a shame Billy ended up killing her through her own foolishness. I need the loo. Stop worrying. I don't think they'll ever talk. What do they have to gain?'

Matt crept down the stairs. He opened the front door; his world began to spin out of control. He gripped his head, a hand at each side, unable to believe the conversation he'd just heard. Sean and Lydia, making love upstairs, his partner behind bars, Billy's ashes in a vase on Lydia's living room mantlepiece. It had all started from a phone call. Lydia wanting to catch Billy with another woman so she could divorce him and be with Sean. He'd pretended he loved Mia when all the time he was seeing Lydia. Planning on being together.

Matt stumbled, falling against the wall, his mind racing, his body weary and exhausted. He reached for the car key in his jeans pocket, feeling like he was going to vomit any moment. He sat in the driver's seat, his body twitching, a rash developing on his chest. He composed himself, then drove away.

The End

Thanks to everyone who pinged over a selfie.
Can you spot yourself below?

AFTERWORD

Thank you so much for choosing Selfie and I hope you enjoyed it.
You can sign up to my mailing list and keep up to date with other projects I have planned.
I'll also send you a short story for free.
Just go to:
https://www.stuartjamesthrillers.com

Special thanks to the Facebook groups who continually promote my works and support me so much.
The Fiction Cafe.
Tracy Fenton and her wonderful book club, TBC.
The Reading Corner Book Lounge.
UK Crime Book Club.
Donna's Interviews, Reviews and Giveaways.
Mark Fearn. Book Mark.
Also to the incredible book bloggers who have supported my journey so much and to all you wonderful readers and authors.

Also massive thanks to Sam Missingham, Adam Croft, Alan Gorevan and Lindsay Detwiler.
And lastly, special thanks to Zoe O'Farrell, Chloe Jordan, Kate Eveleigh, Donna Morfett, Emma Louise Bunting, Michaela Balfour, Kiltie Jackson, Mark Fearn and all the readers who requested an arc of Selfie.
Your support is forever grateful.
You really are amazing and I can't thank you enough.
Thanks to my wonderful family for all your patience and support. I love you all so very much.

Creeper is coming soon.

A husband and wife documentary team move into an old farmhouse and hear about an urban legend.
Someone from your worst nightmare.
A person who it's said, watched the residents of Painswick late at night and may be responsible for a string of missing women.
As they investigate the story behind it, they begin to suspect Creeper could be very real.

BOOKS BY THE AUTHOR.

Turn The Other Way.

The House On Rectory Lane.

Apartment Six.

Stranded.

Make sure to sign up to my newsletter for an insight into my future thrillers and what I'm working on.

https://www.stuartjamesthrillers.com

Follow me on social media.

Twitter: StuartJames73

Instagram: StuartJamesAuthor

Facebook: StuartJamesAuthor

TikTok: StuartJamesAuthor

Thanks again for reading Selfie and please make sure to keep in touch.

Thanks so much.

Stuart James.

Printed in Great Britain
by Amazon